Photo: Renate Klein

Susan Hawthorne grew up on the dry western slopes of New South Wales. She works in publishing and academia and writes fiction, poetry, drama and a wide range of non-fiction. A feminist activist for more than thirty years, her latest books *Wild Politics: Feminism, Globalisation and Bio/diversity* and *September 11, 2001: Feminist Perspectives* (co-edited with Bronwyn Winter) reflect on the parlous state of the world. She has a passion for aerials which she indulges in as a member of two circuses for women in Melbourne.

Other books by Susan Hawthorne:

Poetry
The Language in My Tongue (1993)
Bird and other writings on epilepsy (1999)

Non-fiction
The Spinifex Quiz Book (1993)
Wild Politics: Feminism, Globalisation and Bio/diversity (2002)

Anthologies
Difference: Writings by Women (1985)
*Moments of Desire: Sex and Sensuality by Australian Feminist
        Writers* (with Jenny Pausacker, 1989)
*The Exploding Frangipani: Lesbian Writing from Australia and
        New Zealand* (with Cathie Dunsford,1990)
Angels of Power and other reproductive creations
        (with Renate Klein, 1991)
Australia for Women: Travel and Culture
        (with Renate Klein, 1994)
Car Maintenance, Explosives and Love and other lesbian writings
        (with Cathie Dunsford and Susan Sayer, 1997)
CyberFeminism: Connectivity, Critique and Creativity
        (with Renate Klein, 1999)
September 11, 2001: Feminist Perspectives
        (with Bronwyn Winter, 2002)

THE FALLING WOMAN

Susan Hawthorne

SPINIFEX

Assisted by the Literature Board of the Australia Council

Spinifex Press Pty Ltd,
504 Queensberry Street,
North Melbourne, Vic. 3051
Australia

First published by Spinifex Press, 1992
Second edition 2003

Typeset in 10/12 pt Garamond Light
        by Lorna Hendry, Melbourne
Second edition by Claire Warren, Melbourne
Printed and bound by McPherson's Printing Group
Cover design: Deb Snibson

National Library of Australia
Cataloguing-in-Publication entry:

CIP

Hawthorne, Susan, 1951–
    The falling woman.

    2nd ed.
    ISBN 1 876756 36 5

    I. Title.

A823.3

Creative Writing Program assisted by the
Literature Board of the Australia Council, the Federal
Government's arts funding and advisory body.

For Renate

Author's Note

Parts of this manuscript have been previously published, in different forms in: (magazines) *Hear, Sinister Wisdom* (USA), *Cargo*; (books) *Soft Lounges, Difference, The Writing on the Wall, Inner Cities, The Exploding Frangipani* (NZ), *Body Lines*.

I would like to thank the following organizations for their support: The Victorian Ministry for the Arts, for a research and travel grant that made it possible for me to complete the manuscript; to Penguin Books for unpaid leave that enabled me to take up a position as Adjunct Professor in the Women's Studies Department at San Diego State University, California, making it possible for me to finish writing what I'd begun so long ago.

When a book spreads itself over many years there are many individuals to thank. Thanks go to various unnamed people for their support and encouragement throughout. Particular thanks are due to Kaye Moseley who has seen it through every draft; to Robyn Arianrhod for discussions on physics; to the women in the writers group in San Diego for support during the writing of the first final draft; to Diane Bell and Gill Hanscombe for insightful feedback at a crucial time, and Suniti Namjoshi for the title; to others who have read it in various drafts in particular to Primrose and Hugh Hawthorne, Jackie Yowell, Cathie Dunsford, Beryl Fletcher, Susan Sayer and Sara Hardy. Many thanks to Suzanne Bellamy for the cover sculpture, to Lariane Fonseca for photographing it, to Deb Snibson for the cover design, and to Lorna Hendry and Claire Warren for the typesetting. Especial thanks to Jane Arms for her sensitive and thorough editing. And finally to Renate Klein who has given the kind of support every writer dreams of.

I am an electrical impulse. I discharge at random across a synapse, at the threshold of a seizure. Grand mal. Idiopathic. Without warning.

She cries out. *I dance.*

She waves her arms about, falls. Her pupils dilate, teeth bite into the tongue. *I am dancing.* Her face is the blue of cyanide. *I rampage.* Her muscles contract. She convulses. Saliva mixed with blood dribbles from her mouth. She has lost consciousness.

The sun rose, stretching its petals across the horizon.

Estella fell. She fell into blackness. An electrical explosion took her out of consciousness to the edge of annihilation.

The sun was high now. Everything etched sharply. Her mind reached out into the almost blinding sunlight, crossed the bridge spanning night, and headed into the void.

Vision

1

Time looks impossibly long at a beginning and shortens as one progresses through it, around it. Estella's heart is singing. Everything is happening at once. Olga is with her at last and they are driving out into the unknown. It's been so long. Estella thought she'd never make the distance.

They are leaving what they know, but all they know goes with them. They are leaving behind the familiar smells of the cities and pavements for the dry dusty heat of the bush.

Blowing up beside the window, the dust permeates everything. The car throws up so much dust, there is nothing but dust behind them. Because of the dust they feel as though they are approaching their goal, but there is still a long way to go.

Behind them the sun, shining through the dust, spreads like gold threads.

Olga has fallen asleep, her body confused by the shifts in time, thinking it is night. Estella wants to wake her, to tell her all the things she hasn't told her yet. All the things she has wanted to say in these long months of separation. Olga sleeps on. Estella looks at her and, feeling the light touch of imagined fingers on her skin, sits back, stretches her legs and sighs.

A flock of galahs lifts in a scattered way from the road, flashing their musk feathers. It's harvest time and the roads are littered with grains of wheat, oats and barley from the trucks travelling to the silos and railway sidings. Estella brakes to avoid hitting a straggler.

Olga wakes as the car lurches forward and cries out in sleepy delight at the sight of galahs. She turns to Estella and flashes a smile that wipes her out. It erases all time, erases the waiting, the aching that they have endured, carrying their relationship on the thin lines of letters and telephones.

The light changes and pink is beginning to shine through the clouds. They're not far from the lake. As they drive along its edge a pelican runs breast forward across the water and lifts off the ground like a jumbo.

Olga, her hair the colour of ochre in the late sunlight, is leaning out the window, staring across the lake. She is musing on thoughts of love, and remembering the dust and rocks of Zakros, the Aegean blue sea and the long days of work. Dust seems universal.

They drive on in silence, each trying to create some order in their chaotic lives: departures, arrivals, departures. And now this journeying towards a new place. The drive will be long, like stepping carefully along tunnels that lead to secret shrines at the centre of the earth. But this is a surface journey, no tunnels, just dusty tracks, oracular birds and the criss-crossing of lines of memory.

They stop under a red river gum and stretch their bodies into the pinkened twilight. Wallabies look up from their grazing, gaze a moment, before continuing to eat. A duck stands by the water's edge, quacks a few times and flies off. The lake is still and mauve. The trees dip their leaves towards the surface like expectant fishing lines, never quite reaching, a teasing of trees.

Olga is searching for something warmer to put on; Estella has begun chopping onions on the slatted picnic table. Their eyes meet as Venus, reaching for the water, dips down through the leaves. Above, the sky is clear and growing darker. Stars begin to show as Estella and Olga cook on the open fireplace. Soon it's Jupiter's shine that is reflected in the lake.

They speak quietly with half an eye on the fireplace. There are gaps and breaks between the words they speak, as

6

though there is a need to re-establish fluency. There is a tentativeness of touch in their words and the hands that reach out.

Moths circle the candle, flying suicidally close, singeing their wings. Across the lake the Southern Cross appears to be diving earthwards. A large red ant is scurrying around the table top, tracking food scraps. Estella hears the heavy breathing of a possum, and tries, with the light of her torch, to spot the shining eyes which gleam like tiny stars among the leaves.

Olga's eyes are drooping, and she rises to go to bed. Estella sits on, turning her thoughts to words on a page and listens to the familiar bush sounds, breathes in the scent and lifts her eyes to see the bright mantle of stars, starlight, as she had known it in childhood.

When Estella blows out the candle she notices the smell of wild boar. The stars are brighter now and she sits for a while gazing up at them. Among the stellar lights she sees one star fall, and she makes a silent wish. She crawls into the sleeping bag, touching Olga's face lightly.

On the day that Stella was born a star fell from the sky. No one saw it because the sky was blue and the day hot. It burnt itself out before hitting the ground and left no mark.

An hour's drive away, a header moved slowly around the paddock of wheat in ever-decreasing circles towards the centre. A hot northerly wind blew the stalks and chaff into Theo's eyes and nose. His mind was on Coral, wondering if the child had arrived yet. He looked at his watch: midday. Then he smelled the smoke, and turned to see a blaze of fire in the half-harvested crop. He signalled the other men to come quickly. They had seen the smoke and two were on their way with wet bags, another on his way to get help.

Five hours later the fire was under control, half the crop was burnt, the fences a blackened memory. The men stood about in the meagre shade, quenching their thirst with strong black tea. They still held wet bags, occasionally beating a smouldering spark that threatened to flame.

A car drove up. Betty climbed out of the ute and walked towards them. 'Theo, you have a daughter, born at about noon.'

Stella's mother told her about her birth. The day was hot, a heat wave. The air twisted in circles and the houses outside the window wrinkled in the heat. Coral lay waiting, her heart tightening in anger. The nurses had orders to be obeyed. No child was to be born without the presence of a doctor, in case of complications, but the doctor could not be found. His absence was the complication. The nurses stifled the birth. They held her back in darkness, in an unbearable state of pain. Mother and daughter, unseparated yet. Eventually the doctor came, late, his lunch still on his breath.

When Coral took Stella home on the seventh day, three-year-old Fiona pushed her up and down the hallway in her doll's pram. Fiona pushed the pram into Coral and Theo's bedroom and opened the top drawer of the dressing-table. She stood on tip-toes and carefully picked out a deep red lipstick and drew a big star in the centre of Stella's forehead.

Stella progressed from amoeba to quadruped to biped with effort, will, persistence. She rose, she fell, she wavered like cloth in the wind. She crawled in circles. She charged, her head stretched forward like a turtle. She bent to pick things up and fell again.

Fiona resented the strange new creature who had turned the routines upside-down. She wanted to play with her sister, but mostly she just sat and watched when Stella slept, or wondered why she cried so much. Why, sometimes, she cried all night. It was as though she didn't want to be here, didn't want to be born into the world. Fiona kept to herself, remained silent. Did not speak her resentment.

They told Fiona that Stella was sick. But Stella didn't look sick. She stared a lot, and sometimes she did seem far away. Most of all it was the changes in others that Fiona noticed. She watched silently as Coral moved about in the mornings, tired and worn out. She woke during the night to hear her pacing, a constant midnight ramble. Sometimes she saw them pass her door, Stella staring wildly over Coral's shoulder. She heard mumbling, exasperated sighs and then her father's heavier footsteps taking up the circuit.

At other times Stella smiled and bounced and moved about the house on all fours as if it were natural to her. And the energy! Stella found her way into everything. She had no fear. Fiona would stare in amazement at her unpredictable sister.

Coral took photographs of her new daughter laughing, in a pram. Stella was propped against a pillow, her face round and her protruding ears stuck down with sticky tape. Coral tried to judge the intensity of the morning light, but it was difficult.

Stella's eyes were open in the dark. She stared, unfocused, watching the patterns. Night brought on wakefulness, discomfort. The patterns spun, slowly, first one way, then the other. Stella lay watching. The patterns, the colours, were pretty at first, but then they began to spin. She began to spin. She panted, trying to keep up, then she cried because she was falling, out of control. Her mother came to pick her up and for a while the world stood still. She listened to the reassuring heartbeat, felt the warm softness of the breast. But then it started again. She felt the world spin around her. Dizziness. Nausea. Every night. Her mother and she would watch the sunrise together. Sometimes Coral slept in the chair in front of the fire. Stella, wide-eyed and fearful on her lap, watched the prancing flames. The terror and dizziness came and went. Sometimes they both slept, exhausted by their vigil. With daylight the strangeness subsided. They slept.

The world around me is dark and warm. I float in a vast wet space. The maternal blood cells and salt crystals form sweeping nebulae. My skin would be translucent if there were light. With half-closed eyes I gaze at the rising constellations.

The muscles contract. I am pushed. I am pulled. An unbearable pressure bears down on me. My skull is crushed. I am choking. The pain begins at my crown and moves nerve cell by painful nerve cell to the base of my spine. There is a moment of repose then all is released.

I am swept along on a stream of blood. There is a sensation of coolness on my crown. I am seized by your hands. I feel the dryness across the top of my body. Your hands grip me. I lie across your belly.

Your arms hold me. I hear words being called like a calling for lost souls in the void.

The sound brushes past me, almost touching. I hear a familiar sound: 'Estelle'. It resonates like an old friend. I reach out. I stretch to catch the echo. The placenta comes away.

I feel the sound of 'Estelle' vibrating as it enters my soul. I cry out. Air fills my lungs. I see the light of the new world. The cool white moon greets my entrance.

I lie on the floor, I drag myself along with my hands. I move like an amoeba.

I hear rhythms, I move to the rhythms you utter. I celebrate the metre of your voice and I dance to the music of your lips.

I lie awake at night and stare at the constellations. The moon floats above me like a white ball. It is so close that I reach for it.

2

Stella was watching a seagull skimming the water along the pier at Manly beach. She was with Iris and her great aunt Alice. 'Want birdie,' she said running up and pulling at her grandmother's dress.

Iris extended her hand, 'Come on then,' she said, 'let's go and have a look.' They headed for the pier and began walking out over the sea. Stella's blue floral dress was blowing about in the wind. She walked between the two old women, holding their hands. Every now and again she would allow her body to go limp and they would lift her forwards high in the air. She liked the feel of that. It was like flying. The pier seemed to go on forever. Her little legs were beginning to tire. Stella hung back, urging them to slow their pace. They took her to the edge and pointed at the fish and the sunlight in the water. She knelt down and peered intently into the greeny-yellow water. She saw a fish, reached for it and fell. The water closed around her like a big bath and fish swam quickly past. And then she felt as if she might explode. The rainbow colours turned muddy brown, all mixed up together. Then something tugged at her, pulled, lifted her above the water, and she breathed again. Iris's face looked strange, her hair framing her face in an unaccustomed way, her features pulled downwards, towards the earth, her eyes, her hair, her funny wet dress.

I dream of heat waves, hot liquid sand running between my fingers. I let it run. Mountains of sand stretch as far as I can see.

I feel the sand pressing between my toes, the grains warm against my soles.

At night I lie under the sky's dome and gaze into the spaces between the stars. I watch the moon setting over the sand, see the sky lighten. Black fades to dark blue and then fades pale. In the east the sun rises red, spreading light over the sea. I fall asleep.

My days are filled with sand. I climb the mountains of sand and watch the sand splay as I run down the dunes.

At night I watch the starlight on the water. With each wave stars wash and disperse as I sit at the water's edge. The waves lick my legs and the spume gathers and disperses.

I cup my hands and let the water pour over my banked thumbs. The wind rises. It snatches drops of water, grains of sand. It blows the water, the sand, into arcs like a scythe cutting air.

You light a fire. You gather driftwood on long beach walks or from the scrub behind the mountains of sand. I watch the flickering flames. Tongues devouring wood.

We celebrate midsummer's night, singing and dancing through it all. Time folds in on itself. The magic fades as light spatters the dark sky. We move as ordinary beings once again and sleep through the stellar dawn, strewn like driftwood thrown up by night's high tide.

There is a photograph taken in Stella's second year. It is of Theo and Coral standing in a paddock that doubles as an airfield. In the background is a tiger moth. Theo, looking at Coral, is wearing flying goggles perched above his forehead. The wind is pulling at the scarf that covers her head.

The sun is lying gently on the water when Estella wakes, tongues of light licking the mirror-smooth surface. She waits for her muscles to move from sleep to wakefulness and rise from the narrow bed in the back of the car. 'You want to come for a swim?' she says too brightly.

Olga presses her fingers over her eyes.

Estella walks towards the lake, leaving mudprints. She steps into the water, shivering slightly. It's colder than she thought it would be, but she keeps walking. Olga watches, leaning on her elbow. Estella's bottom jiggles slightly as she walks. Olga wishes Estella would come back so they could make love, right here, now. Estella sinks to her shoulders in the water and turns around. 'It's lovely once you're in,' she calls ritually.

Estella swims towards the centre of the lake. She stops and watches the waterbirds. Ducks are frolicking near a partly submerged log. Over by the car mallee fowl are wandering under the table. Olga, watching Estella, sees her leap vertically from the water. Something cold brushes against Estella's leg and she swims as fast as she can back to the shore.

'What happened?'

'I don't know. There was something in the water. Water snake, eel?' she says shrugging her shoulders. She walks back to the shoreline and searches the water. Something moves. A fin? She stands as still as a heron, watching. The fin thing moves closer. A fish, a huge fish, not trout though. 'I think there's carp in the lake,' she says, returning to the car. She turns around to look again. The fish is swimming along the muddy rim of the lake.

Estella returns to the car, dripping. Olga reaches out and touches the cool skin and Estella ripples at the first touch of the tip of Olga's finger. 'Come,' says Estella, reaching out, almost lifting Olga into the sun. They stand in a deep hold. Their mouths search for a way to place words on skin, to stretch the memory of skin into sounds curled in tongues.

Olga is lapping up the warmth of the Australian sun on her body, which arches in pleasure. Her moans linger on the edge of her lips, wet with desire. Estella sees a great burst of light as she squints into the sun over Olga's shoulder and when she hears the currawong call it is as though a great tidal wave passes through her body. Words are caught on the tongue's breath and slip silently from their mouths like spittled fingers.

13

They are like the words, the riddles, that come from the mouths of oracles.

Olga shifts the weight from one foot to another and runs her hands over the now warm skin. 'Are you hungry?'

Estella nods.

'Let's have breakfast, then.'

Between mouthfuls of kisses they eat. Sitting at the slatted wooden table once again they watch a lone pelican sailing by majestically. Some cheeky choughs approach the table. Olga tosses some bacon to them. Three converge, white showing beneath their black wings as they hover briefly. One, calling noisily, picks up the bacon and flies to the nearest branch. The others stomp about, beaks open, calling for more. Olga and Estella give in. They feed the rest of their breakfast to the choughs: beak-size pieces of toast, lengths of bacon rind, browned egg white.

Satisfied, they set off, leaving in their wake the detritus of breakfast and a trail of dust that feathers behind them. They drive north to the place where Australian history begins. Other sites, like feathered strings, fan out across the continent. For the Aborigines, there are many places, many origins and an eternity of dreaming.

Estella dreams as she drives. Her mind is chasing an image from the night, but it eludes her, shifty as a shark in murky water. She takes the turn-off to the lake, or rather the after-image of a shore bounded by sharp ridges where once the shoreline eroded the earth. The salt has won, and the wind. The soil has withered to sand and forms miniature gullies of erosion. For the ants that inhabit them, these gullies are like mountains, ridged and peaked by the movement of wind and water.

Olga and Estella walk along the pink ridge of the dune, the sand filtering into the crevices of their clothes, filling their shoes. Behind is the flat pan of the former lake dotted with saltbush; ahead is farmland, flat and dry.

They sit. An uprooted, dried-out goosefoot comes dancing up the dune. It rolls and spins, whirls by and prances off towards the pasture on the eastern side of the walls. Closing their eyes against the wind, they listen to the mingling buzzing of wind and flies.

Flying sand forces them to leave. Olga has sand behind her contact lens and grabs Estella's hand for support and guidance. Beyond the ridge a troupe of emus is stalking towards a waterhole. The wind and the sand have abated on the flat and Olga regains her composure. They follow the purposive line of emus to the waterhole, stopping the moment they reach the top of the bank. Dozens of rabbits, several big red kangaroos, a dingo and an assortment of birds – galahs, Major Mitchell cockatoos and crows – surround the water-hole. They stand and watch, delighted.

Estella and Olga are standing, holding hands. Estella turns her head, looking back to the dunes.

'What's the matter? Are you all right?'

'I was just thinking. This dam, the water here . . . my father used to subcontract and build dams. I was fascinated by it and appalled. All that mud frightened me. I wish I'd had a chance to talk to him. We all thought he'd go on forever. You never count on accidents.'

They watch the dingo leave. The other birds and animals take no notice. The Major Mitchells lean forward to drink. When a rabbit hops forward, the Major Mitchells leap into the air, showing musk pink under their wings. Captured in flight on a photograph the cockatoos resemble an upside-down V, like the Greek lambda.

Coral liked seeing her two daughters together, playing in their different ways.

When Coral tried to take a photograph of them, they frustrated her attempts at concurrence. Coral put Stella on a tricycle. She didn't look up at Coral even when she called to her but stared at the spinning pedals, raising her feet above them.

Fiona was pushing a doll in a cane pram. She was wearing corduroy overalls, a dark jumper, and her hair hung in two plaits. She wouldn't concentrate either and, when Coral finally pushed the shutter, Fiona had a wistful, distant expression on her face.

Stella was two, Fiona five.

3

*My sister, I watch you in the garden. You turn the earth.
You plant seeds of vegetables, flowers, herbs. I sit in the dirt
and watch it fly in great arcs over your shoulders. I trace
patterns in the earth with my hands, trace circles and loops
and spirals. I let the soil sift through my fingers and watch
it fall.*

*Autumn is approaching. The nights lengthen. The soil is
cool and moist. I like to pluck mushrooms from the soil. I line
up all the mushrooms I can find. With autumn everything
changes. The desiccated ground comes to life with the moisture:
the leaves and grasses change from yellow to green and new
shoots appear.*

*More special than the mushrooms are the orchids that
waver uncertainly on their slender stalks. I lie on the ground
and look at them, lip to lip. Some are like insects, or they have
ears like donkeys; others seem to be in conversation, laughing
and nodding in agreement.*

When they wake they lie for a while listening to the yellow
rosellas cracking open the seed pods of the bulloaks. The
ground is carpeted with seedpods, and galahs strut around
eating whatever remains. Crows call in the distance.

Olga is still caught up in thoughts of what she should have done before she left. But there hadn't been time to do more than fax the article she'd finished on the plane to the archaeological journal. Her body has moved through vast spaces, but her mind remains rooted in events of a week ago. Distance takes time to achieve separation. She wonders whether the dispute with the locals has settled yet.

A willy-willy is blowing across the horizon, swirling along its own unmarked track, leaving few traces of its passing: twigs and grass and dust scattered in a random pattern.

Estella is worrying about her mother, vague thoughts about loneliness and health. There's no need. Coral is happy to be back in the city, enjoying concerts, films, theatre and a challenging group of bridge players.

When Olga's mind catches up with her body the journey will be a respite from the demands of others. No phone, no fax, no address. The perfect holiday.

Estella has made the preparations: hired the car, bought the food, pulled out her old camping equipment and packed it all. She also bought maps, but there are gaps – between printings there are some areas not covered by the maps. There are none for two of the areas they are planning to visit. They will have to rely on native wit and a slim hope that the small-scale road map will do.

The unknown has its attractions so long as it isn't unknowable.

The landscape they are passing through reminds Estella of the paddocks, the woods, the garden. She could walk through the garden naming each flower, tree, shrub; pointing out the sandpit, the birdcage, the swing and the rose arbour that led to the chookyard.

Fiona had a green thumb. Always. Her garden was small in comparison to the rest, but it seemed large to Stella. The soil was a rich brown and small green seedlings poked their heads up between the turned clods of earth. Fiona spent long hours weeding and watering. Stella thought it looked interesting, at first. But soon she became bored and would begin flicking soil across the bed at Fiona. Stella liked it only when the flowers were blooming. At those times she would sit and look at the colours: the pink of the valerian, the orange of the marigolds, the bright red of the geraniums behind Fiona's garden.

The horizon opens up into a wide arc of space. The plain is so flat the horizon curves at the edges. Overhead a huge grey cloud hangs like an old army blanket, and lines of sunlight shower down. But it does not rain.

Instead dust whirls up behind the car, soft and red and fine. Like solid fire. Estella is watching the dust rise up in the rear-vision mirror. Their bottoms are jostling on the seats as they drive over the road that has corrugations like a washboard.

'Blue tongue,' yells Estella. The wheels pass either side of what might have been a piece of wood.

'Back back,' says Olga excitedly. 'I want to have a look. You didn't hit it, did you?'

'No, I saw it at the last minute. If it stayed still it'll be all right. Can you see?'

'Yes, stop now.'

They climb out to get a closer look. Olga is prancing around trying to get the lizard to show its tongue.

'*Tannenzapfenechse*,' says Olga.

'What's that mean?'

'Pine cone lizard.'

Estella squats and apologises for disturbing its sleep. The lizard responds by hissing and spitting at her.

Stella climbed the stile into the paddock behind the chook-yard. She wandered aimlessly between the cow pats and the rocks that were scattered across this piece of ground. It had rained the day before and the grass was damp. She kicked at a dried cow pat and watched it shatter as it flew through the air; little pieces of it falling randomly. They seemed to fall more slowly than the stones she dropped from the tankstand.

Then she saw it: a huge mushroom, the biggest mushroom

19

she had ever seen. It had a thick leathery veil and beneath the cap the gills were brown, like chocolate. She pulled it out of the ground and ran back to the house, shouting excitedly as she let the door slam behind her.

'Look. Look what I found!'

Coral peered up from her book and admired the mushroom.

'How about we cook it up for dinner?' she said.

'Yes, let's.'

But the small black pieces that were served with dinner that night bore no resemblance to the grandeur of the giant mushroom. Stella would not eat it.

They enter a small town and drive past houses with climbing roses spreading across the front walls. The memory of rose scent hits Estella. Roses, deep red roses, and those pink and yellow ones that fall apart when the rain comes. The garden was always full of roses, bordering the front path and climbing all around the verandah, and covering the tankstand: red roses scaling the metal supports. Even if you climbed on to the roof these roses would nod down at you. And, if you stood at the back door and looked towards the chookyard, you would see an arbour of climbing roses: red, pink, white, peach-orange. After rain, the back path would be strewn with petals.

Estella remembered standing under the archway trying to listen for the sound of petals falling on the ground. She heard nothing, only the sound of a bird welcoming the rain.

Like the magic coral garden Fiona received for her birthday one year, the image of gardens pervades her memory of childhood. Women would visit one another in the heat of long summer afternoons. Each visit included cups of tea and the ritual showing of the latest flower, shrub or tree that had survived the drought, or the dust storm, or the flood or simply the ravages of time. Estella remembers these gardens too, remembers leaving them with cuttings of hardy geranium, lavender, valerian or some other plant with guarantees of success. She and Fiona would have scampered through the rainbow of a sprinkler, sharing it with a willy wagtail that would dart suddenly at the sprinkler head.

Estella had wanted that coral garden that needed no tending other than the awed attentions of young eyes.

It was Fiona's fifth birthday. Stella wanted to be five too, wanted to be grown up. But most of all, she wanted Fiona's present. It was so full of magic. And the colours! Tiny striking skeletal forms massed in a small container. So delicate! She followed Fiona around all that day wanting to hold the beautiful fragile gift. But Fiona wouldn't let her touch it. She could only look. She gazed at it admiringly, enviously when it was placed by Fiona's bed that night.

Stella dreamed of living in a magical coral garden.

The road straightens to the firm trajectory of the next town. Exhausted by the drive, they decide to stay in a motel in the next town. Screenings from the mines perch on top of table-flat hills, just beyond the edge of the town: the discarded dreams of white men, following the reefs of metal deep into the ground.

Six emus streak into their line of sight, like bulloaks running across the plain. They run parallel with the car, effortlessly keeping up the pace. Olga is bouncing with excitement, like the bobbing feathers of the emus. Finally the birds veer off, following some invisible track.

4

Stella stared. Her eyes glazed over. She fell.

Terrified by the convulsions and confused and frustrated by the response of the doctors, Coral took Stella to Sydney. It was Stella's first ride on a train and she was excited at the long journey. The train pulled in at the station noisily, the light soil blew up and Stella's new red dress blew high. Theo put the case on the train and Fiona leaned out the window waving at imaginary people. It didn't stop long at this small station and soon the station master ushered Theo and Fiona back to the platform. The train heaved and jolted forward. Stella waved her hand out the window watching as Fiona and Theo grew smaller and smaller until she could no longer distinguish them from the background yellow grass.

Coral had brought soggy tomato sandwiches just the way Stella liked them and a bottle of creamy soda, Stella's favourite drink. Stella bounced on the seat until Coral could stand it no longer and distracted her pointing out the scenery. Coral pulled out Stella's coloured pencils and some paper and soon Stella was deeply involved in drawing funny little figures that seemed to Coral to sprawl across the page. As Stella drew night closed in.

It was a long journey, twelve hours of sitting and sleeping and getting up to walk along the wobbly corridor to the toilet.

Coral read, sleeping when she could. Stella slept between bursts of activity. They arrived at Central Station in the clear brightness of an early morning and were met by Dora and Mildred, in Dora's little red Morris.

Stella sniffed and smelled the sea in the air, so different from the dusty smell of the plains. The station was full of people. Stella wondered where they had all come from. They were soon driving through the streets, stopping at the lights, and starting up again, until they reached the shady house in Mosman.

Stella knew that she had to go to the hospital, they'd talked about it for weeks, but nothing prepared her for the sight of so many beds in one room, when they went the next day.

At the hospital they took samples of deep red blood from her arms. They gave her pills to make her sleep. Some of them made her sick, but none made her sleep. Stella steadfastly watched the night through. Only at dawn did she relax and grow sleepy, just as the nurses began their waking rounds.

In the morning Stella went with a nurse to a small room, which was almost filled by a large leather-covered couch. As she climbed the little wooden steps, she smelt the leather and the unfamiliar scents of disinfectants. She watched the nurses, who talked as they worked. When the cold sticky jelly touched her scalp, Stella flinched, she hated her hair being pulled. Then the nurse showed her a red rubber hat, the same colour as a bath plug. And though she promised it wouldn't hurt, it pulled her hair, and was too tight under her chin. She tugged at the chin strap, but no one noticed her discomfort. Stella watched in the mirror as the metal pegs were clipped to the hat. The pegs pulled at her hair painfully. The nurse went over to the big machine crouched next to the couch and flicked a switch. There was a low humming noise. Stella, curious and anxious, tried to see what they were doing, but they told her to keep still. Then they told her that she had to do everything they said, and that it would help her get better if she did. Again, they said it would not hurt. Stella tried to make herself comfortable on the couch, but the metal pegs still pressed hard against her skull. The nurse said, 'Close your eyes. Open your eyes. Close them, open them' for what seemed like an eternity. Stella wanted to open her eyes and see what was happening. When she did, all she could see was long sheets of paper covered with tracks of red ink coming out of the machine.

The nurse gave her some· sweets to chew on while she removed the rubber hat.

Outside, Coral sat waiting for her.

Stella could hear Coral speaking in low tones to the doctor, but she did not understand the things they were saying. Occasionally, they would look her way. A nurse came over to the bed and began to pack up Stella's things, passing comment, from time to time, on some small item. Stella jumped off the bed and ran to Coral, hanging on to her legs, but in a moment she was ushered back to change out of her pyjamas and into a dress.

That night, Coral gave her pills to take before bed, one half of a round white pill and one white capsule with an orange line around the middle. And again at breakfast, and at lunch and at bedtime the next day. From then on, came the daily question: 'Have you had your pills?' She took them. She did not ask. Stella didn't notice. How would she? She knew only that there were pills beside her plate at breakfast, lunch and dinner; that no one else swallowed those pills; that she was not permitted to have staring contests with Fiona. She slept at night, mostly. She forgot the awful dizzy feeling. She forgot the way the world spun and frightened her.

It used to be called the sacred disease, the divine disease. Now it is called the falling disease – epilepsy.

There are days when time falls away from me. I cannot answer questions you put to me. I have no words to answer with. I see things. I know there are names attached to the things. I know I know them. But the names are not there. I have no name. You have no name. You are simply there. My tongue is gaseous. Wordless.

Time brought no certainty for Coral, only a diminishing fear. Most days passed without event. Stella began to sleep through the night. There were days when Coral was anxious and watchful, days when she felt unable to leave Stella alone. But

24

as time passed she reduced her watchfulness and allowed Stella the freedoms that Fiona took for granted. With Fiona at school during the day, Stella played alone when she wasn't following Coral like a shadow.

Stella enjoyed spinning and singing. She would stand with arms spread out then hurl herself into a tight spin until she fell over on the prickly lawn. Afterwards she would lie there and watch the world roll over on itself. The sky rocked. The earth was like a basin. The rose bushes swung against the sky. Her voice followed her.

But music was another matter. She had no flair for melody, or for pitch. When she sang they walked away. They told her to take her drum a long way from the house, or they closed all the doors between her and themselves. She played it as fast as she could and as loudly, paying no attention to pitch or rhythm. She lost herself in noise. Coral regretted having given her a drum, but Stella had asked for it after meeting the little boy at the hospital in Sydney. Coral had thought, had hoped, she would soon get bored with it. But the arhythmic banging continued.

I stand in front of the mirror. I spin. I try to see myself spinning in the mirror. I see passing shadows. My arms fly out to the side like wings. I spin. I see alternating light and dark.

It is like passing my hands back and forth quickly before my eyes. It is like the fast running shadows of a line of trees as I fly overhead. There is a flickering, a flailing, a flying. The mirror captures me flailing, falling. The mirror entraps me, holds me entranced.

My arms fly outspread like galactic arms. I spin in space. I am a spiral in time.

'We've run off the map.'

Estella stops the car and leans over. 'Show me.'

'Here. See, we've run off this one, and we should be in the corner of this one.'

Olga folds the map and pulls out the road map. 'We're getting near this salt lake; we should be able to see it soon.'

Estella takes off in a cloud of dust. Grasses and shrubs stretch to the low hills that are visible to the north and west.

The lake bed is covered with salt bush and goosefoot. On the horizon is a white line of salt and beyond an uncertain wavy blue that might be water. They take photographs of one another: Estella in a Chinese-made bottle green hat, with flaps to protect the neck; Olga shaded by her Hawaiian Club cap, her hair poking through the top like a cockatoo's crest.

The water line seems to be receding. Estella stops and drinks from the water container. She looks around as she takes another gulp of water. The remains of shrubs are webbed over with salt, reminding her of old upholstery. Fine leaf hairs and grass stalks joined together in this unlikely form.

She sat playing in the sandpit, pouring buckets of water over the piles of sand she had made. Stella ran her finger around the base of the castle creating a moat. She lurched forward, her nose scraping across the top of her castle and into the moat she had made. She fell forward. Arms and legs kicked. She might have been shivering, but the day was hot.

Coral looked out the window of her bedroom as she pulled the bedspread up over the pillows, saw Stella lying face down in the sand, kicking. It looked as though she was pretending to be a fish, swimming in sand. But there was something odd about her movements.

She called out through the half-open door. No response. She dropped the cover and went out on to the verandah, calling again. Something clicked. She ran down the steps and across the lawn to the sandpit and picked up her struggling daughter.

Stella had a mouthful of sand. The top of her nose was grazed and bleeding and there was blood dribbling down her chin. Coral, holding her close, carried her inside. The colour of Stella's face was ghastly, a tinge of blue where there should have been pink.

Coral sat in the easy chair with her, wiping away as much sand as she could with her handkerchief. She prised open Stella's mouth and blew air in through her nose. Stella gasped.

Coral watched the colour return to Stella's face, and they remained there until both their hearts had stilled.

Stella couldn't remember how she'd scraped the skin off her nose. It healed quickly, and she forgot about it.

Coral said nothing, explained nothing. Stella didn't notice the gaps in her days. On this occasion, her memory stretched taut to say the words she needed; the rest was insignificant.

A woman walks out of the sea. She walks across the land that appears at her every step. As she moves she listens to the deep silence all around her and feels the stirrings of sound within her.

Soon there are other sounds from the land she walks upon. Throaty calls of early morning birds, the hissing of snakes as they slither through the grass, a dingo barking in the distance, the wind stalking through the trees.

She sings. For each word she sings, a fully grown woman springs from her mouth. Thus is the race of women formed and named. Each woman bears the name she has sung.

I sing my name song over and over, waiting.

Estella is trying to separate out the memories and the fabrications. Which parts of the past are real, which constructed from things Coral has said, or Fiona? Which is true? Does it matter? Will it ever matter? What kind of matter is memory? A matrix of threads. We follow the thread of a memory back to its source. Matrix. Matter. Mutter. Mother.

A thud brings Estella back to the world. A kangaroo has hit the side of the car. Estella stops and leans her head on the steering wheel and feels the world roll away from her. But she takes it again, and climbs out to see if the kangaroo is dead. She leans close, touches the warm body, feels the muscles twitch, but the heart is still.

'I've never hit anything before, bird or animal.'

'It's all right. You couldn't have avoided it. Do you want me to drive?'

'No. I'll drive to the next petrol pump.'

Estella's eyes are glued to the road. 'You look too, won't you?' she says in a worried tone.

'Okay.' Olga reaches over and grabs Estella's hand. 'I'll watch the left side, you watch the right. And especially look at the bushes. That's where that one sprang from.'

Estella is shaken, but drives on, squinting into the sun.

5

Estella pushes at the back door of the car, startling the grey wallaby grazing nearby. The joey tumbles into the pouch; the mother hops a little distance away, turns to look at Estella briefly, and resumes eating.

Olga is kicking her feet around in the sleeping bag trying to find a comfortable position now that she's awake. She gives up and lifts on to one elbow.

They eat a leisurely breakfast moving between reading and snatches of conversation. Olga, inspired by guilt, has pulled out a journal article; Estella is trying to identify the wildflowers near the gas stove.

It is late morning by the time Estella decides to go for a walk and, although she tries to convince Olga to come with her, Olga has other plans: sleep.

Estella sets off with a small supply of provisions: water-bottle, fruit, nuts and a tomato sandwich. She walks along the track beside the creekbed between the eucalypts and callitris – the tree that dominated her childhood. Aside from the trees, a mix of native and introduced species grow side by side. Thistles, sedges and native grasses. She stops to watch a beetle waver on a thin stalk of sedge grass. Nearby, a spider is weaving silk strands between grass stalks. The vegetation changes as she climbs higher. When she looks up the callitris seem to be leaning inwards over her.

She walks quickly but carefully. The path becomes rockier. She stops and looks out across the circular valley below. Farmland at one time, cattle and sheep treading the native orchids into the ground, the valley is protected now, except from the feet of tourists and walkers, like herself, escaping the pressures of city living. A bearded crow caws from a tree and in the distance she hears the chuckle of a kookaburra.

Mountains surround her route to the top. From time to time she stops to gaze at them. There are mosaics of trees and rocks and grass. The peaks are screens of green, red ochre and blue against the clear blue sky.

It was Sunday, golf day for Coral and Theo. Today was the play-off for trophies, and a feast of homemade delicacies to follow.

Stella sat on the lawn, her pet lizard hanging vertically from her jumper.

'It's time to go,' called Coral.

Stella, her hand placed gently over the lizard's back, climbed into the car next to Fiona. Coral set the marshmallow-topped pie on the floor of the back seat, near Stella's feet, and slammed the door. The lizard scuttled down Stella's belly, over her legs and across the pie, leaving little prints on the surface.

When they arrived at the clubhouse, Stella wandered past the table of trophies, coveting floral plates, rose-coloured wine glasses, a watch with gold trim. She went into the back room and pulled out her favourite soft drink, which glowed red, like the wine glasses, in the sun.

She took the lizard for a walk up the hill and sat, looking down, first one way towards the town, then the other. She watched the small ant-like figures walking the mown yellow fairways in a predictable pattern. Pockets of children swarmed across the patch in front of the clubhouse, separating, regrouping, converging again at the swings. She followed the track back down the hill and met Fiona, on her way up, with her friend Robyn. Stella stood by the swings for a while watching the others. She wanted a go too, but no one would mind the lizard.

After a while she walked across the course to the dry creekbed on the other side and sat on an old log, grey like the lizard. Above her she could hear the laughter of adults. She followed the laughter along the fairway to the green. Others followed behind. Each group had its own sound: the associates, the members, the mixed foursomes.

The afternoon drew on, lengthening its shadow across the creek. When Coral passed by on her second nine, Stella joined her and accompanied her to the end of the course.

Back in the clubhouse Stella had another round of Creamy Soda and watched the women set out the food. She stood over the marshmallow pie examining the faints tracks of her lizard. She said nothing.

When she reaches the summit Estella can do nothing but gaze in wonder at the view. A double ridge of mountains, like two giant snakes, extends as far as she can see. She sits eating her orange on the highest rock she can find. She remembers a story from the guide book about heavy-bodied snakes who were unable to move through over-eating. The serpentine mountains seem almost to breathe under her gaze. Beyond is the flat plain with its salt lakes extending beyond her sight into the west.

Stella climbed the ladder to the high tankstand in the paddock beyond the chookyard. The tank was still another twenty or thirty feet above her, even though she was already at least ten feet above the ground. From that height she could look for miles across the flat land. She could see the woods beyond the dam, and the paddocks that stretched for miles on this side of the road. If she turned carefully to the right she could see the machinery sheds and the poultry sheds that belonged to Kevin and Aunty Olwyn, but not their house, because her line of sight was blocked by an overflow tank.

Fiona stood at the base of the tankstand telling Stella to be careful.

'You'll hurt yourself if you fall,' she said.

'I'll jump.'

'No, don't. It's too high.'

'No it's not,' said Stella full of bravado, 'I'll land on my feet.'

She looked for a moment for a safe place to land and launched herself into the air.

Fiona screamed.

Stella did land on her feet, unhurt, apart from a few scratches on her hands.

'See,' said Stella pleased with herself.

Fiona took over as watcher when she wasn't at school and Stella, about to begin in the next few weeks, pestered Fiona about what happened there. They played schools until Fiona longed for the real thing, just for a break from Stella's demands.

Stella, carrying her little school case, ran through the back door, which slammed behind her.

Coral was standing like a sentinel in the kitchen as Stella careened through the door. 'You go back and close that door properly, without slamming it.'

Stella turned, retraced her steps and stood at the door.

'Don't just stand there, open it again,' came the voice.

She tried to open it and close it as quietly as she could, but it squeaked like a baby galah. She returned slowly to the kitchen. Coral stood by the wood stove, ignoring her. Then she turned. 'What have you been doing?'

'Playing schools with myself.' For Christmas she had been given a port, a schoolcase. She had packed her port with a lunchbox, a drink bottle, an orange and her new pencilbox and walked out the front door with it pretending to eat her lunch on the lawn.

When the day came, she was up early and dressed in tunic and shirt. Coral drove them to school. There were so many children, everyone standing in the playground. Stella held tightly to Coral's hand. Fiona had disappeared. Then the bell was rung. A big boy swung on the rope attached to the metal bell. Children appeared magically and filled the quadrangle. Coral pushed Stella towards the straggly line of children at the front, but Stella didn't want to go. She wanted to go home and stood in the line with tears running down her cheeks. She looked over at Coral who smiled and waved and gestured at her to blow her nose and wipe the tears away. Stella pulled her clean hanky from her tunic pocket. Marching music started and the teacher told the girls and boys in the front row to hold hands. Stella didn't want to hold hands with the boy next to her, but in front and behind every hand was taken. Grudgingly she reached out.

He was bigger than her and had grey knees with prickles of blood. They walked into the big room with the pink lino floor. Miss Lambert took Stella's hand and led her to her desk. Stella looked up and said, 'Where's Mummy?'

'She's gone, home.'

'But I want to go with her,' she wailed and new tears fell.

She cried until playtime. She cried all through playtime and was still crying when lunchtime came. She sat with Fiona all through lunchtime with tears falling on her sandwiches. She hated school.

6

Stella was wandering between the tents and stalls at the agricultural show. She and Coral had been to see the cakes and embroidery in the clubhouse. She had walked between the headers and tractors and rippers with Theo. And she and Fiona had visited the animal shed together, talking to the cows and squawking with the chooks, rubbing the noses of horses and putting out their hands to feel the soft horse lips search their palms for sugar. Now Stella had some time to walk around by herself, and she still had the three shillings that Coral had given her when they arrived.

She wondered if she should try to win something by putting ping pong balls down the throats of the laughing clowns whose heads turned from side to side. But she had never won with them and walked on, feeling independent and grown up.

She saw a large crowd gathered outside a tent further along the makeshift alleyway and headed for that. A man was shouting, 'Come and see it. The fantastic feather dance. See the ladies with their boas. Come on ladies and gentlemen. Come in now before you miss the show.'

Stella handed the young man in the booth her one shilling piece. She walked into the tent and sat on the grass right in front of the stage. The tent reminded her of the Royal Easter Show earlier that year when she and Fiona went to a side show where a man in black leather threw knives at a woman, just missing her each time. The tent she was in now had a stage with an old bath tub on little squat legs. At the side of the stage were folding screens, just like her grandmother had.

Music began to play and the crowd behind Stella cheered as a red feather duster appeared from behind the screen on the right side; another one, a paler pink colour, appeared from behind the left screen. There was an eruption of clapping as a woman, rather large and pale, with straw hair, danced on to the stage. Stella watched fascinated as the red woman twisted and twirled behind an umbrella of feathers. Then the pink woman emerged. She was slimmer, with dark hair, and carried three oversized pink feather dusters that fanned out in the middle. As the red one slipped behind the screen, the pink woman nimbly moved the dusters from one hand to another, somehow always keeping her body covered with feathers. Stella wondered if she had anything on behind them. The red woman came on stage again and they danced a duet as the red one climbed into the bath, shielded by the pink woman. As she clambered in there was another round of cheering and clapping, and a man shouted something from the back, which drew laughter from the crowd. The red woman now had a huge feather scarf draped over her shoulders and her body was covered by the bubbles in the bath. The woman leaned forward and extracted a huge brassiere from beneath the foam. She kicked her feet into the air causing rainbow bubbles to float down from the stage. Stella put her hands out to catch one floating down near her. Then, as the woman rose from the bath, covering herself with the scarf, the crowd roared for more. But the show was over and the crowd was ushered out.

As Stella emerged from the tent into the sunlight she stopped to listen to the man calling once again. 'Come and see it. Come and see the best show in the world, the revealing feather dance. Now ladies and gentlemen, a special offer for anyone who can blow up this balloon until it bursts. A free entry for anyone who can do this. Now who would like to see the show for free?'

Stella shot up her hand without thinking.

'Okay, young lady, up you come.'

Stella stood on the plank that had been placed between two 44-gallon drums to form an outside stage. She blew into the big red balloon until it was as round as the full moon, and with each breath she wondered, Now? When it burst, there was a lot of clapping and someone yelled, 'Bravo.'

Stella was given a free ticket to the show. She had already seen it, and as she sat in front of the stage for a second time she decided she didn't want to see it again. But she couldn't walk out the front way with all those people there, and that man again. She moved slowly on her bottom towards the edge of the tent where she could see a gap, big enough for her, between the canvas and the grass. She squeezed her body through the gap out on to the grass on the opposite side from the crowd.

Olga has decided to take over the next day's journey. She wants to return to a place she had visited during her only other stay in Australia. She describes the rock with its paintings of snakes and circles with rays, like sun– or starlight, and draws a picture of it in the dust.

'Like the fossils in that book,' Estella says, grabbing the book and flicking to the page of precambrian fossils. They could be pictures of flowers, or the iris of an eye.

Olga wonders what Christoph would have thought of her coming back here; he'd probably want to come too. The last card he'd sent had been nostalgic for their past travels – to the digs in Israel and Mexico, and the trip they'd taken to Machu Pichu. She'd enjoyed it at the time, but it was past, and the divorce was over and she didn't like belated emotions that were sent as an apology for the lack of them then.

Olga pulls the car up just off the road. 'We have to walk from here. There's no road.'

They go through the mix of trees: the acacia, eucalypts, callitris and the occasional melaleuca.

Estella smells the pine in the air and as she walks through the trees the memory of the place they called The Woods settles on her. She and Fiona had filled The Woods with stories of elves and fairies, and had built cubbyhouses and mia-mias.

They hung brightly coloured curtains and created tiny fenced-in cottage gardens such as they had seen on the tops of lolly tins.

Olga watches as Estella walks, oblivious of her gaze. She likes the way Estella moves, the way she seems to blend with the landscape. But Australia is still so foreign to her. She half expects to see snow-clad mountains rise up when they come to the top of a ridge, but instead there are walls of ribbed red rock, yellow grass and those pine trees that Estella loves so much. Her own childhood had been hemmed in by neighbourly constraint, her only adventure illicit visits to the pig and chicken farm down the road. It was close enough just to walk out the gate and go there without saying a thing. As she approached the chickens – or chooks, as Estella would call them – squawked and made a great racket, and she smelled the heavy scent of pig and chicken and her senses went wild. She loved the feel of soft feathers and the warmth of newly laid eggs in her palm and followed Frau Müller around the shed as the eggs were collected in baskets. Olga would pick one out and rub the egg, still warm through the shell, against her cheek. Now and then Frau Müller would say, 'Here hold this one,' and put a bird in her arms; the feathers tickled her nose. One day when they were feeding the pigs, Frau Müller had said, 'Put your finger in her mouth.' Olga hesitated. 'She won't bite you.' Olga felt the sucking tongue wrap itself about her finger. She didn't tell her mother, but she could still remember the sensual pull of it. Olga thought her mother spoilt everything. She didn't ever want to go home and stayed too long and inevitably her mother would arrive, furious that her rules had been broken once again, furious at Frau Müller for not sending Olga home. Olga would blatantly take the big hand of Frau Müller and walk with her to the door of the shed. Her mother hated their intimacy.

Estella stops abruptly as a bulbous rock shows through the trees ahead. She walks quickly forward and runs her hand lightly over the rock. 'It looks so soft,' she says.

'She's like the Venus of Willendorf,' says Olga, and Estella nods, feeling again the adipose rock. The rock is red, ridged with patches of pale green lichen on the south side.

'And the paintings?' asks Estella nuzzling her cheek into a crevice.

'Further on.'

The trees close in over the path again until they reach the second rock face. The surface is pink and smooth as pigskin. Two snake-like lines run parallel across the face of the rock and nearby two circles are drawn like hills on a contour map.

Estella sees the ridged serpentine mountains of the previous day. 'It's a map,' she says. 'You should have come with me yesterday.'

Stella heard something. She sat quietly in the branch of the willow tree. Then she saw it: a huge black snake. It slithered through the long grass and through the hedge and into the garden. Stella slid from her perch and climbed over the gate. She caught sight of it again and followed it through the orchard and across the potato patch where unexpectedly it veered left, then headed off through the hedge to the overgrown tennis court. Stella had to jump two more gates to get to the tennis court and, by the time she had, the snake had vanished into the long grass beyond it.

I rub ink stick against ink stone. Water and ink blend, forming a thick paste. I paint simple circles over and over again. They change. Those I began with are too careful, they wobble and wander. Those I have just done have an unexpected vitality.

I paint pictures of snakes that coil like wreathed stems. The eyes of the snakes stare out of the pictures, gleaming. They are sharp, bright, frightening.

I dream of Maenads dancing. Snakes wreathing my arms, crowning my head, never striking.

I make a Medusan mask. Snakes coil in thick strands forming braids of hair. I wear the mask on special occasions.

7

Stella fell. Children gathered round, pointing at her writhing body. Mrs White picked her up, still kicking. Someone took her home.

Stella woke, not remembering, not knowing how she got home the six miles. No one told her, though a child said something about her fainting.

Outside it is raining. A hot rain. The sky is heavy with thunder. Lightning slashes the darkness. I see an old umbrella lying against the wall, open it and run out into the rain. I feel the rain falling on my skin, its wet warmth, and I spread my arms wide.

I begin to turn, slowly, move around in a small circle. I feel raindrops splashing against my cheeks and nose. I gather speed. I turn faster. The umbrella, black and round, gathers momentum, and I am pulled by its movement. I am a dancing star, spinning through the depths of space, resonating, whirling into the centre of a black hole.

'Where are the raincoats?'

'In the plastic bag behind your seat.'

Estella leans over from the driver's seat and rummages through the pile of books on wildflowers and feminist theory. She pulls a bright yellow bag out from under the pile. 'Are you sure?' she says reaching deep into the bag.

'Yes, unless you moved them.'

'No, I didn't . . . oh here they are, right at the bottom. Here,' she says passing the purple one to Olga. Estella gets out of the car backwards and puts on the green one. 'Do you think it'll last?'

'It doesn't look too serious. It'll give us time to get things done – like the gas bottle.'

'What's wrong with it?

'The mantle, for one thing, we need a new one and some spares. And I think there's a leak somewhere. I can still smell it. The shop should be able to help us out.'

'Yes girls, what can I do for you?'

They raise their eyebrows at one another.

'We'd like a couple of spare mantles, please, to fit this lamp.'

'Anything else?'

'No thanks.'

Once out the door, Olga says, 'I wasn't going to ask him to fix this after the "girls".'

'It's so fucking infuriating. Makes you want to hit them over the head.'

They laugh and head back to the car. The rain has stopped and the sun on the wet leaves and grass is sparkling.

Estella feels the rush of pleasure she felt on her seventh birthday. Not the presents she received, but the moment of solitude. She is walking on the track to the machinery shed that led to Auntie Olwyn's. She finds a patch of dandelions and sits down, cross-legged, to make daisy-chains for her neck, wrists and ankles. What she remembers is the sun, the yellow of the flowers, the bright blue of the sky.

Estella climbs into the car, behind the steering wheel once again. 'Okay,' she says, 'let's go.'

Stella liked standing on her head. She liked rolling and rolling, over and over. She wished she could do it the way she'd seen acrobats in the circus doing it. But somehow she couldn't find the right point. Every now and then she would fluke a balance for a second or two. Or she'd stand on her head or her hands next to a wall. Even a tree would do. Stella would give anything to be able to stand upside down.

They have repacked the car and refilled the big blue water container. Estella groans each time she lifts it back into the car. 'We'd better get some petrol, there mightn't be any for a while.'

The road is bumpy and narrow but extraordinary in its changes from ochre red, to pink, to grass yellow, to an almost lavender purple.

Patches of mulla mulla give off a shimmery lilac glow in the westering sun. Close up they look more like miniature feather dusters.

'Car coming,' says Estella. A white sedan comes round the outer curve of the road. It slows. A man and a woman. The man leans out. 'There's a big hole right in the middle of the road up ahead. Watch out for it.'

'Is the canyon far?' asks Olga.

'No, but disappointing. Don't know why they make so much of it.'

'Trust a man not to notice,' says Olga angrily. 'You only have to stand near the place to feel it.'

On the slopes near the canyon are clumps of acacia trees, like the olive groves that grow near the shrines to Demeter.

You sing of the old times, singing four words, repeating them over and over. Others join in, and soon everyone is singing.

The chant becomes a mantra. We sing and we forget. We sing and we remember. We sing and we invent, creating new meanings for old stories, old chants. We reinterpret the story, the chant. The words give us one meaning. The words are:

The emus became stars.

41

We know the story behind the simple song, a story of flight and transformation. On the dusty plains of Australia and in the island world of Greece, they tell the same story:

Seven maidens in the form of birds were pursued by suitors. The maidens, as emus or doves, fled across the earth. In desperation they rose high above the earth and became stars, forming the constellation of the Seven Sisters. Their pursuers became the group of stars we know as Orion.

You can see this eternal flight if you look into the summer night sky. As winter approaches the Seven Sisters disappear over the western horizon.

Psappha wrote:
> The moon
> and the Pleiades both
> have set
> The night is half gone
> Time passes me by
> still I sleep alone

The Seven Sisters:
> Alcyone Merope Maia Taygete
> Electra Calaeno Asterope
> Daughters of Pleione.

In her grandmother's family there were seven sisters: Alice, Gertrude, Flora, Ivy, Iris, Dora and Mildred. They were all alive when Stella was born. Her only memory of Aunt Alice was of the day she nearly drowned and of her sitting on the verandah sewing a gingham dress. Fiona had a red one, the blue one was for Stella. They were decorated with white cross-stitching on the bodice and hem. Auntie Gert went to England in the twenties and never returned. She sent presents to them every year, but the clothes were always two years too big for them. Stella only met Auntie Flora once. She was old and thin and frail. Stella looked at her deeply wrinkled face. She was old, beyond imagination. The four younger sisters she knew better. They moved regularly into her life during the Christmas holidays. Auntie Ivy lived in Sydney, alone, her husband dead;

her son with children of his own. Only Ivy, Flora and Iris had married, and only the women lived on. There were no grandfathers, no great uncles. Dora and Mildred took Stella and Fiona to Balmoral, Manly, Taronga Park Zoo. Time with them was full of laughter and high-jinks. They joined in with her games and told her stories. They were young at heart, especially Dora. Mildred had something old-fashioned about her, and a haughtiness. Iris, her grandmother, was tall, majestic. She travelled to far places, and brought back presents. She told stories about adventurous and rebellious children, and about Peter Rabbit who hated porridge and put it in his pocket. Stella, who ate reluctantly, loved to listen to her. She imagined herself with pockets full of parsnips, swedes, cabbage, brussel sprouts. Iris told Stella what Coral was like when she was six, how Coral had used Iris's best umbrella to jump from the roof of the house, turning the umbrella inside out. Iris's stories sustained her imagination. The faded grandmother-purple of irises always reminded Stella of her.

The deep silence of the rocks stretches out to meet them as they approach. Olga is adjusting her hat. Estella has stopped, and is staring at the walls where symbols have been carved into the rock. There are symbols for emu and kangaroo tracks, an upsidedown U and almost perfectly round Os.

I like the shapes of the letters. I like C S O Q. I trace these shapes on the ground. I stand and spin. I draw O. I pretend to be a snake slithering through the grass. I slide along on my stomach and draw S with my body. This is the one I like to draw most. The sound of my name is embedded in this letter. When I draw C I have to be careful to stop before I return to the starting point, which is hard when I am spinning. Q is like an afterthought of O. Sometimes all my Os become Qs. I run round my Os drawing little snakes in their corners. I write your name with my body:

I write U
I write O
I write V
I write M
I write W
I write X

I write your ancient names with my body

I write 〰
I write ◎
I write ◎
I write ◇
I write ▽
I write ⋙
I write ∨

Stella and Fiona were sitting on the bed in the back room.

'Your turn,' said Fiona.

Stella wrote an X in the bottom right hand corner.

Fiona responded with an O.

They had been playing noughts and crosses for hours. Sometimes Fiona won, sometimes Stella. Often neither.

There was scrap paper all over the room, covered with double vertical and horizontal lines and an assortment of Os and Xs.

'It's like kisses and hugs at the bottom of letter,' said Stella. 'I want to be a hug for a while.'

'Okay,' said Fiona, and won the next game.

'Maybe I don't want to be a hug, after all.'

'Make up your mind. It doesn't make any difference.'

'Yes it does,' insisted Stella.

'Okay, you can be a cross again.'

'See,' said Fiona, after the next round. 'I told you it wouldn't make any difference.'

Estella is climbing the hot rock face, camera in hand. She wishes she could go higher, but her arms and body are not long enough to reach the next hold up. She wonders how they ever managed to get up there and reluctantly comes down.

Olga is sitting in the curve of a pink-grey rock that seems to enfold her. A safe place, an entrance perhaps. Estella joins her. Both are carrying bags, women's bags, with their small, intimate and idiosyncratic personal belongings. Estella opens her bag and pulls out a notebook:

I feel a sense of awe at being surrounded by these rocks. Some animal has been here recently and has dug for water under the gravel and sand. There is a small hole with a pool of wetness at its base.

At some time water must have flowed here. Where the water has been it is rounded and soft, like a woman's body. The colours, too, are soft: pink and mauve and grey with a touch of yellow.

The rock immediately in front of me is like smooth buttocks. A few dried leaves have settled into the base of the crack, like a star.

Just beyond the grey-pink entrance is a shallow cave. It's like no other place I've ever seen. Like some sort of vulval entrance to a womb. Sharp red rocks falling like a curtain. Sitting inside it is a thoroughly different experience from the pink folding rock. The cave is a luminescent ochre-red. Sharp and powerful. It's as though the rock has taken on some kind of pain; the pain of childbirth perhaps. It's that kind of power.

The rocks here are layered, like an upsidedown slate floor that's been peeled back to reveal yet another slate floor beneath it. Beside the layered bits are long crystalline rocks hanging vertically around a narrow opening. Who knows where the opening goes, and how far.

Sitting at the edge of the cave, when you look up, all you can see is sky, blue and clear now after this morning's rain. And looking straight across, the rocks climb up to a kind of plateau, where eucalypts are perched.

I would like to stay here, to curl up in the embrace of these rocks, but somehow it seems irreverent.

45

Olga and Estella stand up to leave. They step through the folding rocks and walk along the sandy creekbed, which opens out to a straggly avenue of eucalypts with bulbous growths on their trunks. A small mauve star-flower blooms among the dry grasses.

I am learning to spell. It gives me power over these words. I cast the letters in a certain order. They fall and form a word. They fall and form the sound of a name. Each has a certain sound, a certain look, a certain shape.

I cast a spell over the words I need, I want. I name the world. In naming, in spelling, I catch the world into my net. The world takes on a certain shape when I name the objects in it. The world takes on a different shape when my spelling differs from others. I do not hold the same world at these times. I use the forms of some letters.

I have a spell for my name. It is simply S. I have a spell for your name. It is O. It is XX.

8

Estella is leaning over the billy watching to see if it is ready. She grasps the handle and swings it backwards three times. Olga is pulling at a string, attempting methodically to disentangle the knotty bundle. It reminds her of the painstaking cleaning of shards; eventually the string separates into three strands. She ties it around the box of books she has brought with her, acknowledging finally that she won't be looking at them.

The drive is bumpy and the road winds up and down and around the sides of hills. Estella is reminded of a painting by Remedios Varo of a spiral mountain and wonders whether they will ever arrive. They locate arbitrary destinations on the map, but neither knows whether these places will be where they want to stop.

They pull up in a creekbed. 'Why don't we camp here?' says Estella. 'Running water, a nice flat space. And no pine trees,' she adds, since Olga has been complaining of them all afternoon.

'I'd rather go back up there, where the road turned off. You can see it from here. I think there were campsites and fireplaces.'

'Okay.'

They camp above the creek, where blackened pieces of wood indicate previous campers, previous fires.

Olga unpacks the car, and Estella goes off to look for firewood. She returns with a huge bundle and drops it near the stone ring that marks the fireplace. She is covered with bits of bark and dried leaves. She places the sticks carefully and lights a match to it. The leaves flame, and soon the smaller twigs are also alight.

In tidying up the back of the car Olga has found her knitting. She pulls it out and knits while Estella prepares dinner on the open fire. Estella watches as the fingers move in a pattern as long as the history of humanity. Her grandmother had made a jumper for her, not long before she died, which Stella had worn and worn. In her mind she reconstructs the patterns: a central vertical line of diamonds inside a wide chevron; to each side a square net of crosses in moss stitch; beyond that a double helix. A ridge of purl marked the beginning of a wide band that also had cables running through the band. Estella picks up a stick and begins drawing it in the dust.

'What's that?' asks Olga.

'A knitting pattern,' says Estella.

'I thought you were drawing some kind of map.'

'It's a jumper Iris made for me, from a pattern she said she'd learnt from my grandfather. He was a sea captain and his family for centuries had been knitters and sailors along Scotland's west coast.'

Olga puts down her knitting and points at a chevron and diamond. 'That's an old motif of the bird goddess,' she says, 'and so are crosses.'

Estella has raised her hands forming a diamond shape with thumbs and forefingers. 'We used to do this at demonstrations,' she says, recalling the puzzled faces of onlookers. 'Marriage lines was what Iris called them.'

'Pottery was probably invented by women,' says Olga, 'and it's mostly women who knit. You wouldn't change your symbolic system just because your medium changed, you'd try to figure out ways of reproducing them in the new form. These so-called marriage lines are really images of cunts.'

'To think that my stern Presbyterian grandfather and all his kin knitted cunts on to their jumpers!'

My fingers move in anciently remembered ways as I knot the cord. Such knots formed the basis of writing in China and were filled with sacred meaning. Cutting the knot destroys the memory of the pattern, severs the thread to the centre of the labyrinth.

Fiona and Stella were gathering together all the sticks they could find for the bonfire. It was Empire Day, and Coral and Iris had taken them over to the woods and together they built a pyre. Fiona and Stella collected while Coral and Iris built.

'We want big bits first, then smaller ones, and then twigs,' ordered Iris.

Stella tried to drag a piece that was too big for her. Coral came to help her. When they finished they had a cone-shaped bonfire ready for the night's fireworks.

Theo arrived and added old tyres to the pile. 'That'll give it a bit a smoke,' he said, dusting his hands on his trousers.

When it was dark, Theo put on his red jumper, which he always wore on cracker night, and they drove over to The Woods, well supplied with matches and some extra newspaper. The car headlights gave them some light. Theo was fixing the unlit catherine wheel to a tree. Stella was running around with sparklers in each hand, singing and dancing and sweeping them around in circles and spirals and figures of eight. A tom-thumb went off behind her and she jumped with fright. Theo lit the fire and they all sat back to watch it catch. They sat on a log and watched as Theo lit the series of rockets lined up slightly away from the fire. Stella was delighted by the explosion of colour that burst from each rocket as it soared into the sky. Like a myriad stars falling to earth. Then there was the fountain of light and the final treat was the spinning catherine wheel.

You are teaching me to do cartwheels, showing me how to place my hands one after the other. You tell me to let my legs float through the air, trailing my body. I do this many times. I go over and over and over again.

49

When you demonstrate, your body is long and straight. It turns over, wheeling, forming a perfect circle. You move easily from hands to feet and hands to feet again.

I try to imitate you, but my body bends in the middle, and my feet do not rise perpendicularly over my head. My legs drag through the air, though I enjoy the sensation of being inverted.

I sit in the shade and rest while you tell me of Saint Catherine: she too did cartwheels. Involuntarily. Tied to a cartwheel, she was spun and spun and spun until they thought she was dead. But she was not. They set fire to the wheel and spun it again. The people watched the spinning fireworks, the catherine wheel as it came to be known.

The wheel broke, but she was still alive. Catherine's hold on life was intense. Finally they beheaded her, and from the cut flowed milk.

In the middle of the night. Coral came in, woke them and said she had to go to Melbourne. Iris was sick.

'Don't dawdle,' she said as Stella struggled into her dressing gown and slippers. 'You're only going to Auntie Ollie's.'

'Can't we come too?'

'No.'

They drove the short distance in silence and stood waving at the gate with their aunt.

'Look,' said Stella. She pointed at a star that was hurtling earthward, but no one else saw it fall.

'What was your grandmother like?' asks Estella, remembering how much she had missed Iris. 'Did you like her?'

Olga stares at the fire for a while, seeing the grumpy old woman who had come to stay with them a few months before her death. 'No, I didn't. She was so deeply sad I felt I could never reach her. She didn't play games with me or do the things other children's grandmother's seemed to do. It's only now that I have a sense of how she might have felt. I see it being replayed in my mother. The kind of sadness that drowns the person, that sucks energy. A bitterness against the way life had treated her. No, I couldn't like her. It just gave my mother and I another thing to fight about.'

'What happened?'

'She died. They wouldn't let me go to the funeral. It was as though she'd never been there. No one cried, no one said anything.'

'No, we didn't either. We never talked about death. Even the death of animals. When my dog, Sally, was gone after coming home from holidays, I wasn't told that she had been put down. I wasn't even supposed to notice. I didn't for two days, then inevitably I asked Coral where she was. I was told that she had died of old age while we were away. While she was dying I'd been enjoying myself and I felt terrible about it. But I couldn't cry. After all, I hadn't noticed for two days. But then, a year or so later, when my puppy – a sheepdog – was run over in front of me, I cried and cried. That death bred no resentment, no long-standing sense of not having been there at the right time. I had nightmares about another dog too – a small scrawny brown dog that seemed never to grow beyond toy-dog size – that disappeared and was thought to have been lost in The Woods. I remember searching for her. For years I thought of her whenever I went to The Woods. I imagined hearing her barking and dreamt that she had lived on peas and died a slow and painful death. Fifteen years later Coral told me that she had been shot because of her irritating high-pitched bark. That was probably Sally's fate too, but I've never asked.'

When Christmas came that year Stella asked, 'Where's Iris?'

No one answered. Fiona grabbed Stella's hand and dragged her from the room.

'Don't you know?'

'Know what?' asked Stella in turn.

'About Iris.'

'What about Iris?'

'She died.'

'When?'

'That night we went to Auntie Ollie's.'

'How did you know?'

'Jill told me. She said, "I just heard about your grand-mother." I didn't know what she was talking about. She said that Iris fell off a tram backwards in St Kilda and died.'

'But that was ages ago, in the winter. How come no one told us?'

'I don't know.'

'When I go to Fitzroy Street Iris is always there. She's like a flower broken by the wind.'

9

Shearing time. Stella's favourite time of year, except for summer holidays. She loved the shearing. She spent whole days hanging around the woolshed. The smell. Nothing could beat the smell of newly shorn wool. She covered herself in it. She climbed high into the shed, and hung from the steel rafters. And when she couldn't hang on any longer she let her grip loosen and dropped into the bin of wool scraps. It meant she could do anything. She hung by her legs and swung around and over and along the bars. She imagined being a monkey, and sorely missed the tail that might once have been there. Sometimes she dived, swallow-like from the end of the bin, landing on face and belly, her nose in the wool.

She watched the wool pressers turn mounds of soft wool into hard bales. She watched the shearers with their deft movements shear a sheep in a matter of minutes, pushing the thin sheep down the wooden slide into the dark pens beneath the shed. And she watched as Coral picked through the wool, classing it, directing it to be put into a particular bin for baling. Stella wasn't permitted in the fleece bins. A pity, she thought, since they looked so soft, like tangible clouds.

Shearing meant activity, the strange faces of travelling shearers, and something definite to do after school. The winter coldness seemed to dissipate with the activity and the warm greasy smell of the shed. It was in her hair and skin for weeks at a time.

Weekends brought long days of droving flocks of sheep from the outer paddocks to the woolshed.

'G'wayback,' Stella called to the dog. And Krisi was off, rounding up the sheep. She loved watching her do that. First Krisi circled the flock of sheep, then she would run back the other way, then retrace her steps. The sheep were so confused by this that they began to take the middle path and headed straight for where Kimmy, her cousin, and Stella waited, one each side of the gate. As the sheep passed through the gate a few individuals leaped in an arc – of joy? wondered Stella. Meanwhile Krisi would be off, barking and pursuing the occasional renegade sheep. The last one leapt the imaginary obstacle and Stella quickly shut the gate and was after them. They were going too fast. We've got to slow them down, she thought, they're too hard to control at this pace. Then she noticed Kimmy signalling Krisi to head them off at the corner.

'Phew.'

They had a long hike ahead of them. Eleven miles. Though most of it wouldn't be too difficult since it ran between fenced paddocks. It'll be okay so long as they turn the right way on to the main road, she thought.

Kimmy waited for Stella. The flock had settled into a steady pace. They discussed the tactics they would try. 'It's tricky,' said Kimmy, 'with all that open space and trees too. Why don't you go ahead and stand to the left of the turn, and make lots of noise. And I'll stay behind them with Krisi and send her to you if they get away.'

'Okay,' nodded Stella, who then ran round to the right of the flock and took up her steadying position for the time being.

The first turn worked perfectly. The sheep seemed to smell their direction. And fortunately the traffic was light, only a couple of locals in no hurry to get about their business. They lifted their hats as they drove past slowly, at a pace that wouldn't scare the sheep. Everything was going well. Their pace was slow, but moving steadily. The sheep would have stopped to graze, given half a chance, but there wasn't time for that. Stella walked along beside the flock, lost in her thoughts.

54

The stick she carried swinging about her like the jumping, dancing thoughts that kept her amused.

'Stella.' She heard the frustrated cry of Kimmy, and turned to see him indicating the home lane coming up on the left.

'Oh no,' she muttered. 'Send Krisi round to head them off,' she yelled as loud as she could. Krisi took off. But so did the sheep, startled by the sudden activity.

It was on.

The sheep followed the fence and turned into the lane. Krisi wouldn't be able to head them off now. 'Come be'ind,' she yelled several times, in imitation of Theo, to make sure.

The flock had changed from a quiet, slightly straggly round mass, to a fast-moving, long, narrow line.

Stella climbed over the fence, Krisi at her heels, and headed off across the paddock. She saw a flash of white out of the corner of her eye and looked round to see Coral's car crossing the paddock further up. Stella slowed her pace and watched Coral leap out of the car barely before it had stopped, get over the fence and jump about like a St Vitus' dance victim before the approaching flock. The sheep slowed, paused for a moment, confused, and headed back the other way.

Stella and Coral met half way.

'You looked so funny, jumping about like that,' giggled Stella.

'Maybe, but it stopped them. Get away from you, did they? One of you should have been stationed there.'

'I know, I forgot,' she said.

'You'll be right now,' added Coral, 'I'll meet you as you come past the front of the house, and come down to the shed with you. All right?'

Stella nodded.

The rest was easy. Theo and the men saw them coming and stationed themselves strategically between the flock and the yards.

'Have any trouble?' asked Theo, winking almost imperceptibly at Coral.

'No, not much. But they got away at the home lane.'

He nodded and walked away to speak with the men who were leaning over the fence, smoking.

'How did you spend your time,' asks Estella, 'as a child, other than your visits to the chook farm? Did you go to concerts?' she asks, thinking of Vienna's musical culture.

'Not much, just occasionally with my father. Mostly I read. I'd lock my door, so my mother couldn't come in and take my books away. I'd read for hours. Sometimes friends came over, and then my mother would be all sweetness, until they left. And in my early teens I spent a lot of time in the Naturhistorische Museum, the one with the Venus of Willendorf. I was fascinated by these old things and it was that that took me into archaeology.'

Olga had gone to Berlin to study. She remembers the first time she saw Nefertiti, that one hard eye staring out of a flawless face, and the contrast with the joyful pig goddess that stood in the next glass cabinet. It reminded her of Frau Müller. She had often gone over to East Berlin to see the Ishtar Gate. But what fascinated her most were the different conceptions of time. Counting by the moon, notchings of lunar or menstrual calendars on bone; the base-60 system of the Sumerians that remains with us; and the complicated 52-year cycle of the Aztecs.

'Archaeology has changed quite a bit since then,' says Olga. 'These days they take more account of women's contribution, but the popular consciousness still finds it easier to believe in men from another planet bringing culture than that women invented it.'

I draw the shapes of numbers on the ground. I draw 3 6 9 and 0. Sometimes I draw 8 or I draw it on its side ∞, which is no number at all and every number.

If I stand on the other side of a 6 I see a 9. This tells me something about the way numbers change. They are different from words. Words can shape the world and words can have several meanings, but words cannot be transformed as easily as numbers. An additional letter, or several, may make a new word and it may not. Any number, or any number of additional numbers, always makes a new number. Even half a number, or merely a point, or a zero.

Estella looks at the odometer and mentally subtracts. 'We've only gone nine kilometres. I feel as if I've driven ninety. These rocks and creeks really slow you down. I need a break.'

They pull up near a shallow stream of water. Olga half falls out of the car. There is a steep ridge of horizontal rock to the west.

'I'm so hot,' says Estella removing her hat and dipping it into the water. As she returns it to her head, water spills down over her face and neck. 'Aah, that's better.' She looks up at Olga. 'Hello, galah.' She is laughing and pointing at Olga's combination of pink sleeveless T-shirt and grey shorts. 'All you need is a galah feather, then they'll recognize you for sure.'

'And what are you?'

'A mallee ring-neck.'

Estella fills the drinking bottle with fresh water. 'Want a drink?'

'Mmn, yes please.' Water dribbles down her chin as she drinks. 'It's nice and cold.'

'Better than the hot Coke.'

They sit on the warm rocks for a while staring at the stones at their feet. Estella's eyes move to the wall of ochre following the diagonal strata of rock. Then she looks at Olga. 'You ready to go on again?'

'Yes, okay.'

They head back to the car. Estella bends to pick something up. 'There you are, you can be a real galah now.' She hands a small pink-tinged feather to Olga.

The road is barely more than a track. They have seen no other car for two days. As they bump along their bottoms leap from the seat now and then. Estella watches the changing scenery in the rear-vision mirror.

Olga has poked the feather through the adjustable strap of her crownless cap.

A group of galahs lifts, screeching from a branch over-hanging the track.

'There, look, they've come to greet you, Ol'galah.'

They screech and laugh and jostle about.

'D'you think they understand us?'

Olga doesn't answer, instead, mid-bump she says, 'I think these roads were intended for kangaroos.'

'Fiona, come and play with me,' demanded Stella, when Fiona came home from boarding school for her holidays.

'No, I want to read my book.'

'You're always reading.'

'You could too.'

'But it's boring.'

'No it's not. There are all these interesting stories about other girls in other places.'

'But I can't read that, it's too hard.'

'It's about this girl, Jill,' says Fiona, ignoring Stella's pleas. 'She's got a pony and she's going to ride it in the show jumping. She's a really good rider . . . I wish I had a horse. I would build jumps.'

'So do I,' agreed Stella. 'It'd be better than reading about it. Let's ask Mum.'

'All right.'

Two weeks later Theo and Stella went to pick up Lord Bambi. A racehorse. They were on their way home and singing, 'It's a long way to Tipperary', which Theo always sang when they were driving somewhere together – '. . . *it's a long way to go,*' they sang – when there was a loud crash against the cabin roof. Stella glanced backwards to see the horse on its hind legs and then he disappeared.

Theo stopped as quickly as possible. Lord Bambi lay a few hundred yards back on the roadside. 'Stay there,' said Theo as he got out. But Stella couldn't. She climbed down and went over to where the horse lay. She looked at him, he seemed perfect, unscratched, but he couldn't move. Then she saw his eyes. There was pain in those eyes.

Theo walked back to the truck and lifted the rifle from its secure place. 'Go and sit in the truck, Stel. Please,' he said.

She heard the bang.

Driving home, with the back of the truck empty and feeling defeated, she could not forget the look in the horse's eyes. She wanted to cry every time she thought about it.

They drove in the front gate where Coral and Fiona were waiting expectantly.

'Where's the horse?'

'He fell off the truck.'

There was silence at the dinner table that night.

They are sitting under a tree with a lunch of last night's left overs – cold rice and tomatoes through it, some feta cheese and tahini. Estella lifts the feta cheese towards her and sniffs it. 'I think this feta's dead. I can't eat it. The crows can have mine.' She walks over to the bank and begins breaking it.

'They can have mine too,' echoes Olga.

The creekbed is covered with little spheres of white cheese.

A crow swoops on to the branch of the eucalypt.

'Now, how did it know there was food here?' asked Estella. 'Can birds smell?'

'I don't know, but birds have very good eyes. They were always credited with knowing things long before others. And they were messengers.'

The crow darts towards the cheese, picks it up and flies back to the other side of the creekbed to feed a couple of noisy youngsters.

'Poor mothers,' says Olga, 'babies always want to be fed and they always scream. I don't think I could have stood it.'

The mother crow keeps up her relay, to the ever-increasing noise of the fledgelings.

'I've never been all that fond of crows,' says Estella, 'because I grew up hearing that they were a pest, and I saw what they did to sheep.'

'What do they do?'

'Pick the eyes out of them.'

I draw circles which I divide using other circles. The geometry of the circle is the basis of our existence here, in this valley: the architecture, our measurements of time. The dwellings spiral out from the centre in four rings. It resembles the cochlea of the inner ear, the shell of the nautilus, the shape of our galaxy, the passage of time. We remember ancient forms: stone circles in Britain; carved stone temples in Malta and Ireland; the labyrinth of Knossos.

Stella sat on the grass with Mary who had a jam sandwich that Stella wanted, and so gave her a Vegemite and lettuce one in exchange. Stella's pills rolled along the bottom of her lunch box.

'What's that?' asked Mary. 'What're they for?'

'I don't know, they're just my pills. Do you want one? Here, I'll have the long one, you can have the half one.'

'What do they taste like?'

'They're all right. They don't taste awful like those vitamin pills. Here, try it.'

'Okay then.'

Mary crunched on the half white tablet, turned a sour face towards Stella and motioned to her to pass the cold drink bottle.

'Didn't you like it?' asked Stella incredulously.

'Yuk, they're horrible.'

Stella put the capsule into her mouth and tried to show off by swallowing it without water. The gelatine dissolved and she too was pulling faces and reaching for the drinking bottle.

She gulped some and spluttered, 'The inside of those others is worse. I've never tasted the inside before.' She could still taste the sharpness of her tongue, despite the orange cordial.

Coral had not talked of epilepsy, protecting Stella from indiscretion. And Stella asked few questions. Though there were times when she asked, like that afternoon after school, after Mary's question. While admitting giving away her pills, she had asked Coral what they were for. She'd seen sharing her pills as a proof of friendship and didn't understand the wrath it provoked from Coral. But there was one question she remembered asking, about the S4 code on the label. 'Poison,' said

60

Coral, and although Estella now knew that wasn't right, she had wondered how she was able to take poison and survive.

'There used to be an ochre mine here,' says Estella. 'See that wall there, that must have been part of it.'

Estella gets up and walks toward the huge red wall of rock that rises vertically from the creekbed. When Olga looks up, Estella is half way up the wall, standing on a narrow ledge that looks hardly wide enough to hold her. Sometimes she's like a mountain goat, walking straight up walls of rock, as secure as an animal in its element.

Estella's brightly coloured clothes mark her out against the red of the rock and the blue sky just above. What if she were to have a fit right now? Sometimes she behaves as though she were invulnerable. Olga gets up and walks over towards the wall. She restrains herself. Like Coral before her, she does not say come down. She just waits, watching dragonflies hover over the pool of water at the base of the rock. Estella walks nimbly down a narrow path and leaps into her arms at the bottom.

'Hello, Ol'galah,' she laughs. 'You should be able to fly to the top.'

'My wings are too sore today. I think I'll go and live in an old galah's home, and sleep forever.'

'Look at my hands.' Estella's hands are red with ochre powder. 'It's so soft, it comes off.'

'Did you see the dragonflies?'

'No.'

'See. Red ones and blue ones with orange wings. And there was a skink on this rock just before you came down.'

After a stretch of winding between gorges, the car is now crawling along a creekbed that leads out to the open plain. They have passed a turn-off to a nearby homestead, and go on to be well away from the prying eyes of strangers. 'I'm getting tired,' says Olga after a long silence. 'Why don't we camp in this creekbed?'

'Fine by me.'

'But I'd like to go a bit off the track.'

'There won't be anyone along here, not now.'

'I'd prefer it.'

'Okay. How about under that tree over there,' Estella says pointing along the winding creekbed. Let me go and have a look.' She leaps out and checks the ground for ant nests. 'Looks fine,' she yells.

Olga drives slowly towards the tree. As she is coming over the final small rise of sand, she stops, accelerates, sprays sand, and stops again in a deep rut. 'Bloodyfuckinghell!' she yells, hitting the steering wheel.

'Have another go,' says Estella. The wheels spin again. 'Do you want me to have a go?' she asks calmly, hoping she can get it out.

'Yes, all right.'

Estella tries to get it into low four-wheel drive. She puts it into reverse and moves the gear. 'Here goes.' She presses the accelerator, moves about an inch, and stops. 'Fuck!'

'Try again.'

'But it didn't move. It feels like it's stuck.' She climbs out and looks under the car. 'Have a look here, this bit is stuck in the sand. We'll have to dig it out. Why didn't you put it into the low gear? That's what it's for.'

'I thought it'd be okay in the normal one. Anyway don't blame me, you told me it was okay.'

'I was thinking more about ant nests than getting bogged. I hope we can get it out. Can you unpack the back while I start digging?'

Estella is under the car with the spade. Arcs of sand fly over her shoulder. After twenty minutes she has cleared it. 'I'll have another go,' she says. 'Can you watch and tell me what's happening. If I'm getting anywhere.' She climbs back into the car, starts the engine and slowly removes her foot from the clutch. The car moves, she is feeling pleased with her efforts, and then the wheels spin again, and the car jolts to a stop. 'Fuckshitbloodyhell!' she screams.

The wheels are in even deeper this time, and the car is on a slight angle on the edge of the slope.

Estella is back under the car. Olga is digging with her hands on the other side. 'We need stones and bits of wood, to pack under the sand. I'll keep digging, if you'll do that.' Estella is covered in sand. She is looking at the underbelly of the car, worrying about the angle. What if the car fell sideways. She'd be dead. Broken neck or broken back. She scrambles out, suddenly worried that it could happen. She joins Olga who is collecting rocks and wood.

'It's too dangerous, it could fall. We'll have to get some of these rocks in before we can do anything else.'

'Did you see the sign to the homestead at that junction?'

'Yes, I think it said two kilometres. How far back do you think that was?'

'Oh, about a kilometre or two. Perhaps we should walk there.'

'It's too late now, it'll be dark soon. Why don't we wait till morning? I think we should sleep in the creek tonight. I don't trust sleeping in the car on that angle.'

'Okay.'

'What's for dinner?'

'Baked beans.'

'Fancy us getting bogged on Christmas Eve.' Estella slumps against the tree trunk, watching the sky darken. Olga opens the tin of beans and plonks it in front of Estella. 'Aren't you going to heat it?'

'No. I can't be bothered. I just want to go to bed. I'm so tired.'

Estella digs into the tin with her spoon. 'Not bad, considering.' They laugh.

They make up their bed on the sand. Estella can't sleep. Mozzies bite at her ear. In the tree nearby a jackhammer cricket is doing its best to keep her awake, and the moon is too bright. She is also worrying about the car. Even if they walk, will there be anyone home? She decides to have another go at digging on the other side of the car in the morning.

10

I believe I have the run of the universe. All experience is held within. Everything that is possible takes place within me first. My body is a replica of the universe: within it are minute replicas on hands, feet, ears, nose, eyes.

Each carries within her the seed of future generations, and in her mind the seed of future actions, future realities, dreams that will burst into flower. The germination of a thought may mean the creation of a whole new world, or the loss of an old one.

Each is a creatrix in her own right.

It was nearly Christmas. Theo had promised to take them Christmas tree hunting that afternoon.

Stella and Fiona sat on the bonnet of the Landrover as Theo drove slowly through The Woods. It was their job to look out for a suitable tree. It had to be fairly young, no more than about seven feet, and its shape had to be just right.

Stella enjoyed tree hunting, partly because it meant it was nearly Christmas and all that it entailed – presents, parties, staying up late and the pleasure of Christmas dinner – and partly because the hunting meant going further into The Woods than usual. It was darker here and the trees grew more thickly. She ducked, avoiding a branch. The soft callitris needles brushed her face. Despite the heat, it was cool in The Woods. There were occasional circles of light between the trees, but mostly it was shady. Twigs and leaves crackled as the vehicle wound its way deeper into The Woods.

'There's one,' shouted Fiona. Stella had forgotten about looking.

Theo pulled up and said, 'Where?'

'Over there,' Fiona pointed.

'Hmm, yes, it's a nice shape, might be just a bit tall.'

'No it won't. It's just right,' Fiona said.

Theo stood next to the tree measuring it against himself. It was about three feet taller than him.

'We could cut a bit off the trunk I suppose. All right. Bring me the axe, but be careful, it's sharp.'

As he chopped little chips flew all around him. Stella moved back a bit. She watched carefully as he moved round the trunk. With each stroke the needles quivered. He was nearly through. Stella began to lay silent bets with herself about which would be the final stroke. The next one, she said to herself, but no – not yet. Just before the axe hit for the last time she cried out, 'This one. Timber.' And the tree wavered and fell in an arc to the ground.

They rushed forward to help carry it to the vehicle. Fiona took the top end and Theo the trunk. Stella carried the middle part.

'Now, stand it upright,' said Theo, 'and I'll tie it onto the back here.' He pulled out a rope and began to tie the tree firmly. The trunk rested on the tow-bit and the top of the tree poked up over the roof.

Fiona and Stella perched on the bonnet again and they proudly headed for home. The tree rustled with every movement.

'That's a big one,' said Coral when they arrived.

'I found it,' said Fiona, 'it's not too big.'

They carried it along the dark hallway into the living room, placing it into a bin of dirt. The needles shuddered in the breeze from the cooler. Stella anticipated the familiar tinkle of the decorations.

The tree took up the entire corner of the living room, almost touching the ceiling.

'See,' said Fiona, 'it's just right, isn't it?'

Everyone nodded.

'Where are the decorations?' asked Fiona.

'Here,' said Coral, passing her a large cardboard box.

The annual ritual began.

'Stella will you help me put the paper round the bin?' Coral held a large piece of bright red wrapping paper in her hands. 'You crawl round the back and stick it together.'

Coral held it at the front and passed the sticky tape to Stella.

'It doesn't meet properly at the back,' Stella said.

'That doesn't matter. No one will see it. Just stick the paper to the bin.' Coral added, 'Pull it down on the right.'

'Okay.'

Fiona had already sorted out which decorations she wanted to use and had begun to hang them.

Stella started to help her.

'No, not the ones from that pile, silly,' said Fiona, 'just the other ones.'

'But that won't be enough.'

'Yes it will. You always want to overdo it. This year it's going to look artistic.'

Stella didn't know what to do. 'I'll do the ones at the top.'

'All right, but you have to do what I say.'

'Oh, okay.'

'I'll need the kitchen stool to reach the next bit.' Stella said, 'Come and help me bring it in.'

They went into the kitchen and dragged out the heavy blue wooden 'stool'. It was too big to be a stool, and too small for a table, but it was used to stand on to change light globes, to pin up hems, and they always sat on it when Coral cut their hair.

Stella climbed on to the stool but still couldn't reach.

'I need a chair as well.'

Fiona brought the chair and passed it up.

'Hold it,' said Stella climbing up, agile as a possum.

She pressed one hand against the wall and with the other

tied the red Santa to the top of the tree. The needles bent over with the weight.

'Is that all right?'

'Can you straighten it?' asked Fiona peeved.

'I don't know, I think it's too heavy.'

'Move it down then.'

'I can't. I can't reach to do that.'

'Try.'

Stella stretched a bit further, wobbled and grabbed the chair.

'No. You do it. You're taller,' said Stella, knowing that Fiona's fear of heights would make her give in.

'It'll do.'

Stella climbed down, victorious.

Estella spends half the night lying awake. She watches as stars seem to gather and disperse before her, as though they were not separated by unimaginable light years.

Conversations come and go like clouds, merging with images of wheels spinning and sand flying. Huge wheels spinning and all the women falling off the wheel at different times and places. She sees women standing at the centre – in Greece, Anatolia, Old Europe, Australia – who became peripheral and fell. Fathers and sons rushed in to fill the void at the centre, pushing the women further out. But the fathers and sons had to follow threads to the centre and back. Estella opens her eyes and draws pictures with stars, joining the dots. A star falls and out of habit she makes a wish.

And then there are the trees, she thinks: Christmas trees, Trees of Knowledge, Trees of Life. And now – trees to cut down. When did they forget? Was the change of landscape part of it – the absence of the familiar – callitris had to substitute for the fir tree, but the emotional resonance had gone. The symbols of Christmas persisted on Christmas cards with snow, candles, fir trees and Santa Claus with his reindeer

The words of a Christmas song are suddenly in Estella's mind:

Rudolph the red-nosed reindeer
had a very shiny nose . . .

She hums her way through though she can't remember the
rest of the words. She remembers how, on Christmas Eve,
before bed, Coral always put out Christmas cake and a bottle
of beer for Santa, and carrots for the reindeer, just as the
people of Samiland did, who had fed the spirits of Christmas
in this way for millennia.

She also remembers worrying that Santa would not complete his rounds, after all if he started in England, it being so
much nearer the North Pole, it'd be late by the time he reached
Australia. And she worried that he might have trouble getting
down the chimney. But the snow and the reindeer posed no
such problem, she accepted the mismatch of realities. She
knew he existed. She had seen him once, one Christmas
morning when she was very young. She, Fiona and Coral had
eaten breakfast with him on the lawn. Her belief persisted
until Fiona proved, beyond all doubt, the trick. Even then, the
memory tugged at her and was so much more powerful than
the pull of rationality. But Fiona was too embarrassed by her
gullibility and protected Estella from her own power to
believe in the unbelievable.

It is light when she falls asleep.

Olga wakes, as an early bird stalks through the leaves and
bark making rustling sounds. The sun shining through the
leaves of the eucalypt nearby makes a dappled pattern on the
ground. Estella is still tired as she's hardly slept. But Olga rolls
over chuckling to herself, 'Happy Christmas, possum,' she
says, taking Estella in her arms. 'A big christmas cuddle for my
digging goanna.'

'I'm so stiff,' groans Estella sleepily, folding herself into
Olga. 'But I decided while you were snoring that I'd dig some
more this morning. An unconventional Christmas, eh!' she says
stroking the skin. 'But before I do that . . .' her fingers running
along the inside of a thigh, 'Nice to have a double bed again
. . .' and their mouths are wet on one another.

Eventually they pull themselves out of their creek bed and Estella puts the billy on for some tea, picks up the spade and resumes digging.

'Okay, moley, it's time for breakfast,' calls Olga. 'Don't kill yourself. We can always walk.'

'I know, but what if no one's there?'

'There will be, it's Christmas morning. Who ever goes out on Christmas morning?'

Estella knocks the top off her boiled egg and eats.

'Maybe there really isn't any point in me digging more. Why don't we collect a few more rocks and pieces of wood and then head off.'

'Yes, it's going to be stinking hot today, judging by the temperature now.'

On Christmas morning Stella always woke early and would rummage through the pillow case for the long-awaited presents from Santa. There was more excitement in them than those from aunts and cousins.

That Christmas a two-wheeled bicycle leaned up against the wall. Santa must have received her letter after all. She had addressed it to: Santa Claus, The North Pole, and had written URGENT in the top left-hand corner.

She crept into Fiona's room, waking her with a well-judged 'accidental' noise and told her to get up. Together they walked the bicycle out the front door, down the steps and out to the drive. But the gravel made the bike slide. They crossed the road and headed towards The Woods where the track was hard-baked earth. Fiona held the bicycle while Stella pedalled.

'Don't let go,' screamed Stella.

Fiona ran and Stella pedalled. It was hard work for Fiona. She soon suggested they go back.

As they approached they heard loud music. Stella realised the sound could only be from the house. But who could play the piano like that. And what piano?

Fiona and Stella walked in and saw Coral sitting at the piano, also pedalling.

'It's a pianola,' cried Fiona.

'Santa must have got your letter too,' said Stella.

They have been walking for an hour. They have just left the creekbed and have reached the boundary of the homestead. The land here is flat and open. Sheep have trodden down all the native plant growth, and the earth is covered with sheets of dry yellow grass.

'A fire would rage through here. Nothing to stop it.' Estella is thinking about the grass fires they had had at home. She remembers being covered in soot after running along the edge of the paddock with a wet bag hitting at sparks that seemed to combust spontaneously with each draught of wind. 'We used to burn off to stop fires, but not all farmers did, and sometimes the fires came before you'd had a chance to burn them. That's what the Aborigines did too, it prevented wildfire and meant there were always different levels of growth. New growth sprang from the fire, which opened seed cases that'd been dormant for years and gave everything a fresh start. It's a pity it's taken so long for us whites to stop and listen.'

'I wonder what the country will look like in, say, another two hundred years. Do you think enough trees will have been replanted? Do you think the rainforests and deserts will regenerate?'

'I hope so. It's too late for some things, but not to heal others.'

The homestead is on a hill just across a wide hollow. 'It looks well kept,' says Estella. 'At least there are trees around the house. Let's go in the back gate.'

'It doesn't look as though anyone's home.'

'Yes there is, the generator's on.' Estella walks around the verandah, which is covered by a deep green shade net that makes the house seem cool. She knocks on the door. There is a shuffling sound inside and the door opens into a dark room. A woman, middle-aged, with squint lines around her eyes stands there. 'Sorry to bother you on Christmas morning, but we've got ourselves bogged in the creek nearby, and we were wondering if you might be able to help us.'

'How far away?'

'Oh, about six kilometres. It's taken us about an hour to walk here.'

'Well, you'd better come in and have a cold drink of water before we do anything else.'

'Yes please. That'd be lovely.'

They follow her along the verandah to the kitchen. The woman pulls a plastic bottle of cold water from the fridge. Olga and Estella gulp down the first glass. The woman refills them immediately. 'Thanks,' they splutter and begin the second. 'We still had some water left in our containers, but it got pretty hot while we were walking here,' says Olga.

'You were lucky it wasn't hotter. People have died round here walking for help at this time of year.'

'Well, that's why we set off early,' Estella says, rather too defensively.

'Now about this car . . . oh, this is my daughter, Alice.'

'Hi.'

Alice nods a hello.

'The car?'

'We got bogged last night. Estella has dug around it, but it's on a bit of an angle and I think we need to be towed out.'

'It was too dangerous,' says Estella.

'How far, six kilometres, is that right?'

'About that.'

'You stay here, I'll go and find a rope. I should be able to get you out with the Toyota. Is it a four-wheel drive?'

'Yes.'

The woman walks out, followed by her daughter.

'Thank the goddess for that water,' says Olga.

'It was nice of her not to ask us anything until we'd finished drinking.' She pours herself another drink and sips at it.

'Are you ready to go?' the woman asks, returning with a thick rope over her arm and a plank of wood. She has changed from her thongs into heavy boots.

'Yep, we're ready,' says Estella standing.

Alice and the woman climb in the front, Olga and Estella in the back.

Estella leans forward. 'Have you lived here long?'

'Eighteen years.'

'Alone?'

'Most of it. Dick drowned, fixing the pump in the dam, nine years ago.'

'Farming's a dangerous business,' says Estella. 'My father died in a tractor accident when I was fourteen. Poor Mum had a hard time of it for a few years, but she kept on, like you. Do you have help?'

'Yes, but it's holidays at the moment. I can manage most things by myself, and Alice is a big help.'

'The car's over there, just beyond that tree,' says Olga, pointing off to the right.'

'Down there? I thought you meant near the waterhole a bit further on.' They drive in. She stops the car, shifts into low gear, and continues. 'Well you have got yourselves in a dicky position. Now, I need to get over there in front of you.' The car feels as though it is floating along the sand. She turns, 'Do you want to drive it out, or will Alice? We've done this together before.'

'Alice can do it, that's fine by me,' says Estella.

'Me too.'

The woman pulls up on the flat in front of the car. 'You got a spade?'

'Yeah, sure.'

The woman digs fast and expertly. She has a wirey frame but is strong with it. 'Alice, get that plank out will you?' Alice nods. She hasn't said a word yet. 'And the jack, while you're at it.'

Estella and Olga stand by as the woman raises the car on the jack. 'Okay, Alice, push that plank under there. Now add some of those rocks under it, to give it a firm base.' Estella jams the rocks in. 'Do we have the chain in the car?' she asks, turning to Alice. Alice walks off, opens the back of the car, and returns with the chain. 'Think we need this,' says the woman more to herself than anyone else.

In the meantime, Olga has cleared away the boxes from in front of the car. They are ready to go.

Alice climbs in. The woman climbs into her car and starts it up. 'Not too much throttle,' she yells to Alice. Alice nods.

The woman is backing. The car is moving forward slowly. The plank cracks, as the car rolls off it on to the sand. The chain slackens. The car is out and moving of its own accord. Olga is taking photographs. 'Documentary evidence,' she says. 'Nobody will believe us otherwise.'

Estella's face is almost breaking with a wide smile. 'Thank you, so much. We really do appreciate it,' she says at the window of the woman's car.

'Don't ever turn the wheels like that, on a slope, in sand. And keep moving.'

'The low gear,' asks Estella, 'I'm not really clear on how to use it.'

'Change into it before you get into the deep stuff, and you can always let the tyres down, with a match. You know what I mean?'

'Yes,' nods Estella, remembering Theo doing just that.

'If you want a swim, there's a waterhole just down the road. It says NO SWIMMING, but you look like you need one.'

Alice has detached the chain from the tow point, and gets in beside her mother.

'Thanks again. Have a Happy Christmas. We'll follow you out.'

Estella gets in, puts the car into low gear, and floats along the sand behind the other car. As they reach the road, all wave. The woman heads back to the homestead and Olga and Estella drive on.

There was a party at Auntie Betty's on Christmas Night. Everyone was there, dressed in their best clothes. The men, out of their work clothes for once, showered and shaved. Most were still busy with harvesting that would begin again on Boxing Day.

Stella headed straight for the kitchen. She knew there would be creamy cakes and other sweet delights there.

A group of women stood in the kitchen, talking and smoking. Her Uncle Bill came in and offered beer or spirits. Coral, a beer in her hand, was standing talking to Mrs Brummel.

'Have you finished yet?' asked Coral.

'No, but not much more to go. Just the big wheat paddock near the house. What about you?'

'I think it'll be a while yet,' replied Coral. 'That rain set us back. I just hope that Theo can get it done before we go on holidays . . .'

Stella grabbed a fairy cake and ran outside to join the other children. But there was nobody her age, apart from a couple of boys. She decided to go and listen to the grown-ups talk. She moved from one group to the next, picking up food and getting the occasional mouthful of beer from Theo or one of her uncles.

The teenagers had taken over the gramophone. She could hear the music playing and though she wanted to dance she felt too self-conscious and so sat by the window instead and peered through the curtains. They were dancing to 'Rock Around the Clock'. She watched amazed as her cousin leapt on to the hips of a boy, slid between his legs and then seemed to fly through the air. 'Come and see this,' she said to a couple of younger girls. The three of them crouched by the window, hands over their mouths and giggling as the girls were lifted into the air, showing their underpants.

Stella decided that when she grew up she would dance like that.

The next day Stella asked, 'Carmel, teach me to rock 'n' roll.'

Carmel went over to the bench and switched the wireless over to the commercial station.

'Hold my hand. Now, feel the rhythm of the music and go with it.'

Stella danced around, too vigorously.

'No, you don't have to jump so high. Make your steps smaller . . . Have a rest for a minute.'

'Fiona?'

Fiona began to dance with Carmel. She fell into the rhythm easily and soon looked as though she'd been doing it for years.

'How come you can do it?' asked Stella enviously.

'I don't know.'

'Carmel, I want to do it so I can fly through the air like they did at Auntie Betty's.'

'What did they do?'

Stella explained as best she could what she had seen.

'All right, hold both my hands. Now leap on to this hip.'

Stella leapt, and as she did Carmel's hip moved sideways and Stella landed on it.

'Now the other side.'

She leapt again.

'Okay, through the middle.'

She slid on the lino floor between her legs and then was lifted up and out.

'Let's do it again,' said Stella beaming.

'All right, then Fiona can have a go.'

You say that I have a talent for chanting, for dancing. You are teaching me new things. Lines are drawn on my body. Around my nipples. You draw a double spiral, like a 6 and a 9 end to end on their side. Around my navel another simple spiral.

I feel the brush of fingers forming a pattern down my spine. I feel the dampness of wet ochre. A double serpentine helix winds about my spine.

You are teaching me a spiral dance. I spin. I whirl. I spiral. My arms form spirals in the dance. My legs dance a spiral on earth, lifting dust. I feel myself turning in the spiral, my whole body transformed, spiralling warmth, from the base of my spine to the crown of my head.

You exclaim. You say you have never seen such a performance by a novice. You do not know that this is the way I see the world. Spinning. Spiralling. This is my natural habitat.

Fiona was home for the half-term holidays. She and Stella were in the orchard. Stella sat in the branches of the orange tree and passed oranges to Fiona from time to time. Stella made a perfect white circle against the orange with her thumbnail, then carefully removed the skin so that the peel hung spiralling from her hand. She hung the peel over the branch on which she was seated.

Fiona, with her back against the trunk, was surrounded

by a scattering of small irregularly shaped pieces of peel.

Stella wished that, just once, Fiona would do something adventurous. Climb a tree, swing from branches, dive into the dam, do a wheelie on a bicycle, walk a 44-gallon drum along the lawn.

Fiona wished that Stella wouldn't be so childish and stupid. Why didn't she grow up? Why didn't she care about how she looked, what she said? Why didn't she think?

Stella wrapped her hands round the nearest branch and leapt as near to Fiona as she could.

'Oh Stel, cut it out.'

'Why?'

'Cos it's stupid.'

''S not stupid.'

'It is so, you baby.'

'I'm not a baby.'

'Yar so.'

'Not. You . . . you stink.'

'God you're childish.'

Stella grabbed her orange peels, hurled them at Fiona and stormed off mumbling, 'Am not,' under her breath. Tears were already beginning to gather in her eyes. She couldn't work out why their orange feast had suddenly turned into a row. She stood on the bars of the back gate and just stared. The wind on her face dried her tears quickly. She climbed the gate, and a second one and walked across the paddock towards the wood pile.

The wood pile, made up of trees felled when the land was cleared around seventy years ago, was one of her favourite places. The wood was grey with age, but she could still see the circles of years inscribed in it. She climbed up the easy end and sat on the highest piece of wood. She stared at the wood between her knees, at the circling pattern on the wood. She traced the form with her finger, occasionally losing her place, then went back to the beginning and started again. She tried not to look ahead, tried to keep her mind at finger pace, but it was too hard. She gave up in frustration finally and returned to gazing at it. Oops, not allowed to stare, she remembered, and broke her reverie.

She began to feel bored. Stood up, feeling herself very tall in that moment, and went looking for Fiona. Fiona was reading. Stella hovered for a moment before deciding it was no use. She turned round and went to her own room. She climbed on to the bed and sat swinging her legs back and forth. She was sulky now; now that Fiona was occupied and it was getting too late to go outside again. She could hear Coral making cooking noises in the kitchen, and the sound of Theo in the shower.

I'll go to the toilet.

She sat there for a while contemplating the French caption to the picture of an old-fashioned little girl on a pottie. She could never remember what it meant, even though she'd been told, and she certainly couldn't see what was supposed to be funny about it.

'Stella.'

She jumped to her feet and pulled up her pants.

'Coming in a minute,' she yelled.

She ran through the sleep-out, her bedroom and the living-room to the kitchen.

'Could you set the table, dear?'

Stella hesitated.

'But go and wash your face and hands first, will you?'

She nodded.

The bathroom was steamy. Theo was drying himself. She looked at his large, strong body.

He leant over and put the plug in the basin. 'Don't waste water, Stel,' he said and turned round and picked up his singlet and khaki undershorts.

'Why do you always buy Dad those awful khaki pants?' she asked when she returned to the kitchen.

Coral turned round and smiled, more to herself than to Stella. 'I don't. He bought them. At the end of the war the army was getting rid of things. They were cheap. He brought home eight hundred pairs with him. He'll never run out.'

Stella thought it was a bit like the wood pile: more than anyone can use in one lifetime.

As they drive towards the waterhole, Estella tells Olga about her first trip to the boarding school when she was nine and Fiona twelve. 'I walked with her through the big old echoing buildings and tried to imagine myself there in three years time. The idea was exciting,' she said, 'and I didn't mind her going, although I soon noticed her absence in the long afternoons after school. I really missed her taking care of me, in a way. And the chores, there seemed to be so many more. I hadn't realised how much she'd done. A couple of times I forgot to pick up the bread from the baker, the meat from the butcher. I wasn't used to thinking about them.'

They are relieved to be on their way again. Though the thought of lying around in the creekbed for a day or two rather appeals to Estella. She imagines lying under the eucalypts, drinking billy tea, reading, simply disappearing from the world.

'This must be it,' Olga said and pulls off the road to the gravel. They get out and Estella stretches her back like a swan. It is a permanent waterhole, used for stock, and so the bottom is composed of fine mud and shit that Estella tries not to think about as she lowers her body into the water. She doesn't put her head under the water, it is too thick with green swirling things to contemplate.

'It's like soup,' she yells as Olga tests the water with her toes.

Olga splashes towards her, like a duck running across the surface of the water. 'Don't splash me with that filth,' says Estella good humouredly, 'or I'll just have to splash you back.'

'It's like vegetable soup, with bits,' says Olga sinking up to her ankles in the mud. Olga lifts one foot above the surface of the water. It drips green slime.

'Woman emerging from primordial mud,' Estella says in a deepened voice, lungeing towards Olga. 'It's just like the dam we had at home, in which we swam and fished for yabbies with pieces of raw meat tied to the end of a length of string. But it wasn't as green as this,' she says, leaning back and kicking both feet into the air.

They move slowly shorewards, trying to avoid the deepest patches of mud as they scramble and slip up the shallow bank. They sit down under a sapling eucalypt and wait for the mud on their feet to dry and crack in the heat.

11

Stella dreamed. A terrible dream that came back to her again and again. Theo was building a dam. The bulldozer gouged a great hole in the earth. Mouthful after mouthful was piled up around the edge, forming the dam wall. In the dream Coral and Theo were both riding on the yellow bulldozer which had 'Caterpillar' written in big black letters on one side. The clay was dung brown. It was wet. As the Caterpillar crawled along the wet clay on its big circling iron tread, it began to sink right down into the clay, taking Coral and Theo with it. All that remained were the tracks into the mud.

The car has passed through the wall of the mountains several times. They drive out to the plain and looking back see the lines of rock scratched along the surface, like lines of bricks in a wall built by giants. The plain is dry and flat and studded with rocks. Then they pass back into the arms of the mountains through another gap, another gorge.

A bird following the car's progress would see a squiggly line passing between high walls of rock, like a child's finger following a maze, or an ancient Troy town traveller. Estella remembers the circles Iris had traced on her palm when she began, 'Can you keep a secret?' Was it a memory of some secret at the centre of the labyrinth? Nowadays only rats run mazes.

They stop at a shop in the middle of nowhere to buy an icecream, and chops for dinner.

I play with mazes beginning with a simple one. The red ink of my pen coils its way slowly to the centre. There are more complex mazes: one resembles the half moon in the sky, another a seated woman. The last has several possible entrances but only one track leads to the centre. I trace the routes with my eyes before I put pen to paper.

The car stops between two walls of rock, where once hunters became stars, leaping into the sky to escape the fire that pursued them. They became the bright pointers of the Southern Cross.

Estella is gazing at the peaks, looking from one to the other, trying to reconstruct the story of the hunters against the rocky walls rising on each side of her. 'You know,' she says, 'on the map this place is marked as abandoned. By whom? Seems to me there's plenty of spirit left here. But there is a wall . . .'

'We're used to walls, in the west. When I was living in Berlin, I ceased noticing the wall after a while. At first I thought about it all the time, felt hemmed in by it, and I used to cross over into East Berlin regularly just to escape that feeling. It wasn't them that was enclosed by the wall, it was West Berlin. And we were all frantically denying it. It wasn't until I came here that I developed a sense of space, of needing the wide open spaces. Maybe that's why so many of us visit the desert. It's a way of healing ourselves.'

The bell rang and everyone piled back into the classroom. It was Wednesday. Social Studies. They were learning about Daisy Bates.

Mr Clayton told them that she was a heroic lady. He said that she had lived with the Aborigines for thirty years and had learnt to speak eighteen Aboriginal languages. And she always wore long dresses. This last fact took Stella's attention for some time as she imagined walking around in those long, heavy, black garments in that heat, and out in the desert where there was no one to make you dress like that!

She returned her attention to the class to hear him speak of the Empire, the Queen and the government's duty to a dying race.

Stella looked up at the painting by Albert Namatjira that hung in the classroom alongside the portrait of the Queen. Her eyes flashed across the landscape that was so familiar to her. The gum tree in the foreground, the red soil dotted with yellow grass, the blue hills beyond. Not so very different from the countryside nearby. She glanced briefly at the pale face of the Queen (she saw a slight resemblance to Coral there, or was it just the hairstyle?), the crown sparkled upon her head and her white fairytale dress stood out against the blue curtained backdrop. She looked from one to the other weighing up the two worlds.

There were certain days of the year that even school days bent to. Anzac Day was one of the days when the school closed. Stella was dressed in her special white dress that had been Fiona's a few years previously. She found her red cardigan and pinned her red cross badge to it. She watched Coral iron the white veil that would be pinned to her hair just before it was time to leave. It would fall out otherwise.

At breakfast she looked at Theo. Usually he was dressed in work clothes. This morning he wore a dark suit. Above his lapel pocket was a string of medals. She could never remember what they were for.

They left the house at half past nine. She had to assemble at school first. Theo and Coral dropped her off, Coral straightening Stella's veil before kissing her. The school ground looked strange with the boys in soldier khaki and the girls dressed in red and white like nurses.

They assembled at the school gate and began the march to the Main Street, where they joined the rest of the marchers and headed for the School of Mines, which doubled as a Town Hall. Men from all over the countryside were dressed in their best suits, and most sported at least one medal. Stella smiled at Theo's array of medals and felt happy to be his daughter. She looked for Coral and saw her standing with the other women. She had been in the army, why didn't she participate in the march?

The final marchers came to a halt and the service began. She enjoyed the familiarity of the service and the poem they had rehearsed at school. She liked the rhythm.

They shall grow not old, as we that are left grow old,
Age shall not weary them, nor the years condemn.
At the going down of the sun, and in the morning,
We will remember them.

Stella stood in silent awe as the trumpeter played 'The Last Post'. The silence that followed was filled with the ghosts of dead men. She tried to think about Theo's cousin who had been killed, but no picture of him formed before her eyes, she had never known him. His name was written in gold on the Roll of Honour, like so many others, but he was only a name. Instead she wondered about Uncle Jack. She knew he'd been a P.O.W., but that didn't explain his strangeness. Her mind rambled on to other things. She would ride her bicycle down to Auntie Betty's, and watch the ducks and turkeys. She might even get afternoon tea if she went at the right time.

Lest we forget.

Everyone chanted. Then the wreaths were laid. Most had a relative or knew someone who had died in either the first or second war.

Soon they were milling about, exchanging greetings and comments about the unseasonably chilly weather, small-town gossip stifled for the moment in reverence for the dead.

The men climbed into vehicles to pay their symbolic respects to their comrades by the laying of wreaths in the local cemetery. The cortege proceeded slowly down the main street and disappeared out of sight.

'Have you ever seen an Anzac Day march?' Estella asks.

'No. I haven't. I've heard about Anzac Day, but last year was the first time I'd been here at that time of year. Do you remember what we were doing?'

'No. It's ceased to be important to me, except in an anti-way. I took an English feminist to an Anzac Day march once. We were all dressed in black to mourn the women who'd been raped or killed in war. It was really weird, because simply being there was a threat to the established ritual. There were men in uniform all around us. Policemen formed a kind of inner ring. Soldiers were gathered in groups beyond them. One woman held the wreath and moved towards the policed rim, in the direction of the shrine. They arrested her. The wreath was passed to another who repeated the movement. She was arrested. As each woman was arrested the wreath was passed on. We were standing near the centre watching as all the women were led quietly to the paddy wagons.

'There were hundreds of us,' says Estella, continuing. 'I was still there when they played 'The Last Post', which always makes me remember Uncle Jack. I still wonder what they did to him in Changi. Finally the wreath was handed to me. I walked forward, just as all the others had. Policemen took me by the wrists and elbows. But it isn't that that sticks in my mind. I looked at the young army men in uniform, and for a moment into the eyes of one young soldier. He must have been eighteen, or twenty at most. He returned a look of such intense hatred and suppressed violence that I reacted by walking straight ahead and raising my chin slightly as if he were about to punch me. Then I was pushed into the paddy wagon, which was dark. Arms reached out to grasp me and I sat pressed in close to two unknown women who held my hands.'

'So how long were you in jail?'

'Just a couple of hours. Long enough for them to take our names and so on. But we weren't charged.'

We talk of Cassandra. Belief is as important as knowledge. For what is knowledge if no one believes it? There have been many times when destruction could have been avoided, when the future was glaring at people. That was the fate of Cassandra, though her ears had been licked by a serpent, no one would believe her prophesies.

They laughed at her story of the wooden horse – and the city fell. They laughed even as they died.

There have been many Cassandras. Many of us.

Stella liked to go and watch when Theo killed a sheep. A 'killer' was culled from the flock, three of its legs tied with green twine, and heaved into the back of the ute. She wondered whether they knew they were soon to be killed. And, although she had some compassion, it did not bother her that this sheep would soon join the potatoes on her plate.

Stella walked next to Theo through the orchard and climbed the gate, even though Theo had opened it for himself. She had watched him sharpening his knives in the laundry and could still hear the metallic sound in her ears.

The sheep lay on the ground in the shade of a huge eucalypt. It seemed relaxed, despite its tied legs. Theo bent over the sheep, grasped its head firmly in its hand, tipped the head back and quickly slit its throat. He continued to hold back the head while the blood spurted from the severed artery. He rested it on the ground and Stella watched as the blood trickled into a pool among the leaves and dirt. The untied leg kicked a couple of times, the others merely flinched. When the blood had drained from the neck Theo untied the legs and cut through the hide of a back leg. He removed the skin from the leg by alternately cutting and punching. Then the leg was broken at the mid-joint. Soon there were four bluish-white stumpy legs poking out from the body. He then began on the torso. Again he cut the connecting tissue and lightly punched it away. Theo lowered the winch, hooked the sheep by its back legs and raised the winch again until the sheep's head hung about two feet above the ground. Bit by bit he removed the hide, working meticulously, as though what he did was an art form. He cut and punched the hide until it finally came away from the body and then lifted the hide over the fence palings to dry. Stella was still watching intently. She gazed at the bluish body swinging in the afternoon light. The leaves created a lovely dappled orange effect at that hour. Now came the exciting part. Theo dipped his knife in the water and deftly slit the belly. As he did the innards began to slide. They moved and gathered, moved and gathered, then hung precariously for a moment before Theo made the last cut. They fell, almost slithered, into the bucket. Now she could see the inside of the sheep's body. The bladder, the heart, and the lungs were severed and dropped into the same bucket. Then in a separate container, an enamel bowl from the kitchen, he put the kidneys and liver. Coral would make lambs fry and steak and kidney pie with these. Finally the head was removed from the body. The carcass was splashed with a little water and lifted down from the hooks. Theo carried the carcass slung over his back, along the path through the orchard and then lifted it into the meat-safe on the back verandah. It would hang there overnight and be cut into usable joints the following day. The dogs ate the head, heart, lungs and innards. The hide would be dried on the fence, then hung over a branch of the gum tree with others. Later they would be sold to a tannery. Nothing but the blood was wasted.

As Venus dips behind the lip of the hill, Olga begins to make dinner.

'Do you want any help?' asks Estella.

'No, not yet. I thought I'd marinate these chops in some oil and chilli and garlic first. Maybe in a little while you could put on rice or potatoes.'

Estella returns to her book, which she is reading by the light of the hurricane lamp. Soon the smell of food cooking proves too distracting and she goes to help.

They eat watching the stars brighten as the sky darkens through deep blue to indigo black. Estella has found the distinctive red glow of Mars and points it out to Olga, who always confuses the false cross with the Southern Cross.

'Look, there's a satellite,' say Estella.

'Where?'

'Up there, it's just approaching Mars.'

'I've lost Mars.'

Estella stands behind Olga and points her finger at the sky. 'Can you see it?'

'Mmm, I think so. It's moving fast.'

'I remember when the Russians put up the first sputnik, we went outside and watched it pass. I thought it was magic, and Coral was so excited by it. But I haven't seen one for years. The city lights are too bright.'

'The same happened in Europe too. Everybody went outside to look. It just seemed so amazing. But I also remember wondering why? What's the purpose? The beginning of being a Luddite, I suppose.'

'I remember worrying that the satellite would get lost up there with all those stars.'

Olga chuckles. She leans over and kisses Estella's neck. 'One star, two stars . . . who needs sputniks?'

Vibration

12

The cicadas were chirruping loudly when Theo, Coral, Fiona and Stella drove into the school grounds on Stella's first day. Not long before, Stella had dreamt about going away to boarding school and playing the piano in a huge empty room. What she remembered most clearly was the long lines of parallel polished floorboards.

Theo lifted the suitcases out of the boot and carried the two heaviest. Stella and Fiona carried one each. They went up the wide spiral staircase with its polished bannisters, which Stella immediately saw possibilities of sliding down.

Fiona, accustomed to the routine by now, went to look at the room lists. 'You're in this room here.' She led Stella into a room with four beds. 'Take this one,' she said.

'No, I want to be in the middle,' said Stella.

'You'll regret it.' Fiona pulled a soft striped towel from the end of one of the other beds. 'Here, you might as well start with the nice towel.'

Coral had vanished into the housemistress's office. She was taking a very long time. Theo had discreetly gone back downstairs and Stella waved to him from the window. He was sitting on a stone wall in the sun, and she ran down the stairs and joined him.

'Have you got everything?' he asked.

'Yes, I think so.'

'Here,' he said, pulling a two dollar note from his pocket, 'just in case you need anything. Don't tell Mum.'

'Okay. Thanks.'

Fiona and Coral appeared at the door, 'Let's go and have some lunch,' said Coral. 'We'll drop you back later in the afternoon.'

When they came back, the other three new girls were there. Two were sitting on their beds watching the third unpack. Stella noticed immediately that the nice striped towel was now at the end of another bed.

'Excuse me,' she said, 'but this is my towel.'

'Finders keepers,' said the other girl.

'But it was on my bed.' Stella knew this was not quite right, but it hadn't been on the other girl's bed either.

'I know,' said the other girl abruptly, 'let's have a tug-of-war.'

Stella looked at her, she wouldn't win, but she would try. Each took an end of the towel and pulled. Stella pulled with every ounce of strength, but she was soon pulled across the line of the floorboards. Reluctantly, she let go of the towel.

Coral came back. 'Stella, come with me.' Stella was glad to be able to do something, to go away for a while. 'You'd better meet Miss Foxglove, she's the sister here; I've explained to her about your pills, and that you have to have them twice a day. Now don't you forget.'

Stella nodded, but wondered how she was ever going to remember without Coral to remind her.

Every morning and every evening Stella went to the sick-bay to take her pills. She felt embarrassed, but mostly no one said anything. The morning queue was a meeting place and Stella learned a lot listening to the older girls talking about themselves. There was always someone who would walk in casually, ask for a packet of Modess, and just as casually walk away down the corridor tossing the bulky packet in the air and catching it.

Stella could never imagine herself being that blasé about anything.

'Who's next?'

'Oh, just me,' stammered Stella. She took her pills in her outstretched hand and filled the glass at the sink. She tried to take the pills surreptitiously, but she always felt that the others watched and wondered.

All four of them had crushes. Ginny started it by talking about her favourite older girl, Satchmo with the deep voice, and soon each had picked a favourite. Polly was courting Ratty. They looked so odd together – Ratty tall and thin as a pole, Polly heavy and squat. Diane had latched on to Peggy, whom they had surrounded and dragged into the room one night after lights-out so Diane could kiss her. Stella had just been given a lock of hair by Wendy.

Several times a week the older girls would buy them ice-creams at the corner shop, or would help them with home-work. It wasn't until she mentioned it to some day-girls that Stella realised that this was not as ordinary as she'd thought it was. After that she kept quiet about what went on after lights-out.

They were telling secrets. They always talked for a while before they went to sleep, but Stella sensed that tonight was different.

'I wet the bed,' Polly said. Stella knew that. Ever since her first night, Polly's bed had had to be changed, and Stella had seen the rubber sheet that had been laid beneath the cotton one. She accepted it as Polly's secret, even though she felt resentful about the towel. She knew how hard it was to say some things.

I'm partially deaf in my left ear,' Ginny said.

'How'd it happen?' asked Stella, genuinely interested.

'My brother poked a knitting needle down my ear and it pierced the ear-drum. I had to go to hospital, and it took ages because there had been lots of rain that year and we got bogged at the bottom of the drive.'

'Does it still hurt?'

'No. What's your secret?'

'I take pills.'

'What for?' asked Diane, the doctor's daughter.

'To stop me from getting over-excited.' The phrase had been suggested by Coral as an answer to this question.

'What does that mean?' persisted Diane.

'I don't know. No one knows. Only the doctor and my mother.'

'But doesn't your father know?'

'No,' said Stella, suddenly worried that Theo might know whatever there was to know. He can't, she thought. Coral said it was only between her and the doctor. It must be something pretty bad. I don't want him to know, she thought suddenly. She went back in her mind, remembered all the times she had visited the special doctor in Sydney. No, Theo had never been there. He always dropped them off and drove away with Fiona to do something else. She had been to the doctor every year as far back as she could remember, and it was always just Coral and herself. He can't know. He never asked any questions afterwards. He would, if he knew, she thought.

She remembered the time in Cronulla, a month ago, when she felt dizzy after dinner. Coral had taken her up to bed, given her her pills and told her that she had been testing her to see if Stella could go without them. Stella shuddered involuntarily. She had not liked that dizzy feeling.

Theo hadn't heard Stella tell Coral that she felt 'funny' that time either.

She was amazed that Coral could keep a secret like that. It must be something really terrible, she thought again.

'No,' Stella replied, 'he doesn't know.'

She wanted to cry and wished that Diane would say what her secret was, although she didn't really care any more. She turned over to face the other way and slid down into her bedclothes, so the others wouldn't see the tears in the corners of her eyes.

Stella was sitting in prep doing her homework. She'd been feeling a bit strange for a while. Like she wasn't there, or that the world around her was separate from her. She felt displaced. It was getting worse. She felt nauseated. Would they let her go back to her room if she said she felt sick? By the time she stood up to ask, the roof had lifted and it was as though she were a bird floating high above the world. She wished she could come down.

'Miss . . .'

'Are you all right?' asked Miss Blackbird.

Stella pulled herself back into her body. 'No. I feel sick.'

'Jenny, can you take her over to see Miss Foxglove.'

'What's wrong?' asked Jenny after they were out the door. 'You look awful.'

'I don't know, I feel kind of dizzy.' She couldn't explain. It reminded her of how she'd felt at Cronulla, but it wasn't quite the same. As she walked, her mind seemed to be dancing off to other places, like a helium balloon on a long string.

When they reached the sick bay, Miss Foxglove wasn't there. 'Why don't you go to bed,' said Jenny, 'I'll tell her when I see her. Will you be all right?'

'Yes.' Stella put on her pyjamas and went to bed. She lay there for a while wondering what was happening. It was hard to explain how suddenly everyone was a million miles away. Dizzy wasn't the right word. It was a bit like those frightening visions she sometimes had before falling asleep, of fat dots swallowing thin dots and getting bigger and bigger all the time. Like the numbers in her head that sometimes got out of control, growing so big that you couldn't say what number it was. Like the way she felt sometimes when she looked up at the stars. If you started counting you got lost. The world was just too big.

I lie awake at night staring up at the sky, full of fitful nightmares. Constellations gallop by. In another moment I see the Pleiades, running back and forth across the ecliptic. In part I am there too, lost in the spaces between the stars, travelling light years, crawling through eternity.

I am a creature made up of dots (like stars in the furthest reaches of the galaxy). I am the dot, and yet I am outside it.

93

I panic finding myself so alone, hear the whisper of a distant electron, panic again.

The spaces around me diminish. The world falls on me, stars collapse. I am jostled by the crowd, smothered. I dance on the floorboards, breathlessly. My body dematerialises in front of you and, as you reach down to touch me, your hands pass through my torso, lifting me into light.

I am flying and falling, flying and falling. The electrons beat. I fall through a dark tunnel past a thin black gauze into your arms and light shines through my eyelids.

We eat well when we go foraging. Sometimes we travel for many days. We sniff, taste, eat as we go in search of pituri. An outcrop marks the gully where it grows. We climb the gravelly rise and slide down the inner wall on our bottoms, and pass between a narrow gap in the rocks into a large open chamber; shrubs grow on the slope above it. We pick tops and leaves which make us sneeze.

We hang the plants to dry in the chamber. The leaves are hung with bell blossoms and the chamber seems dressed for an occasion.

Your tales carry us even further than our weary legs. You take us to places beyond the desert and the sea and to times beyond our memory. Sometimes I sleep and the stories weave with dream images.

We walk through the bush collecting medicinal plants. The bark we scrape from the stringybark tree we use for stomach ailments. We use melaleuca eucalyptus birch sandalwood oak callitris and the acacia.

Soon the trees will flower and there will be honey. We go out searching for honey in the warm spring days. The native trees are flowering: the acacia, the eucalypts. We search for hives in the hollow trees and look for hovering wasps that are attracted to the honey and easy to see. I see wasps and the bees dancing their complex directional dance; their bodies swinging back and forth in the sunlight. I dance through the scrub after the bees and find myself at the base of a big eucalypt.

'Come,' I say, and take you by the hand. You climb the

tree, inspect the hive and extract the honey and combs. The women have brought smoking wands of damp wood to drive the bees from the hive.

You fill the containers that are passed up to you by a long chain of ascending hands. We lick honey from our fingers and return home chanting the bee song as we dance.

You tell of Melissa, sweet-tongued and dark, her gift of poetry to the woman who slept near her cave and who, upon waking to wax-sealed lips, broke the seal and sang. One night the poet dreamt of Black Melissa, her shoulders wrapped in a shawl of black bees. The sound of their unearthly buzz struck terror into the poet's heart.

Melissa said, I made you a poet and you have never written me a single song. The poet died a few days later. Some nights after her death an old woman, a friend of many years, dreamed of the poet who sang a song of Black Melissa, as mistress, as ordainer of mystical rites, as golden rain. The old woman woke and sang her friend's last song. As she did she saw the shadow of a dark undulating form. She too died within a few days. Her friends were puzzled by the black honey upon her hands and the wax that sealed her lips.

To the east lies a huge flat expanse that leads to the salt lake. They decide not to go there, but to drive north towards the place where the giant snakes emerged long ago. They stop to watch corellas screeching in the trees near the road. A group drinking from a water trough rises as a single wing and flies to a tree further away.

Low hills lounge along the horizon turning into mirages as they flatten out. Olga and Estella turn off for a walk through the gorge that lies just off the main road.

Unlike the plain, trees grow in the shelter of the rock walls. A native orange tree is beginning to fruit, but is too green and hard to eat. The long filaments sprawl like exhausted lovers across soft yellow petals. Estella touches the leaf of a small mauve flower with a star in the centre, which is soft as velvet.

'Look at the grevillea,' says Olga pointing to a tree covered in red flowers.

'It's mistletoe,' says Estella. 'A native one. It looks like grevillea.'

Olga insists it is grevillea.

Estella points to the leaves, and insists that they are mistletoe. As they walk on Estella says. 'It's the leaves that are distinctive.'

'Maybe,' grumbles Olga, touching the juicy leaves.

'Mistletoe's used to treat epilepsy. Though I've never used it. You really have to know what you're doing with mistletoe. It's powerful stuff.'

The mistletoe in this sheltered valley is growing at the expense of everything else.

They walk on. Some trees are covered with what looks like huge balls of hair. As though some giant has brushed her hair over the tree and left it sitting there in great grey tangled knots.

'This place is weird,' says Olga. 'It's as though it's some sort of parasites' paradise. Everything is thriving at the expense of something else.'

'Mistletoe is also great for kissing under,' says Estella, drawing Olga towards a tree.

Returning upstream, Estella jumps from rock to rock. Olga, more sedate, walks on the track alongside the creek. There is a crisp silence in the trees, broken only by the occasional bird and the jarring sound of the car's engine starting up.

13

'Where's the mat?' Estella is about to close the back door. 'Everything will be filled with dust.'

'Hanging on the tree.'

Estella pulls the mat from the branch and spreads it over the boxes of food and books and they drive off along the bumpiest road yet. Dust rolls behind them like a thunder cloud. Beside the road are serrated peaks, walls of rock that look like some giant creature has bitten huge chunks out of them. Serrated peaks. The rocks are red as though blood and ochre have been mixed.

'Do you think that if we got out there and danced on those rocks for a long time, we would begin to bleed?' Estella says.

'I don't know. Why would you want to do that?'

'I just wondered.'

In a far away place beyond the plain, many days journey from here are The Singing Rocks. The rocks are said to be full of magical power: unaccountable things happen to those who travel there, and travellers are rare.

The rocks were traditionally inhabited by the snake people, a spiritual people who spent much of their time in ritual. The power of the rocks ensured their success in every endeavour. No one from outside the country ever entered the rock chamber without invitation. They were greatly respected by all the people of all the lands for their task was to disperse and gather the dream. They sang constantly and when they sang the rocks sang with them, echoing, amplifying every voice.

One day they were gathering in the dream in order to disperse it. Every woman present was marked and painted with circles, lines, spirals of white, red and black earth paint. They sang and danced and played the sticks with hands carved on the ends. The sound thundered around the chamber but beyond the rock walls it was silent.

A solitary traveller approached the silent mass of rocks that sat pensively like an enormous pregnant woman. As he moved into the arms of the rocks the sound rolled over him, pressing him back against the wall. The women saw him cover his ears with his hands, the sound ceased and his face blanched in terror. The women turned their unsympathetic gaze upon the one who dared to break the spell of their song.

He did not turn to go as he should have, but stood and stared as though his feet had taken root. They moved forward like a serpent, surrounding him, staring him into terror and death. His body fell on the hard earth and they carried him beyond the walls of the rocks and left him there.

The women resumed their ritual, but they no longer sang. They hissed and the rocks sang.

You say The Singing Rocks are inhabited by the daughters of these people, the snake that terrifies in silence, and that at certain times the rocks sing with the lost voices.

Stella was sitting in the front row of the chapel with twelve others. It was a confirmation class. The minister, a handsome dark-haired young man intense with belief, was instructing them in the catechism. Stella's concentration had wandered. In her mind she wound a piece of red wool around her thumb and little finger and made patterns: diamonds, inverted triangles, pointed stars, crowns and others where the wool formed complex twisting patterns.

'Stella. Did you hear what I said?'

'No, Sir.'

'How do you expect to get through your confirmation classes?'

'I don't know, Sir.'

'Well, if you didn't hear the question, no doubt you don't know the answer either.'

'No, Sir.'

'Well Stella, the question was, Do you have any questions? Next week I expect you to know what we've covered today, and that you will know how to respond to the catechism questions. That will be all.'

Stella didn't go back. She decided it was a waste of sunny lunchtimes. She didn't want to be confirmed anyway.

But she did take communion once. Estella remembers the day vividly. It had been a test of faith and of god's power. Would she be struck down? She walked down the aisle towards the altar, knelt, eyes cast down. As the minister approached she prepared to take the wafer, just as the girls had instructed her, 'This is my body . . .' and then the wine, 'This is my blood . . .' She waited, then rose and returned to the pew. 'Have mercy upon us,' intoned the minister. Inside she laughed, she had taken god in vain and nothing had happened, no one had noticed. A sense of triumph filled her.

As it gets darker, grasshoppers and a large praying mantis come to sit in the circle of light from the hurricane lamp and the candle. Olga puts her hand out and the mantis crawls on to it.

Estella gazes at the supplicating limbs. Olga places her hand on a nearby log and waits for the mantis to move.

They sit watching a long time in silence. The fire makes their faces warm, but the air is cold away from the fire.

They walk out of the circle of light towards the trees that surround the campsite.

'Urgh,' says Estella, stopping suddenly. 'What's that?' She steps back and shines her torch at the tree. As she does a golden orb spider pounces on a moth. They stand, like disinterested gods, and watch as other insects, attracted by the light, suffer the same fate. With each capture the web becomes more ragged, gaping holes torn where silk is used in the bundling.

I see you travelling through the stars carrying a compass and sheets of paper that bear strange marks. They could be mathematical formulae or an ancient script. There are lines curving in many directions, dispersing and scattering, then fusing again.

I observe as you play with numbers. You shift figures from one place to another and a magical transformation takes place. The world is created anew with each new equation. I want you to explain it to me.

You say that an equation is a story, and a story an equation, a representation of reality. Some representations are more exact than others, but all our answers are approximate. Those that approach reality work. They have an impact on the universe.

I watch in silence. You shift an integer from one side to another. I query the separation. You say everything changes, everything shifts. The two sides are like twin particles. One is stable, enduring, eternal. Two are dynamic. Two can dance. Twin particles create the universe. Twin lips create new words, new worlds. The two sides of the equation are dynamic. They are the writing on the wall, the hieroglyphs.

In the late afternoons, between five and six o'clock, they showered. Stella sauntered to the bathroom with a towel wrapped around her and stood in the steamy room waiting for a door to open. When it did she went in, closed the door and stood waiting as the girl under the shower finished washing her hair.

She looked at the girl's body. Her breasts were large and she had dark, almost brown nipples. Stella was fascinated by the variations in bodies she saw each afternoon in the showers. Her own body was small. Her breasts hardly buds on her chest. They were just beginning to grow, and were large enough to make it impossible for her to wear skivvies. She tried to imagine herself with breasts as large as the ones before her.

What would hers be like, and how on earth would she ever get used to them? She found a lifetime of breasts ahead of her unimaginable. As it was, the bumps showed, and she felt embarrassed. It didn't matter in the showers. No one seemed to notice but, when she went out, or went home for holidays, she noticed the change, and so did others.

At night, after lights out, they practised kissing on one another. The new girl had told them about tongue kissing. She demonstrated first on the mirror, and then on each of the others in the room. It tasted funny. But there was also something pleasurable about it. She described how you didn't kiss with your mouth closed, you didn't peck, you allowed your lips to relax, but not too much, and then, with an open mouth, kissed. It was difficult. Sometimes teeth knocked against one another. Sometimes the other lips seemed too hard. At others it was too slobbery. How to find the exact combination? What if they did it wrong when the time came for the 'real thing'?

The day was hot. It was early November. They were home for the term break that extended over Cup Day weekend. Fiona was making herself a dress. Theo was up the paddock.

Coral came in carrying a *Life* magazine. 'Stella, I want to talk to you.'

Oh no, thought Stella. 'Can I finish my chapter?' she asked, hoping Coral would say yes and then forget about it.

'No, it's important. It's about your pills. I want to explain to you why you take them. I think at thirteen you're old enough to know.'

'But you already told me. Before I went away to school. You said they were to stop me from getting over-excited.'

'That's partly true,' said Coral, 'but there's an article here that tells you a lot more about it. I think you should read it. Come and ask me about it if you have any questions.'

Stella looked at the page, which had a large black-and-white photograph of a scientist standing next to a machine, like the one that crouched in the doctor's office in Sydney. The article was about epilepsy. Not a very nice word, she thought. But she knew nothing about it.

There were two main types, she read: petit mal and grand mal. She decided she only had petit mal, because grand mal was seizures, and she did not remember having had them. She did remember the time she had found herself on the other side of a fence, without remembering having climbed through, but she thought that must have been petit mal, a little sickness.

The article mentioned Dilantin, the pill with the orange stripe around the middle. But not the other one, Mysoline. At least she wasn't taking barbiturates. They sounded awful from what the article said, but for some people they were the only thing that worked. She was glad she only had a mild case of epilepsy.

When she finished she said to Coral, 'I've only got petit mal, haven't I?'

'Well, no. When you were little you had several . . .' Coral seemed to have trouble with the word. 'But you haven't had any since you were about six or seven. Dr Silberman thought you might grow out of it, and you may yet, but he said last time that the EEG showed that you still need to keep taking your pills.'

There did not seem to be much more to say, but then Coral began again.

'It happened when you were being born.' Her voice shook. 'The doctor wasn't there when he should have been. They put pressure on your head, to stop you from being born. It was very . . . unpleasant, painful. The nurses told me later he'd been at lunch. I had no trouble with Fiona. I'd chased a fire-engine down the street just ten minutes before she was born. It could have been easy with you too.'

She stopped.

'Oh,' mumbled Stella. She didn't know what to say.

'Does Dad know?'

'Yes, of course. What made you think he didn't?'

'You said that only you and the doctor knew.'

'Did I? It was just a manner of speaking.'

'Do any other people know?'

'No. Well, a couple. Peter Black knows. He was the one who first suggested you might have . . . epilepsy. He suggested I take you to see Dr Silberman.'

'What about Auntie Betty?'

'No.'

'Auntie Ollie?'

'Yes, she knows. I had to talk to someone.'

'I suppose.' Stella wished no one at all knew. She felt exposed and vulnerable. And although she liked her Auntie Olwyn, she felt that the next time she saw her it would be like standing in front of her without any clothes on.

Stella and Fiona returned to school on the train that afternoon. She said nothing to Fiona about her talk with Coral, only wondered whether she knew. Stella was reading, *Who Walk Alone*, a novel about leprosy. She cried until Fiona took the book out of her hands and said she wouldn't return it until she calmed down a bit. She didn't have the courage to ask Fiona. She tried to regain her composure, but it was all mixed up together. She felt as though she was carrying an invisible burden. Suddenly everything looked different, her perspective had changed somehow.

She decided to keep her secret firmly to herself. But she did wonder what the other girl who took Dilantin thought about her. Perhaps she didn't know yet. Neither revealed the other's secret. Nor did they speak about themselves to one another.

That night, when she went to bed, she could think of nothing else. The words 'epilepsy', and 'epileptic' went round and round in her head. They formed a kind of chant. 'I have epilepsy . . . I am an epileptic . . .' She tried to make the words sound better, but they were like a poison. The words were poisoning her system. She felt different, separate, other, as though the world was not made for her.

14

'Come in, Stella,' said the housemistress, Mrs Murphy. Stella walked in and saw Fiona, sitting in a chair. She was drinking a cup of tea. What's going on, thought Stella. Mrs Murphy never served tea to girls. 'Would you like a cup of tea?' Stella thought she'd better have one. 'Yes, please.'

'I have something to tell you both. It's not easy, and I wish it could be otherwise.'

They both looked at her.

'Your mother rang half an hour ago. I'm afraid your father passed away in an accident.'

Stella saw the yellow Caterpillar sinking into the mud.

'Your mother was distressed and we didn't speak for long. The tractor rolled. He was killed instantly.'

Stella watched the Caterpillar sinking through mud and water, tears rolling down her cheeks.

'Would you like to spend the night in the sick-bay?'

They shook their heads. Fiona stood up and moved towards the window. She looked out into the garden to the huge old trees and focused on the fallen leaves in the circle of light from the window. She didn't cry but turned around and said gently to Stella, 'Come on.' They walked towards the closed door. Mrs Murphy, behind them, said, 'Come and knock on my door during the night if you need to. A taxi will call for you at ten to eight in the morning. I've booked tickets on the train for you. Sleep well.'

As they walked through the door, they knew word had gone around. Other girls looked at them with pity, and turned away. Fiona turned to Stella. 'Let's go down to the common room.' They walked down the back stairs and into the large room with its soft chairs and lounges. Fiona closed the door behind her.

Stella wiped her eyes. 'Why?'

'I don't know.'

Stella saw the Caterpillar again. This time it flew into the air, turned and landed in a cloud of dust. As it flew a small figure like a rag doll seemed to fly off it.

'Here,' said Fiona, passing a hanky to Stella. 'Blow your nose.' Stella looked at Fiona and couldn't believe she wasn't crying. Stella wanted to curl up in a bed and pass out.

'Do you think you'll be able to sleep?' asked Fiona.

'Mnn, naybe.' Stella's words rattled in her nose.

'Are you all right to go upstairs?'

Stella nodded, and blew her nose noisily.

Everyone stared at them.

Stella was aware of the red tear tracks under her eyes. When she walked into her room the others stopped talking. Two girls stood up and left. Stella pulled her case down from inside the cupboard and started putting clothes into it.

'When are you going?' braved Ginny.

'In the morning.' The tears began to roll again. Stella couldn't stop them, but she kept packing.

Ginny pulled out her toothbrush and left the room. Soon they'd all gone. It was easier to be alone. Stella closed the case and put it on the floor at the end of the bed. She remembered Theo sitting on the wall, the first day she came to school. Miss Foxglove appeared in the doorway. 'Here are your pills,' she said. 'I thought you might forget in the morning. I'm so sorry to hear about your father.'

Stella nodded. 'Thanks.'

'Would you like a drink of hot milk?'

She shook her head, and tried to shake the tears back into her skull.

Stella pulled her toothbrush out, squeezed on the tooth-paste and walked to the bathroom with the toothbrush sticking out of her mouth. Nobody attempted to share her basin tonight. She returned to her room, which was still empty, and crawled into bed. She got up again and turned off the light. When the others returned, they whispered, assuming she was asleep. But Stella lay there a long time after the settling of their breathing.

We sit in the freshness of the day's end. You say whatever occurs to you. You make observations about the inner world, the world between, the twilight zone. You say that birth and death are not as different as we imagine. You say there are miniature deaths. You describe the falls, the breathlessness, the cyanosis of the skin. You say knowledge and ignorance are relative, that nothing is absolute. You say the world is in constant flux, that there is a single process, that change is incessant. You say that beginnings and endings are merely arbitrary points, markers that allow us to comprehend the world. You say that these markers are not visible to some. I know what you mean.

You say that sometimes the effect is destructive, sometimes not. You say that these people are considered mad or mystic. For some there are no markers between past and future. For such people tomorrow is as clear as yesterday. Tomorrow is a memory. You say we should value these capacities. We should learn to read them just as we learn to read letters, or faces, or bodily expressions. You say the future is comprehensible to all.

The six-hour train trip was dreadful. Fiona was silent. Stella kept dissolving into tears and then feeling embarrassed by the stares of the other travellers. She tried to read, but she kept missing whole chunks and had to go back and re-read the pages. She stared out the window at the flashing trees, the flat paddocks backed by blue hills, the areas covered in Patterson's Curse purple. She got up and walked to the buffet car and bought chocolate. When she listened to the turn of the wheels her mind was brought careening back to Theo's death. She couldn't imagine getting there and Theo not being there, not ever being there.

Coral's friend, Grace, met them at the station.

'Where's Mum?'

'At home, dear. She didn't feel able to make the trip.'

'Oh.'

Grace threw worried looks at them and then bundled them into the car. It was a long silent drive. In the glow of the late afternoon sun it seemed impossible to Stella that anyone could be dead, and certainly not her father.

The road was mostly straight and the few oncoming cars were visible miles in advance, with their tails of feathered dust. As they entered the drive Stella's stomach lifted and fell. She held herself, and the feeling passed. She opened the car door, and the pink of the oleanders before her seemed to lift into the sky for a moment, then settled, shining, glowing with life. Coral, who stood at the top of the steps, seemed to shrink and expand. She moved forward and Fiona and Stella ran up the stairs and held her to them. Stella sank into the feeling. Fiona stiffened and pulled away.

Stella looked at Coral and saw her face, lost in the shadow of the wire door frame. Both turned away. They went inside and sat at the table with tea and biscuits in front of them. No one ate much and there was little to say. Stella wondered where Theo was, but she didn't know how to ask.

Grace stayed overnight. She prepared dinner for them and kept the chaos from overtaking the house. Lying in bed, thinking about Theo, Stella heard Grace and Coral talking. She got out of bed to join them, but paused before opening the door. She could hear crying and words. She went back to bed and lay there gazing out at the night sky. She wished she were a star and far away from all of this.

'This would be the ideal place for fossils,' says Olga, as they jostle along the bumpy track. 'Let's stop and have a look.'

Estella and Olga walk along the edge of a crusty mud bank. Olga stops, picks up a stick and pokes the bank with it.

'What are we looking for?'

'Brachypodes.'

'What're they?'

'They're like shells – they're actually an earlier form of modern shells left over from the time when this was sea.'

'An original way to gain immortality – land in the sand and wait for a few million years to pass.'

Estella starts poking at the bank too. They move slowly along, stopping to look carefully at something before discarding it. Estella, pausing in imitation of Olga, has only a vague idea of what she is looking for. 'What about this one?' she asks.

Olga stops, looks, looks up at Estella, 'I think this *is* one.' She drops on to her haunches and places the mud on a handkerchief. 'Must be beginner's luck.'

Estella is filled with a sense of childish joy. Olga makes noises to herself in German while examining the fossil and passes it back to Estella, who curls her fingers around it and walks on, musing. 'Do you have a desire for immortality?' asks Estella.

'No. When I'm dead, I'm dead,' Olga says finally, adding with a smile, 'Immortality is a patriarchal plot.'

The road to the hot springs is bumpier and rougher than either had imagined possible. They stop from time to time. Once, when they stopped they saw rock wallabies perching in the crevices of rocks high above them. The wallabies sit and gaze out over the valley. One wallaby, startled by their presence, bounds down the sheer rock face.

'Wouldn't it be wonderful to be able to move like that.'

'I'd rather be a screeching cockatoo flying over a rainforest,' says Olga.

They drive on across a flat area that leads to more rocky hills, more valleys. Estella, who is driving, has shaky legs some of the time. Each time she reaches the summit of a new hill, she grips herself for the descent. She talks to herself silently. Slowly. Not too much brake. Watch that hole, that big rock. The car wobbles to the bottom and they go on, Estella breathing out a sigh of relief.

There is a sign that warns against drinking or swimming in the radioactive water. The stream near the hot springs is narrow and overhung with the long thin leaves of eucalypts.

Estella dips a toe into the stream. 'It's hot,' she says, surprised.

'Of course it is. That's probably why they wanted to turn it into a health farm in the thirties. They thought radioactivity was good for you then.'

They walk towards the pool. Estella puts her toe in. 'God, this is even hotter.'

Two round rocks crouch near the pool. Estella has removed her other shoe and is standing on top of the rocks, one foot on each, peering down into the green-yellow pool. Her feet absorb the heat of sun-warmed rock.

She climbs back down to ground level and stands by the pool. Beneath the sulphur surface are tiny pinnacles of deposits growing up from the floor of the pool like miniature stalagmites. Tiny red fish swim between the pinnacles. It is like the ocean floor, only much smaller.

I dream of you standing on a hillside surrounded by white arum lilies. White swans with burgundy wings fly overhead. You are teaching me to fly. I swoop and dive at your insistence. I can hardly see you through the misty whiteness. Colour is annihilated by white on white. Only the green stems and leaves of the lilies make your form visible. I sweep past you and hear you say, 'In China white is the colour of death.'

When she woke it was bright again. She could hear noises in the kitchen. She rolled sideways and landed on her feet. Then she remembered the funeral. They ate breakfast, and dressed in their best clothes and left far too early.

The day was full of waiting. Waiting for the time to go; for Coral to come out again; for the service to start and finish. Waiting for all the people to stop saying nice things about Theo and for the people to go home, which took all day. Stella cried and sang and watched as others wept. She stood watching the coffin go down the aisle, half expecting the lid to lift, to find that none of this was real. She watched as Fiona and she stood watching. She ate cakes. She went out into the garden and sat on the swing. Leaning back, the world turned in a circle, an all encompassing bubble. She swung in an arc, back and forwards, like a pendulum. She went with it as the amplitude of the arc decreased. Hardly a movement was left in it. She sat there, limp, and waited until it was over.

I catch sight of a movement. A black fluttering movement. I see it now – a black moth that hovers briefly, then flies out of the room and is gone. The earth reclaims her own.

*Kunapipi Persephone Ereshkigal
Kali Hella Mu Olokukurtilisop
Kybele Mawu Hecate.*

During her fourteenth year Stella lay awake, stiff with fear, for months. Each night when the darkness came she didn't want it, she didn't want to sleep. She woke from dreams that kept her awake again. She woke with tears on her cheeks. She woke screaming several times. She couldn't always remember it. A deep terror took hold of her: she was afraid that this would go on forever, that she would always think of death before she slept and her life would stretch before her, a road of fear. It wasn't confined to night terrors. Sometimes during the day she had flashes of terrible things happening to people she knew. She worried that thinking them would cause them. She dreamt one night of her best friend drowning in a pool, her skin flayed on her back. The next day she hardly dared to look at her friend. In her mind the images – of Theo sinking into mud, of her best friend drowning, of Theo flying through the air – became jumbled. She tried to forget them, to eliminate them, but the images were too strong. She fell into them unwillingly and they pulled at her like quicksand.

As the night deepens and the stars begin their nocturnal dance you tell me the story of Kali.

You say that Kali is called the black mother of time. You say that three-eyed Kali sees all, no temporal divisions exist for her: past, present, future lie exposed before her gaze.

You say that the people of India loved and feared her for, although she is the force of raw destruction, new life wakens from her carrion dance of death and, that once her terrors are confronted, Kali frees her devotees from all fear. Kali draws together all opposites. Kali is as black as the sky above, but the whites of her eyes and the string of white skulls around her neck shine like stars in a night sky. She is the erupting violence of the volcanic fire, the fertile soil at the base of the dormant volcano, the gentle sleep of extinction. Her dance, like the volcano, brings life and death. She dances the world into existence, then tramples its corpse.

You say that she brings us our dreams, that she passes freely through the veil that separates the two worlds.

15

Estella, still wrapped in her sleeping bag, announces to the morning that she is bleeding. Olga mumbles something about a dream she is having and falls back to sleep again.

Estella jiggles her way towards the bathroom box and falls off the narrow seat, finally waking Olga.

Olga, seeing the awkward position Estella is in, laughs. 'Do you want a tampon?'

Estella nods and raises herself slowly, groaning and holding the hip she has landed on. She scrambles out, one hand clutching herself. Blood drops on the ground. Olga tosses her a tampon.

They pack up and leave the hot springs and the smell of sulphur behind them. Although it's not clear quite where the road out goes, they decide to drive on, instead of returning the way they came.

'When my mother told me about periods,' says Estella, 'she forgot to tell me about the blood!'

'Oh, I knew about the blood,' says Olga. 'We called it *Tante Rosa*, Aunty Rosa.'

'Then,' said Estella, 'I thought I was sterile (that's the word I thought), because I was sixteen before I had to use those rotten surfboards.'

'A New York friend once told me they used to call pads

"mouse mattresses". Like something you'd see in a surrealist painting.'

'Unclean,' hisses Estella.

It was 5 AM. Stella woke up to the movement of the white cat on her bed. The cat should not have been there. It was against the rules. But the five of them had managed to keep her in their room for the last five days.

Stella had befriended the cat over a period of several weeks, sneaking food out from the dining-room in her hand-kerchief: bits of roast beef, breakfast sausages, the occasional piece of fish or chicken. At first she thought the cat was getting fatter because of the food, then one day holding her, she felt something move inside. She turned to Ginny who was with her and said, 'Feel this.' Ginny did and they decided she must be pregnant.

When they told Diane later she ran her hands over her and said, 'Yes, definitely.'

It was after that that they watched carefully and it wasn't long before they had all agreed the cat should come to sleep in their room.

They carefully set up blankets and towels in the fireplace behind a big chest of drawers and suddenly became model boarders, agreeing to turn the light off quickly for fear that the cat would miaow and give away her presence.

Stella sat up in bed, and in the half light patted the white cat. She began a painful-sounding mewling and Stella drew her to her in the hope that she would stop. It was then that she felt the wetness and saw the patch of blood on her bedspread.

The others had woken and Stella said, 'She's bleeding.'

'She's ready then,' said Diane. 'She'll give birth soon.'

'What'll we do with this?' asked Stella, pointing to the dark patch.

'Just say you got your period in the night,' suggested Ginny.

'I wish she'd miaow more quietly,' said Stella. 'Do you think it'll happen before breakfast?'

'Maybe. It depends how many there are. Perhaps it'll be over when we get back from church.'

Stella and Ginny went to wash out the bedspread, but there was still an awful mark there after they'd scrubbed for ten minutes. They agreed to stick to their story for everyone, just in case word went round about the cat. But they also agreed that one of the fifth formers, whom they could trust, should know, in case they needed support later.

Stella was so excited she could hardly wait for breakfast to finish. She hid some bacon in her pocket and ran up to the room to see if there were any kittens yet, but there weren't, and there were still none when they left for church at 10.30 AM.

The service dragged, and the sermon seemed to go on forever. The walk back to school seemed long and dawdling. They rushed to the room and immediately heard the high pitched sounds of kittens. They pushed a chair up against the door and pulled back the chest of drawers. There sat the white cat proudly fussing over five kittens. Diane ran to get Kate, the fifth former, but Diane's indiscretion soon meant that they were besieged by a crowd of girls outside the door, wanting to see the kittens. Ginny, in an attempt to discourage them, said through the door, 'But there's lots of blood. You wouldn't want to see it.'

Blanche's reply came back, 'But I'm going to be a nurse. I need to see blood.'

Such a crowd could not be ignored and soon Mrs Murphy was there, saying, 'What's going on?'

'Nothing,' chorused everyone, and dispersed. There were some things that were understood.

Inside, they pushed back the chest of drawers and spread themselves nonchalantly across the beds.

Mrs Murphy burst through the door. 'What's going on here?'

'Nothing,' came the predictable reply. But then a kitten squealed.

'Nothing, my hat,' said Mrs Murphy, walking towards the fireplace. She pulled back the chest of drawers, 'What's this then?'

'A cat,' came Stella's innocent reply. 'Please, Mrs Murphy, please let her stay. It's too cold outside. They'll all die.'

Mrs Murphy stood a moment, hunched over the edge of the drawers, 'Well, all right, but just till tomorrow. I'll ask Mrs

Mac to find them somewhere warm.'

They spent the rest of the day accepting visitors in limited groups, to peer at the cat and her kittens. And when she was moved into a warm spot near the heaters in the basement the next day, Stella kept up the visits with the bacon, sausages and other titbits.

'I'm getting worried,' says Olga. The view before them is of flat stones extending as far as the range of blue hills in the distance. 'I'm worried we'll get lost. Do we have a map for here?'

'No, we've run off it, at least, we've run off the detailed one. We should be somewhere near here.' She points to an open area of white on the road map.

'That's really helpful,' says Olga.

'I think we just keep going. This track's got to go somewhere. I mean you don't have a track if it doesn't go somewhere.'

They drive on.

What appears to be flat land turns out to be a series of hills. Just as a dotted line seen from one angle can appear to be joined, so with this stretch of land. Only the tops of the hills are visible and because they're all the same height it gives an appearance of flatness. The car goes up and down the hills, the track gets bumpier and Estella has to detour around the edges of erosion gullies that break the track.

Three hours into the drive, Estella pulls up on the top of a ridge. 'Shit, do you think we'll get down there?'

Olga climbs out and walks down the slope. The track is strewn with boulders, and two vertical gullies meet in a hole at the bottom.

Olga signals to Estella to keep to the right. Estella sits a minute, puts the car in gear and edges to the rim of the slope. It looks almost vertical. Slowly the car creeps down. A huge rock lies on the track just ahead. She veers to one side and drives over the rock, using its height to keep the car level. At the bottom, she stops.

Her legs are shaking. She opens the door and climbs out. Her jelly legs collapse under her in relief. 'I hope there aren't any more like that,' she says, as Olga helps raise her from the dust.

'You were great,' says Olga.

'This time.'

Estella bends forward, her nose at bent knee level.

'What're you doing?'

'Just checking. I thought it might have come through with all that bumping.' She pulls at the elastic of her shorts and peers down into her knickers. 'Thought so.' She finds a new tampon. 'I wish I'd thought to bring a sponge. Much easier out here.'

They drive on chatting about the rocks and the bumps and discussing exactly where they might be.

'I wish these bumps would stop. It's really shaking me up. It's bad enough having my period without having to jolt my way through it.' She pauses for a moment to screw up her face as something cramps inside her, and then continues. 'Do you remember the conversation we started once, over dinner, at Karen's place?' says Estella. 'We wanted to know what others called it.' They begin shouting the words to one another as they bump along the rocky road: 'George. Max. The Curse. Charlie. The Rags. On the rags. Henry. The monthlies. Auntie Rosa. The Visitor. Periods. My friend. My friend is visiting. A letter from a girlfriend. My little friend. My aunt is visiting. George is visiting. Henry's visiting. Max is visiting. Charlie's visiting. That time of the month. Spot. It. The deadly reds. I'm bleeding.'

Estella has almost folded herself over the wheel with laughter. 'Ooh, it hurts,' she says. 'Don't make me laugh.'

Olga has puffed out her cheeks with unlaughed air and, while looking at Estella, slowly releases the air through a small hole formed by her lips making farting noises.

Estella copies her, gradually changing the noises. They continue making air and lip noises at each other, eventually breaking into nonsense words.

'Nunununu nu,' says Olga.

'Nunu to you too,' says Estella hardly moving her lips.

And so it goes on from one nonsense to another, to pass the time until they find their way out of this place.

The track continues to be bumpy. Estella has driven the entire distance and is getting into the swing of boulders and gullies. She has to have three goes at one uphill slope, eventually choosing the track with its gullies in preference to the slippery slope of stones at the edge.

'You know,' says Olga dismally, 'I think we're on the track that goes right around the perimeter of the mountains. I think we should take the next turn to the right and try to head for the main road.'

'But why would they do that?'

'To maintain the fences probably. And to keep the sheep and goats out of the park.'

'I suppose so.'

Twenty minutes pass before a track veers off to the right, twenty minutes of bumping up and down the endless hips and dips in the earth's surface.

'Let's try it,' says Estella turning off. The road flattens out as they drive through the fenced paddocks. After a while the track peters out altogether. 'I'm going to follow those wheel tracks through the grass,' she says. Only the certainty that ahead of them, somewhere, is the main road, keeps them going even when no track at all is visible and they've detoured around so many gullies to make any notion of a straight line nonsense.

Ahead they see a fence. Olga gets out to open the gap, a wire gate. She pulls at the wire, untwisting it, but she can't get it through the hole in the post. Estella stops the engine and gets out. 'We'll have to cut it,' says Olga.

'Here, let me have a go.' Estella pulls and tugs and twists and gets one wire through, but the other is stuck. 'Okay, let's cut it,' she says giving in.

Olga drives through the gate. 'Don't worry about it,' she calls to Estella.

'Come on. We have to fix it. You can't open a gate and just leave it. The farmers round here will stop people like us driving through here. And rightly so,' she adds righteously, remembering Theo's complaints about city people. She gets the foot of the crowbar into the looped wire at the base and manages to retie the wire slightly differently but knowing it will hold.

Ten minutes later they reach the road. They leap out to stretch themselves and dance along the edge of the road, kicking up dust and stones.

'Uh oh,' says Olga wearily. 'I think I'm bleeding too.' She puts her hands down her pants. 'I am. Maybe you were right about vigorous movement. Maybe it does cause bleeding.'

They camp in a creek bed at the side of the road and watch the full moon rise into the sky.

I dream. We are walking and there are two of us. The land stretches to the horizon. Your belly is large. We travel and speak, we travel and sing, we collect plants and, as we consume them, we give them names.

Each day you are slower, and heavier, until your belly drags along the ground. We must stop and find a place to rest. Waves move across your belly, forming ridges and there is blood on the ground.

Your daughter is born on the ground, lies in blood on the ground. In time we walk on across the flat land that stretches to the horizon. Your belly is empty, flat, but the bleeding continues and you leave a trail of blood. Blood and earth mix. As you are weak, I build a shelter for you, and you rest in its shade. We all rest.

From the shade I see a movement, the flicker of an eye, a tail, a mouth. You are too weak to move, too weak to travel. The snake regards us, moves her tail and approaches us. She wants to devour us, to engorge her belly. She wants us.

My sister.

Her daughter.

My self.

I rise. I dance. I dance like the wind, like the water, like the leaves on trees, like the stars in the sky. I dance. I dance like the brolga on the plain, like the snake in the waterhole, like the fish in the sea.

The snake, is entranced. She ceases her approach.

I dance. But I am tired. I call to you, my sister. 'Dance with me,' I say.

You dance. We dance together.

I must rest. I am tired.

You dance. You dance and bleed. You bleed and the snake approaches. We dance in turns.

I dance.

You dance.

I dance.

You dance.

When I dance the snake stops. When you dance the snake approaches.

There is blood on the ground.

There is blood on the ground.

There is blood from her. I dance in fury. I dance in rage. I begin to bleed.

There is blood on the ground.

Blood on the ground.

There is blood from me.

We dance.

We dance together.

We bleed.

We bleed together.

There is blood on the ground.

Blood on the ground.

Blood from you.

Blood from me.

Blood from us.

The snake opens her mouth. She devours us. The cry of the child. The cry of the mother. I cry out.

There is blood on the ground.

16

On the winter solstice the walls are hung with harlequin mistletoe, with its long-lipped scarlet flowers.

We sit in a circle around the dimly lit room. A soft susurring of breath fills the room. A voice spins and turns, bouncing across the room, coiling around my mind. A voice of another timbre, sailing high, enters the circle. It continues while a third voice dips beneath it. Another slides between them. My voice enters the circle too and I hang on to it, playing the vocal chords. The sound intensifies. Echoes of voices bounce around the domed room and are lifted into the dome. Voices rise like eagles wedged in hot air. The room might lift, such is the strength of the chorus. Voices weave their own paths. While the pattern of sound is constantly changing, an underlying rhythm connects the whole.

I lift, losing all sense of being seated and my mind floats high above. I look down and see the sound rising in circles, waves rolling before my eyes. The sound is softening, slowing down. I am floating like a feather down the dying streams of sound. Only a few voices remain. They echo in the emptiness. One solitary voice slices the silence. It is silent. A deep green silence envelops me. All breathe slowly, even the walls.

Stella dressed for chapel. It was the first Sunday of the month, which meant an evening chapel service in addition to the Matins service they had already attended at the local church. She was peeved, since she'd been enjoying the book she was reading. Stella decided to slip it into her skirt band and take it with her. No one would notice. And if they did, she could count on them saying nothing. There weren't many who would choose to attend if they didn't have to.

They climbed the stairs in an orderly single file and sat in their usual places. She liked the interior of the chapel. There were no stained-glass windows here, but the contrast of the white walls, the rich red velvet curtains behind the altar, and the royal blue carpet thrilled her sense of colour.

She sat uncomfortably, her book digging into her. She lifted it a little and folded her arms over it. She couldn't begin reading until the service began. Instead, she sat and listened to the organ, turning every now and again to watch Miss Breely play – hands and legs all a-go – as though she had grown extra limbs for the purpose. She looked at Fiona sitting in the choir stalls at the back of the chapel. Part of Stella wished she could sing well enough to be in the choir, but then she wouldn't be able to read. As they stood to sing the first hymn, Stella pulled *Brave New World* out and put it inside the covers of her hymn book: 'Take ectogenesis. Pfitzer and Kawaguchi had got the whole technique worked out. But would Governments look at it? No. There was something called Christianity. Women were forced to go on being viviparous.'

What does that mean? wondered Stella. Something to do with life, probably from the Latin *vivo* – I live. But she could get no further.

Everyone knelt. The droning intonation of the curate's voice was punctuated by the congregation's responses.

Stella moved as the service dictated: standing, kneeling, sitting as required. She read:

'Even Epsilons are useful. We couldn't do without Epsilons. Everyone works for everyone else . . . '

Around her voices chanted from the Magnificat: 'For he hath regarded: the lowliness of his handmaiden.'

'"I'm glad I'm not an Epsilon," Lenina said with conviction.'

Stella's thoughts echoed Lenina's sentiments. Unconsciously she joined in with the final phrases of the Magnificat: '. . . as he promised to our forefathers, Abraham and his seed, forever. Glory be to the Father and to the Son: and to the Holy Ghost. As it was in the beginning, is now, and ever shall be: world without end. Amen.'

She sat back and mused over her book, wondering what it would be like to be a happy Epsilon, a semi-moron. What does it mean to be happy? She remembered how grief-stricken she'd been when Theo died; how she'd thought she would never be happy again. And yet on the whole she was, although sometimes she found it hard to believe that it had happened. He had always been a distant presence in life; in death he was simply more distanced. It was Coral she felt for: the hardships, financially and emotionally, that had followed his death. The last year had been even more difficult than usual, what with the drought. The promised trip north, to cheer them up, had never happened and they'd spent the Christmas holidays dragging through the days of unrelenting heat. But Coral was tough, at least on the outside, and she had made a good fist of her hardships. Stella wondered if Coral was happy now. Is happiness simply an absence of boredom? She thought, I'm bored in church, because it's always the same. How can people keep on going for years on end? What did it satisfy in them? It seems more like the sleep teaching in *Brave New World*.

She sat up with a start and smiled, pleased at her thought. She began reading again.

The hushed silence distracted her. The curate was putting on a record! He stood up and said, 'Psalm 51, if you want to follow the words.'

Stella returned to her book again.

A single voice pierced her attention. She looked up and waited for it expectantly. She sat in rapt attention, listening to the voice alternating with the choir. But it was that voice that carried her, lifted her out of her surroundings.

In the silence that followed the *Misereri*, the curate said a prayer and the girls filed out, subdued.

Olga and Estella are sitting in the creekbed, eating breakfast. The morning light is bright and sharp. The trees offer some shade, but the air is hot. Seven eagles are circling in the sky. One fledgeling eagle is sitting on a high branch of dead wood making a noise like the beginning of a kookaburra's laugh. There is a maniacal edge to its laugh.

Estella wonders what her life would have been like had she lived in another time, when there was no way of controlling the fits. Would she have been like Dostoyevsky's idiot: half mystic, half mad? Her fits would have marked her out for different treatment: witchcraft, reverence, madness. Fear creates such distortions. There had been times when Estella felt the pull of the labels, wondered about sanity and madness and concluded that she was saner than just about everyone else. Wondered about possession. She had come to understand the charge of that: a body falling, shaking, gasping for the strangled breath as if about to die, and then, through a veil of confusion, returning to life. And, like the mythical traveller to the underworld, she remembers nothing. Time folds away and does not re-open easily. She remembers the stunned looks on the faces around her when she comes to after a fit, remembers the void in her brain, wondering where she is, what she might have said. If she were religious it would be easy to call it divine intervention, or perhaps a relative of the laurel-inspired seizures of the Delphic priestess.

She wonders just how people in an earlier time felt. The mad and the revered and the reviled. Like the paradox of the snake: symbol of evil in one time, in one religion; or divine, the snake that licks clean the ears and ushers in prophecy, in another.

Estella can see herself and Julia at Delphi when she was twenty-two. They were visiting the Castalian Spring, at the base of the sanctuary. She remembers making a clicking sound with her tongue, like a death rattle or the sound of a rattle snake, and she wonders what had inspired that. She and Olga have spent long hours on this journey pulling out the recurring images of snake and bird. Estella retelling myths, Olga placing them in an archaeological setting, finding more and more examples of snakes and birds in ancient

123

cultures around the world. They laugh at the thought of Estella being possessed.

You lead me to the cave. We spend the night in silence, sitting on the cold rock floor. The silence of death enters. Stone silence. Wind silence. I follow you into the heart. One hand against your flesh, the other against the stone cold walls.

Much later I see a form, a figure in an alcove. The figure of a woman. She is snake-mouthed. I watch. I see the tongue flicker, twist, trying to form words. I hear her sibilant whisper

spirit sister

spirit sister

spirit sister

The whisper becomes a chant, endlessly repeated and with each repetition the sounds change. The same and yet different.

I extend my hand, try to touch her. I see the tongue flicker, then darkness presses forward rushing into the light, extinguishing it.

I am back at the entrance, watching the sunlight spread. I watch it ink its way into the cave, forming strange patterns as it moves towards us, slow as a winter snake. I remember the light, the drowning darkness, the snake-mouthed woman.

'Better to be possessed than mad,' says Olga.

'Not always. Depends on the time. Possession wasn't always divine and they'd do barbarous things in some cultures, like trephining.'

'What's that?'

'Ancient medicine. They cut a hole in your head to let out the bad air or the evil spirit.'

They were playing Scrabble. They had bent the rules so that every player had to make up a word and then had to give a convincing meaning to it.

It was Stella's turn. She put down T-W-I-N-K.

'It means "toilet", as in going to the twink.'

'I've got a great one,' said Janet excitedly. s-p-a-v. 'V on a triple letter score.'

'What's it mean?' Stella thought this was always the best part.

'It means throwing a fit, as in "he's having a spav". And you can use it as a noun too, as in "what a spav". You know, thick, a bit like a dag.'

Stella was silent as the rest laughed at Janet's dictionary-like examples. 'I don't think I want to play any more,' she said yawning, trying to pretend tiredness.

'What a spoil-sport. Just because Janet got a triple letter score.'

'No it's not. I'm just tired.'

'What a spav.' They all laughed as Stella left the room. Their not knowing didn't make it any easier to forgive them their insensitivity.

Stella was standing on her head in the centre of the gymnasium. She spent a lot of time there. 'How long is it?' she asked from her inverted position.

'Two minutes,' said Judy.

Stella lowered her legs slowly to the ground. 'Here, help me drag these mats into line, I need to practise my sequence.' Stella was competing in the gymnastics competition. She enjoyed throwing herself at the mat, turning in the air and balancing on various parts of her body. It gave her a sense of control over her body's movement through space.

She ran lightly towards the mat, leapt on to her head and hands and spun to her feet. Her body moved immediately into the next position, like a river in flow. She turned slightly sideways, and as her hands touched the ground her legs followed like a wheel turning. Then slowing to a balance, one leg raised and hand grasping her ankle, she leaned forward like a stork. Her body moved to the memory trained in the muscles. Balancing on her head again, she lowered her legs, in a jack knife and suddenly spun like a top on to her feet. It was as if she had springs in her head. She stood quite still a moment, as she knew she must at the end of the sequence.

When she wasn't in the gym, she was reading. She discovered in *The Republic* that Plato recommended gymnastics, and she was delighted that Plato wasn't as hard to read as she'd been led to believe. She read history books and novels. Among her favourites were *Coonardoo* and *To Kill a Mockingbird*. She began to notice her power to remember increasing. She'd stumbled on it one night when she hadn't had time to study for a history test. After lights-out she went into the bathroom and sat on one of the toilets madly memorising for the next day. She wasn't confident, but knew, when she sat the test, that it all seemed to be there. She got an A. After that, whenever she had a test she memorised just before going to sleep, using the silence of the bathroom, late at night. She got As in Chemistry and in English, as well as another in History. That year they gave her the progress prize, a dubious award, since it implied early failure. Even more rewarding than the prize was the apology she got from the headmistress.

The day they announced the prizes, no one was listed for her class. She asked Miss Hunter afterwards who'd got it. She shrugged and said, 'You'll find out.'

When the morning break came, another girl came up and said, 'Miss Montford wants to see you.' God, what've I done? thought Stella. It had been a long time since she'd spoken with the Head, though she'd been nice to Fiona and Stella when Theo had died.

She arrived breathless in the secretary's office. 'Yes,' said the secretary.

'I got a message to come and see Miss Montford.'

'Not looking like that you don't.'

Stella looked down. Her jumper had three holes in the front, and her skirt was rumpled. It had never been very good since Coral, as a strategy in economy during the drought, insisted the pleats be taken out of her old skirt and the material be re-used for the new style skirt. Fiona had transformed it into the new style one summer holiday. Stella felt ashamed, but she couldn't change her skirt.

'You'd better go and borrow someone else's jumper. Be quick, the bell goes again in five minutes.'

She ran down to her classroom, and practically pulled the

jumper off Judy's body. 'Quick, I need it. It's just for ten minutes. I'll bring it back.' She ran up the stairs two at a time and paused for a minute outside the door to get her breath back.

'That's better,' said the secretary. 'You'd better go in. She's waiting for you.'

The bell rang for class as Stella opened the door.

'Come on in, Stella. How are you?'

'Fine thanks, Miss Montford,' answered Stella, trying not to betray her breathlessness.

'Why didn't you come up after assembly.'

'What for?'

'The Progress Prize.'

'You didn't announce my name.' Stella could hardly believe it.

'Yes I did.'

'No, you didn't.'

'Let me have a look.'

Both were still standing.

'I'm sorry,' said Miss Montford finally, 'your name's not here. It should have been.'

'That's all right,' said Stella magnanimously.

'Tomorrow morning you will wait for Mrs Barrington at the front gate. She'll accompany you to the bookshop, where you can choose a book or books to the value of twenty dollars. You'd better go back to class. You'll be late.'

'Okay,' said Stella, who turned at the door and said, 'Thanks.' She flew down the stairs leaping the last four steps and landing lightly.

She bought a copy of *The Idiot* by Dostoyevsky.

To the left of the road, not long after they leave, there is a mountain shaped like an eagle in flight. It looks as if it is about to take off, but it is caught in the rocks on either side of its wings. Grounded.

Stella and her roommate, Mandy, often talked for hours after lights-out. Sometimes it was about the books they had both read, or about the big things, what they wanted to do with their lives; sometimes it was the stars in the sky, or the moonlight streaming in that prompted their conversations; occasionally they spoke about death.

The beds, which were close together, were sometimes dragged together, and they would gaze out the window and talk until there was no talk left.

One night, Mandy kissed her. They had kissed before, but this was different. Stella returned the kiss, softly. She put her arms around Mandy's shoulders and drew her into her bed. They touched and touched again and again. Their nipples rose, erect. Stella reached down into Mandy's pyjamas and twirled her finger lightly through her hair. She was wet.

'Want a ciggy?' Mandy said suddenly.

'Sure. You got any?'

'Yes, in the drawer.'

'You got matches?'

'I think so.'

Stella lit Mandy's cigarette, and they leaned out the window, to avoid leaving a betraying smell.

'I hope Miss Montford isn't walking her dogs tonight,' said Stella. 'I got caught on the stone badge at the front of the school one night just because she was out walking the dogs. I thought I'd be expelled. That was before you came.'

The conversation drifted into thin strands.

'I guess we'd better go to sleep,' said Mandy finally.

They pulled the beds apart and slept.

It never happened again, but Stella never forgot it either. Mandy snapped at her abruptly the following day. It seemed an ending, though Stella wished it were otherwise.

I touch my breasts. I run my hands over my nipples. They become firm, like raw ripe peas. I move my hands over the contours of my body. I tense the muscles of my belly. They form a symmetrical pattern of small ridges. I feel the muscles flex and relax. I run my fingers through my pubic hair. I touch the labia majora that hangs slightly. I feel the folds of skin around and between. I brush my hand against the inner part of my thigh. The labia swells. The hair is wet. I press my finger between the lips, into the warm mouth. I feel the little bulbs just inside the entrance. My finger is held there. I contract my muscles. They press firmly around my finger. My finger presses tip to bud. I caress my nipple. I feel the blood move towards the surface of my skin. My fingers and toes tingle. The muscles in my arms and legs relax and flex. I watch the play of colours near the surface of my skin. I play. I touch. I stroke. I continue to touch my body. I drum my fingers on my chest, belly, thighs. I pass my fingers through the wetness of my cunt. I thoroughly enjoy myself.

17

'Bloody hell. Feels like a flat tyre.'

Estella leans out her door, as far as she can, 'Yep. The back tyre is as flat as a tack.'

'Well, now's when we test our survival skills.'

'I guess so.'

'I'll go and look for a stone to rest the car on. She walks about twenty metres along the road and yells back, 'Look at this. Perfectment.' She lifts the stone, which is as long as her arms and about as wide as her two hands at their thickest parts. 'At least we stopped near a decent one,' she says, carefully placing the stone behind the tyre. 'Someone up there must be barracking for us.'

Olga gets back in the car and slowly backs it on to the stone.

'Whoa,' calls Estella, who then pulls out the tyre-changing equipment. Lying on the ground behind the wheel she places the jack under the support and winds the jack handle slowly. 'Oops,' she says, 'better loosen these nuts first.' She lowers the jack again. She pushes hard against the nuts. There's no movement. She has several goes. She tries pulling, knowing it won't help. 'You have a go.'

Olga repeats what Estella has done. Both are swearing at the nuts and the stupidity of the men machine-tooling them in workshops with no concern for the driver who has to undo them.

'How far back was that homestead?' asks Olga.

'It was 196 on the odometer. Nine kilometres then.'

'I guess we take the chance and walk it.'

'The tyre's fucked anyway. Maybe they'll have a spare. I don't fancy driving the next 200 kilometres without a spare. Or without anyone knowing where we are.'

'Okay, let's go.'

They gather water, sunglasses, sun screen, hats and a book each, and head off along the road.

Nine kilometres is a long walk in hot weather even if the sun is past its zenith. Olga and Estella pace themselves to match the heat. From time to time they pause to drink or to smear more sun screen on their shoulders, arms and noses.

'You've got flies all over your back,' says Olga. 'Do you want me to shoo them off?'

'No, leave them there. I don't mind them freeloading. It's better than having them landing on my nose. Maybe they're lost souls looking for a place to stay.'

Olga is less generous to them. She shakes her head several times and waves her arms about. But after a while she forgets and the flies land again, covering the back of her T-shirt.

As they walk they talk about the birds, the heat, the occasional stone they pick up. They wonder many times how much further it could be. Towards the end they begin to think that the house will be around every corner, over every rise. Estella is making private bets to herself: next corner; next hill. But it is a long time before it is.

Finally they see the house on a hill that is much higher than they remember. As they approach a flock of sulphur-crested cockatoos screeches into the air and lands further away. A long water trough is the attraction; some still stand on the edge of the trough, leaning forward to drink in delicate sips. A sentinel squawks loudly, and the rest rise like a single organism and fly to the nearest tree, which they have stripped of foliage.

'You knock,' says Olga, when they reach the door.

'Excuse me,' says Estella to the man who opens the door, 'I hope we're not interrupting your afternoon, but we have a flat tyre about nine kilometres down the road. We could change the tyre, but unfortunately the nuts have been machine tightened and we can't move them. Would you be able to help us?'

'Sure. Come in.' Children scatter as Olga and Estella walk into the living-room. A small girl, blonde and bright runs up to Olga and says, 'You want to see what I got for Christmas?'

'Yes,' says Olga. 'Why don't you bring it here?' The little girl runs out.

'She hasn't had a chance to show anyone since Christmas,' says the woman, also blonde.

The little girl runs back in. 'Look.' She hands Olga a hair-dryer.

Estella can hardly contain herself. 'Kids are amazing, aren't they?' she says to the woman. 'You have a giant hair-dryer right outside the door, and what do they want?'

There are three children, and they are so pleased to have visitors that it sounds like there are ten. All three are talking simultaneously. They don't want answers, simply the sound of their own voices.

'I think Pete's just gone to get the gear ready,' says the woman. 'I'm Carole, by the way.' Olga and Estella introduce themselves. Pete comes back in.

'Do you think,' says Estella, 'we could have your telephone number? That way we could ring, say, by noon tomorrow and let you know that we've reached the town. We've only got the one spare, you see.'

'I might have a spare out there. What're you driving?'

'A Toyota.'

'I'll go and check.'

Olga and Estella are filling themselves with water.

'Would you like something to eat?'

'No, we're right, thanks.'

Pete comes back. 'No worries. You ready to go?'

'Yep. Ready as ever,' says Estella.

The three children are yelling, 'Can we come, can we come?' Pete gives in to the pressure. The kids climb into the open utility back, just as Estella had done when she was a child. They leap about in the back, spitting into the wind, their hair streaming back from their foreheads.

'Quite a walk,' says Pete.

'Yes, we don't usually walk so far in the city,' says Olga. 'But it wasn't a great hardship, though I could have done with fewer flies.'

'No chance. Not out here,' says Pete. 'It's their homeland, you know.'

They reach the car and the kids tumble from the back even though they've barely stopped. They prance energetically about as their father kicks at the wrench. 'They're bloody tight,' he says as he loosens the last.

'We know,' Olga and Estella chorus.

After changing the tyre, he loosens the nuts on all the other wheels. 'Well, kids,' he says, turning, 'we'd better get home so I can put the spare tyre I have on this wheel frame.'

'Okay, we'll follow you,' says Olga, climbing into the driver's seat.

They sit and watch, along with Carole and a couple of dogs, as Pete changes the wheel. He bashes the hub out and then checks the new tyre and tube that's to go on, wetting it, looking for bubbles. Estella is reminded of the many times she watched Theo change car tyres, truck tyres, tractor tyres and her own bicycle tyres. She figures she could do it if she had to but is glad that today it isn't necessary. Pete bashes the wheel hub into place, lifts the tyre and bounces it a few times.

'Thanks a lot,' says Olga. 'How much do we owe you?'

'Let's say, twenty-five?'

'Are you sure? Are you including your labour?'

'That'll cover it,' he says.

Estella is rummaging through the purse. 'We don't have any change, so how about thirty?'

'Okay, if you insist.'

'Are you sure you don't want to stay?' says Carole. 'We've got a couple of spare beds in the workers' cottage, which we don't use really. You could stay overnight and join us for tea. We have turkey and salad left over from our New Year's dinner today.'

'Thanks,' says Estella, 'but no, we'll go on. We're a bit behind schedule anyway.'

The three children have run outside again and are standing waving with their parents as Olga and Estella head off once again.

Stella was given her itinerary for the trip. In two and a half weeks thirty-three school girls and three teachers would travel from Port Hedland to Darwin. She went round excitedly and got everyone's signature, a kind of beginning souvenir.

Stella was so excited about flying. She felt like a bird looking down from her window seat. A natural hoarder, like Theo had been, she collected souvenirs from the planes and the hotel they visited on the first day. She had sugar, tea and coffee sachets, a towelette packet, a paper napkin, her air ticket, a laundry list and writing paper from the Walkabout Hotel.

Their first night camping out under the stars was less than perfect. Stella was freezing and kept waking up. When she did she wished it would hurry up and get light. Between patches of sleep she lay there keeping up her old habit of trying to count the stars, which was easier when they were framed by a window: out here it went on and on. When morning finally came she was glad to get up and outdid the rest by leaping into the river and swimming across to the other side.

They spent the day looking for rocks: tiger eye and asbestos. Stella found a huge piece of asbestos with long blue silky fibres. She thought about the asbestos plates they put under the bunsen burners at school and wondered how it was possible that something so beautiful could be turned into something so mundane. She packed her asbestos stone in a safe place, and from time to time would draw it out to touch the silk threads.

The days were filled with driving and singing and climbing out of the bus to fossick for stones or to photograph flowers and rocks. In the mornings and evenings the jobs were rotated among three groups: wood and water; cooking; and bed erecting. Once completed they were free to do what they wanted. At Broome Stella went for a long walk by herself along the wide beach. She sat and watched the waves that had pounded in her ears the previous night. She paddled in the shallows, watching her toes appearing and disappearing in the foam. She wondered what it would be like to live up here and collect shells, like the old woman with the huge shell collection, whose place they had visited yesterday afternoon. Or to live in Marble Bar, in those awful houses, with no trees, out in the middle of the hottest place in the country, and only the beauty of the Bar itself to sustain you. Home seemed in the midst of a metropolis by comparison.

That afternoon they visited the old prison tree outside Derby – a huge boab, with a trunk shaped like a balloon, and a small opening in one side, like a gaping wound. They said it was a thousand years old. She tried to imagine what that tree had seen, but all she could imagine was the crowding of criminals around the curved walls inside the billowing trunk.

Stella was standing in grass as high as her knees looking at the high range of black rock that reared into the sky. An old reef fossilled was what Miss Morton had said. The rock was sheer and pinnacled high above where Stella stood. She walked towards it and touched it, as though she was handling something sacred. It was sharp. She ran her fingers lightly across a pointed section just to see how it felt. She picked up a stone and tapped it. It rang. It made her feel eerie, which seemed odd standing in bright sunlight. As she turned she noticed a swarm of tiny black bees flitting between the spires of rock.

She climbed back on the bus and stared out the window as they moved away from the strange fortress of rocks.

As the bus drove on the girls in the back seat began to sing:

One man went to mow
Went to mow a meadow
One man and his dog Spot, a bottle of pop, sausage roll with sauce on top
Went to mow a meadow

Everyone joined in. They reached the last verse, which they yelled rather than sang:

Ten men, nine men, eight men, seven men, six men, five men, four men, three men, two men, one man and his dog Spot, a bottle of pop, sausage roll with sauce on top
Went to mow a meadow.

The bus reached Tunnel Creek in the late afternoon, and after they had set up camp Stella and six others went for a swim in the river. All except one were from the country, and felt at home swimming in creeks and rivers in the bush. They dispensed with bathers and went skinny dipping. Stella thought there was nothing better than feeling the water wash around and through her body.

The next day they walked in hundred degree heat through Windjana Gorge, rock walls soaring above them. Bill, the bus driver, said he knew where there were some rock paintings. They had the choice of sunning themselves by the river or going with him. Most chose the sandy beach and swimming. Stella kept the pace of the walk fast, walking ahead of the party, and then waiting in the shade as they caught up. It was a long walk, but worth it, thought Stella, when they finally reached the cave. Just above their heads were two paintings, mostly red ochre on brown rock, along with some white. Stella mentally followed the outline of the two kangaroos. She wished she were taller so she could touch the rock. Instead, she touched the rock wall near her. It was cool. None of them said much. Stella squatted near the line of sun and shade for a moment, her neck craning back. They walked back and swam in the cool water near the big rock, where the others, now tired of sunning themselves, waited.

They lunched back at the campsite and Bill took them on a second walk for the day into Tunnel Creek. The creek at this point buried itself in rock, passing right under the black fossil rock of the Napier Range.

As they entered the cave they stopped a minute to allow their eyes to adjust to the dark. They walked forward. The roof was like waves. 'Don't go out there,' lied Bill, 'there's quicksand.' They held one another's hands for reassurance in

136

the dark. Bill took them to what he called his Jewel Palace. They scrambled one by one into a small cave above the water, dry and firm. When he struck a match, the walls shone like silver and diamonds mixed. Stella wanted to stay forever in the cool quiet of the cave. But that wasn't possible and she half slid from the cave, and the next in line climbed in while she waited in the dark. Occasionally she thought she saw something move. She heard fluttering. 'Bats,' said Bill when he joined them and they headed back into the sunlight, which glared at them as they emerged.

The bus left Tunnel Creek the following day, headed for Geikie Gorge. It wasn't far and they were all looking forward to it. But the bus broke down. Bill crawled under the bus and came out with the news that the centre bearing on the rear wheels was broken, and he reckoned it would take about three hours to fix.

Stella, Jan, Pam and Bill crawled out from under the bus. 'It's fixed,' said Stella. Stella and the others were covered in grease.

'God, look at you,' said Pam.

Stella looked. She had two round circles of grease on her breasts, and another, a little lower. She looked up, 'You can talk,' she said, wiping her greasy hand across her forehead.

'We'd better wash up,' said Bill, offering them kerosene. They scrubbed as much grease from them as they could, but Stella's yellow top would never be the same.

They reached Geikie Gorge just as it was getting dark.

The next day they travelled up the river in dinghies. The water was clear and reflected, mirror-like, the rocks and trees along the edge. The white limestone has been sculpted, leaving small grottoes and hollowed out clefts in the rock. In some places they were like the pillars of an old church.

After lunch Stella sat on the small beach reading. She heard something move in the grass and moved quietly towards the sound. A small Johnson crocodile was sunning itself on a log. She reached out and grabbed it behind the head, as she'd done with her pet lizards at home. It was about as long as her arm. She looked at its teeth which were sharp, but small. The crocodile squirmed, but she wanted to show the others. Then she let it go again, and it swam out into the stream.

For Stella, the rest of the trip paled against the beauty of Windjana, Tunnel Creek and Geikie Gorge. Even the gorge at Katherine. Although the cliffs were more sheer, it lacked the beauty of isolation. She could see around her, all the other people who had come to look. She thought she'd like to come back some time, perhaps alone.

Flying back from Darwin, she slept and dreamt that she was a bird swooping over the plains, circling in the rising air above cliffs, sitting high in the branches of a tree and laughing.

Stella finished her exams on her birthday. She couldn't tell how she'd done. She knew she had crossed out one right answer and replaced it with a wrong answer in her Biology exam, but she thought she'd probably got through okay.

She went to stay with Fiona for a few days. She knew she could do whatever she wanted there. Her friend, Mandy, came with her. On their first night they got drunk together on a flagon of claret. They turned the furniture upside down, sat in the sink, and laughed until they were almost sick with it. Fiona was furious.

Although they both felt terrible the next day, they went out and drank some more. And they walked around the city, telling each other ridiculous jokes.

They rang their boyfriends from a public phone and arranged a date for that evening. The two boys took them to a pub, and then they went back to Bruce's house in Carlton. It was a dingy house with small windows opening on to grey rooms, and a staircase so narrow Stella wondered how they'd managed to get the double beds upstairs. Bruce and Mandy took one room, Mark and Stella the other. There was no mattress on the bed in the room that Bruce had said they could use. Mark spread a blanket and a sheet over the wire mesh of the bed. It wasn't comfortable.

Stella had decided tonight would be the night, before they'd come here, and now she felt unable to change her mind, in spite of the discomfort. They went through with it, and although Mark was careful, she didn't enjoy the pinching of the wire mesh beneath her.

'Did you have an orgasm?' he asked, afterwards.

'What's that?'

'Well, you'd know if you had,' he said cryptically.

18

Stella went to dinner on her first night in college, wondering if the food would be as bad as it had been at school. It was, but at least she could choose between several things. She'd heard that there was to be some sort of initiation that evening, with the boys from the other college. Nobody seemed to know what would happen. Or if they did, they weren't letting on.

She went upstairs, and read until the time came to leave. All the girls left together. They walked to the boys' college, not far away. Some of the second and third year girls were sitting among the boys in the common room. Then they closed the door. The girls were kept outside in the corridor, and were called in one at a time. I shouldn't have come, thought Stella, as the first was called in. But it was too late, boys stood guard at the doors at the end of the corridor. The second was called. They tried to hear what was going on, but the sound was muffled. The first hadn't come out. Was she still in there? Did she go out another door?

'I don't want to be here,' said one of the others.

'Me either,' said Stella. 'But there's no way out now.'

They looked at the boys stationed at the doors. 'Do you think they'd let us pass?' said Stella.

'We could try.'

'Do you think we should charge, or just walk out?'

'I think we should run at them and dodge under their arms.'

'You want to do it?' asked Stella.

'Why not?'

At that moment the door opened and the third was called in. It was terribly quiet in there.

'Okay, when they look away we'll go for it,' said the other girl.

They waited a few minutes, then the boy nearest them looked out the door. They both charged at him as fast as they could. They got past him, but three others were at the next door. One grabbed Stella, and she bit his arm, but he hung on. The other girl, who was a bit bigger than Stella, was being held by the other two boys.

'You don't think you're the first to try it, do you?' said one of the boys.

Neither answered. They were dragged back to the waiting point, where the others stepped aside, not wanting to be associated with them. The door opened and they were pushed inside.

'A bargain this time,' said one of the guard boys as he pushed them in.

One boy, dressed in his gown, sat on the largest chair in the room. One of the older girls sat next to him. Around them were a lot of other boys, and a sprinkling of girls. The older girl whispered something to the boy in the gown, and then laughed to herself.

'Shall we begin?' said the boy.

All of them nodded.

'Two for the price of one, eh? Okay girls, relax. We don't mean you any harm. You thought we did, didn't you?'

Neither girl responded.

'Talkative too, I see. If you just do as we say, everything will be fine. You with the red T-shirt, turn around.'

Stella stood there. She didn't move.

'No manners either. I asked nicely. TURN AROUND,' he yelled.

She stood still until a boy stepped forward and made her turn.

'A bit big,' she heard someone say.

'A bit small in front,' said another.

'Hairy legs,' said a female voice.

'Okay, Fatty, now your turn,' the boy said to the other girl. She didn't turn either, until they made her.

'Great tits,' said a boy at the back.

'The only thing they've got between them though,' said the boy in the gown. 'Who's going to start the bid?'

'Twenty-five cents,' said the boy from the back. 'For Tits.'

'Am I bid any more? Four tits for the price of two.'

The room was silent.

'What a bargain,' said gown.

'Might be more trouble than you bargain for,' said a voice from the side of the room. 'Must be lesos if they've got hairy legs.'

'Going . . . Am I bid another ten cents . . . Going . . . Gone.'

They were ushered out the back door, where they were forced to sit and wait.

'God,' said the other girl, 'you were so gutsy. I think I would have turned round when they said to, if you hadn't refused. I'm Harriet.'

'I'm Stella. God, it's so awful. I don't know if I want to stay after this.'

'You have to. What would I do? I'm on a scholarship. I have to stay. You will, won't you?'

'Yeah. I guess so. I have to too. My mother thinks it's too dangerous to live in a flat. God, if only she knew.'

They could hear laughing through the door. Harriet turned to the other three girls. 'What was it like for you? Did they bid for you?'

'Sure. It was fun. I got ten dollars.'

'Really?' said one of the others. 'I only got six.'

'I don't want to know what they bid,' said Harriet. 'I want to know why you liked it.'

'I don't know. It didn't seem too bad,' said the second, 'I mean, they said some nice things.'

Harriet was getting angrier, she turned on the third, who'd been silent up till then. 'What did you think?'

'I . . . um, I didn't like it much, but, um, I didn't really think it was terrible, I just thought maybe it should have been different, you know, nicer. I mean, after all, it's our first night here.'

'Well, I reckon we should kick up a stink,' said Harriet.

'Me too,' said Stella, who felt braver in her actions than in her words.

The next day Harriet and Stella and a couple of others, including the third girl, Anne Marie, went to the head of the college.

She said she agreed with them in principle, but thought that since it was over it was best not to make a fuss. It was meant in fun, she said, and asked which boys were rude. Harriet and Stella tried to explain that it was all of them, and it was the fact that they had egged one another on. The only one they could name was the boy in the gown. She said she'd try and get him to apologise to them.

He never did. He just made sure everything was harder for them. They gave up wasting their time on it after a while. The only good thing that had come of it was their friendship.

Stella and Harriet went everywhere together. They would meet in the caf at lunchtime after their classes and talk and drink coffee, and talk more. They spent hours sitting in one another's rooms talking, sometimes reading. Stella stayed up all night with Harriet, to help her finish her first assignment which was running late. They went ice-skating together and would dance together on the rink as the music played through the tinnie speakers. They picked up a couple of boys at the rink who would later pay for their coffee. They laughed about it afterwards, since neither really liked the boys, but it was useful.

At Easter Stella went to stay with Harriet's family in the country. They went to the lake and Harriet taught Stella to water ski. Stella loved it, but her arms ached terribly the next day.

When first term finished, they were separated for three weeks and wrote one another long letters about what they were doing, which books they had read and their newest insights into the world. Harriet wrote saying she thought she'd fallen in love, with a boy she'd met at a barbecue at the Water Skiing Club. She wrote pages about how she felt. How this had never happened to her before.

Back in college, their life continued on in much the same way. Sometimes at lunch they'd be joined by others they'd met in their classes, or Anne Marie would sit with them and bring her friend Lorraine. Anne Marie had moved out of college and shared a flat with Lorraine not far from the university. Stella visited them sometimes, listened to the loud music and shared a joint or two. She liked their flat and wished she didn't have to stay in college.

One day Anne Marie asked her if she'd like to stay there and look after the flat during the second-term holidays. Stella wrote and told Coral that she wouldn't be home after all, that she had somewhere to stay, and it would give her a chance to go to the library and do some work. Then Lorraine dropped out and Stella moved in with Anne Marie.

She went to see Harriet in her room on the first day of term.

'Turncoat,' yelled Harriet and slammed the door in her face.

'Harriet, please. Let me in. I want to explain. I don't see why you're so angry.'

Harriet opened the door. 'You promised to stay. And you didn't even have the guts to tell me.'

'I tried to ring you, but you were always at the Water Skiing Club. I didn't think it made any difference to you any more.'

'Well, I couldn't ring you back, could I?'

'No, that's true. Maybe we'll get the phone on, but we can't afford it just now.' They were both silent, still standing in the doorway. 'I'm sorry,' said Stella finally. 'You know I hated it here. It's not as though you can't visit me. Do you want to come to dinner?'

'No thanks. I've got work to do tonight.'

'How about lunch as usual?'

'Maybe.'

Stella went and sat at their usual table in the caf. Harriet didn't come. Not that day, or the day after. After a week, Stella gave up and went home for lunch instead.

They have left the rugged ranges behind them and are diving headlong into flatness towards the west. The land seems to spread out, like melting liquid, around them, and the colour of the road has changed, to a light brown colour, that seems to reflect the sense of over-exposure from light, like the washed-out colour of an old sepia photograph.

The first town they come to is asleep, no doubt sleeping off the effects of yesterday's drinking. They see notices for a New Year's Day celebration on the verandah of the pub. A few strips of broken balloons and some coloured streamers blow in the hot wind. They drive on, leaving the town to sleep off its hangover.

The vegetation has shifted back to the grey green of salt-bush. The flatness is broken in the distance by a pinky-purple mesa. As they drive the forms and colours of the mesas change. Some are like pyramids, with their tops cut off; others more like the conventional table.

They have been silent for a long time, gazing at the open panorama of a horizon that extends the full three hundred and sixty degrees.

'Stop,' screams Estella suddenly. 'Go back.'

Olga starts backing, 'What for?'

'The sign. Did you see the sign?'

'No.' She is squinting at the rusted metal sign next to the road. 'What's it say?'

'LESBIANS ARE EVERYWHERE.'

'Even in the most unexpected places,' says Estella, 'including inside.'

'Huh?'

'Harriet,' says Estella. 'Even inside Harriet, though she didn't want to admit it. Nor did I at first.

'I truly did not understand why Harriet was angry with me, when I left the college,' says Estella. 'I do now. She felt betrayed. But I thought this boyfriend was all that mattered. I hadn't met him, but she would go into long descriptions of him and rapturously describe his every feature. Much later, after we'd finished at uni, well I was still there, but she'd finished, she told me she'd made him up. That was when I felt betrayed. I asked her why, of course, and she said it made her feel more normal. It was too late by then, and I knew that if that was how she felt, then there wasn't any point anyway. And there'd been Steve and others in between.' Estella fell silent. 'I still miss her sometimes. We were so innocent. I mean, at that stage, it didn't even occur to me that I'd been in love with her. Strangely, it was Steve who noticed it.'

'Not so strange really. You probably talked about her, in the same way she'd talked about the fabricated boyfriend.'

'Yes, probably.' She paused for a moment. 'We must be getting near the lake, all this salt.'

'Look at that little hill over there,' says Olga. 'It looks like snow in the desert.'

Stella thrived on the freedom of living outside of college. No more regimens. No more having to lie when she came in late. No more grey food. She even had her own sheets to sleep in. There were always lots of people at the flat, loud music and conversation that roamed beyond the bounds of formal subjects. Sometimes they stayed up all night, drinking and smoking, and then they'd sit on the line of bricks that separated the flat from the footpath and watch the sun rise over the buildings. It was a night like that, when she met Steve. He came with a friend of Anne Marie's who introduced him as Steve, the poet. And that was how he thought of himself. He wasn't a student, he thought he was above all that. He worked, sometimes, on the railways. He said he could write more poetry during work there than anywhere else, except maybe in the public service.

Stella liked his irreverence, and especially liked it when he began to write poems dedicated to her. One morning, after a party, he brought her a poem:

I might have called you Salomé
(she too could dance).
Except she danced for gluttonous men.
And you, you danced alone
with only one veil, your scarf,
to flash through the air
like lightning.

146

When the academic year came to an end, he stopped going to work for a while. Instead, they lay around, or they'd go for long rides on his motor bike to the beach or to the country, or to visit friends of his.

Stella got a job for a while, selling encyclopaedias. She memorised sixteen pages of sales' pitch in a day at the beach. That bit was all right. But she couldn't go through with the selling. On the day when she was meant to be promoted, because she'd had one successful sale, she and Steve decided to go to Sydney instead.

'It's too far to ride,' said Steve. 'Why don't we hitch?'

They set off at five. The first ride, in a truck, took them over the border to Holbrook, a town with wheat silos and two 24-hour petrol stations for the truckies driving through over-night. But then they got stuck. The truckie insisted on taking a break. He invited them in to meet his mate who ran the petrol station and then drank beer until the sun rose. Stella refused to go any further with him. She'd thought, at first, that a break meant sleep. She got Steve to come outside with her on the pretext of looking at the sunrise, and they left. The rides were erratic. Sometimes it was only a matter of minutes between rides, at others, hours. The best was the Rolls Royce that picked them up outside Mittagong. It was midnight when they finally arrived in Sydney.

They slept for a couple of hours on newspapers in a half-built house and then went to the beach, where they slept again, until the shops opened.

It rained that afternoon and all of the next day. So they stayed in a hotel in the Cross and hitched back to Melbourne the next day. A truck picked them up in Liverpool and dropped them in Melbourne at 5 AM the following day. They went back to Stella's place and slept.

Anne Marie returned from her parents' place, and so did all her friends.

'Want to try some magic mushies?' said Tim, who had long blonde locks. 'A friend in Queensland sent them to me.'

They all had some. And they all felt sick. But someone said it would be worth it. Someone turned the music up.

Stella watched as the walls began to crawl and bounce and

147

become like coloured marbled paper. She lost all sense of time and laughed a lot. She went and lay on her bed and watched and watched. She heard, as though far away, the voices of others. When she looked towards the sound, she could see no one. The room had expanded into a huge dome. The carpet extended like a gibber desert to infinity. She heard birds and saw something fly, as she turned her head, just the wings. Someone screamed, and there were birds sitting on her; crows pecking at her skin, which had become blotchy and red with the pecking. Then she was sitting with someone who had hair like an elf. He said something and she replied with a voice that didn't belong to her. He pointed and she saw friendly round people all around her. They were smiling so hard, she thought the tops of their heads might fall off. They smiled like the clowns who swallow ping pong balls at the shows, with mouths like roses, opening and opening, petals peeling back forever and ever. She said to the flower heads, 'You're so pretty, I think I'll have to die.' She turned to the one with elf hair, whose hair was writhing towards the light bulb, 'It hurts, when it's so beautiful.' He nodded and lay back on the carpet to dream. She knew, because she could see the dreams hovering like clouds over him. They were all laughing again and she laughed until the room shrank to its usual size and the flowers no longer danced in the vase. She went to bed and dreamed illogical and senseless dreams. When she got up to make a coffee, sleeping bodies were spread on every bed, couch and space of floor. She made eleven cups of coffee and went to sit on the bricks.

There are rivers in my hands, my fingers are webbed like a delta. My arms have become wings and I am a witch soaring on magic flying ointment. Others fly near me – Hecate, Circe, Medea, Sappho – and their words burn into my flesh. I am tattooed with the words that killed them:

> *witch wicce witga vitki wit wisdom wise woman*
> *incantatrix lamia lesbian saga maga malefica*
> *sortilega strix venefica herberia*
> *anispex auguris divinator janutica*
> *ligator mascara phitonissa stregula*

'Look at the lake!' says Estella. 'It's really here, and full of water!'

Ahead lies a vast expanse of water, stretching right across the horizon, like a huge bird with outstretched wings. Sandy beaches edge the lake and salt crystals glisten pinkly in the fading sunlight.

They get out and stretch their bodies. On a bank that reaches into the water, pelicans stand in profile against the sun, some spread their wings, or scratch their backs with long beaks. Other birds are wheeling overhead.

Olga and Estella, in a single movement, drop to the ground and sit to watch the dying day's activities, overwhelmed by the magic of water birds in the midst of the desert.

Long ago, you say, a huge bird came to this land. She came, her feathers rich with spirits. She flew across the land and from time to time a feather fell from her body and where they fell rivers flowed. She flew until she reached a place with rock walls that rose high all around, a place of shelter. As she landed she fluttered her wings noisily and the spirits were thrown from her feathers.

Feather fine, some broke the earth and water flowed forming a huge pool; some slipped into the cracks of the rocks. There they remained, emerging only to dance with the wind, or to gaze longingly at their sisters the stars.

The bird travelled on to other places but always returned to the place of her first landing. Whenever she returned she watched the spirits dance. But each time she returned they grew fainter and fainter until one day she returned to find she could not see them at all. She could hear only a faint tapping sound like dancing feet on rock.

The bird chipped at the rock with her beak. She pounded the pieces into fine powder, by curling her toes around the chipped fragments and dancing. Then she mixed the powder with water and began to paint the spirits back into visibility with the fine line of her beak. When she was done she was surrounded. They all danced kicking up their legs. Rocks leapt from the walls, dust was raised in willy willies, spinning

149

eddies formed in the water. And so they danced and danced.

The bird travelled no more but remains dancing with her companions among the painted rocks beside the clear pool.

19

The lake is dark and still. Two moons, one a golden reflection of the other, lie on it. Indefatigable fingers of light reach out across the water.

Sound registers in the inner ear as dawn trembles on the edge of night. A dawn that brings a sky flaming red, like a girl's first menses. As the light lifts I curl into the hollow of your belly, feeling the wave roll over me before it falls into scattered oblivion. We drift between sleep and wakefulness, slipping from night into day, and we waver like lovers on the edge of making a commitment.

Estella wakes to the sound of birds. She lies, listening, wondering if Olga is awake. The land emerges into visibility in the water-colour morning light. She moves her hand, lightly brushing Olga's leg. Olga opens her eyes and smiles. Their bodies fall into one another: hands and legs and cheeks and lips meeting. Olga feels the surge of waves breaking through her half-dream state as Estella's hands find her. Her body anticipates the movement of fingers and she lifts, almost flies, to meet her. Her mind is filled with just one word – you, you, you – as fingers and lips meet and the sounds of dawn wash over them, lulling them back to sleep again.

Stella was up unusually early for her. She and Steve were going gliding. If they were to be there by nine, they had to leave home by seven. He was coming to pick her up, and she moved around the flat quietly so as not to wake Anne Marie and Mike. She took her breakfast out on to the bricks and sat there watching the sky lose its tinges of red. She was thinking about the last sunrise she'd seen, only a few weeks earlier. She hadn't been to bed at all that night. She and Steve and Anne Marie and Mike and Tim had sat around all night watching the music stream from the speakers in waves of green and red, and flashes of yellow. They compared the colours they saw with the pitches they heard. When the sun came up someone had said, 'Look, the music of the spheres.' They had all laughed and wondered what record god was playing to create a sunrise like that. But today, the sky was silent.

She sat in the car at the airfield and stared at the page of her book, reading over and over the same lines. Her chest had become unbelievably tight. She'd been waiting all day for a ride. But members always had first option, and it seemed that children of members and spouses of members could also jump the queue. The problem with Steve was that he let everyone else walk over him, and consequently over her too. The airfield was windy and miserable and she was sick of sitting in the car. But she knew that if she went over to the clubhouse, no one would bother to tell her when her turn was up. So she sat on. She preferred her solitude to the company of the club crowd.

She continued to stare at the pages of her book, but her anger interrupted the flow, and she kept having to go back, or she lost her place, or she lost interest in the disjointed prose. It was as though the book was staring back at her, refusing to allow her to comprehend its meaning.

There was a tap on the window and she almost jumped out of her skin in fright. She wound down the window. 'Your turn next,' said the man.

'Okay, I'm coming. How come I had to wait so long?'

'Just one of those days,' he said, not even bothering to defend himself.

Stella's anger was renewed by her powerlessness to respond. She shrugged her shoulders and stood next to the man with the flight sheet.

Gliders were coming in every five or ten minutes, as the day's flights drew to an end.

'You'll get the sunset run,' said the man. 'Nothing better than that.'

As if that made up for a whole day's wait, thought Stella.

Steve came up behind her, patting her on the bottom. 'Ready?' he said.

'I've been ready for hours,' said Stella grumpily. They walked to the glider and got in. Stella pulled the safety belt across her and clicked it in. Steve climbed in behind her.

They were towed into the air, and then they were on their own. Once the tow plane had left it was quiet, except for the soft whistle of the wind. Stella opened her window and put her arm out, touching a wisp of cloud as they passed through it.

'It's almost as good as being a bird,' she said.

'Want to really feel what it's like?' said Steve from behind.

'Yeah, sure.'

They seemed to stop in mid air, the nose pointing to heaven. Then they dropped. Stella thought she'd left herself behind somewhere. The ground was now spinning above her. She fell inside herself. And then it stopped. The spinning stopped and the ground and sky returned to their places.

'Want some more?' said a voice.

'Yes. In a minute, when my stomach finds me.'

'More of the same, or something different?'

'Can you do a loop?'

'Sure can. We'll just get our height up again.'

Stella looked across towards the hills and saw an eagle soaring upwards in a thermal at almost the same altitude. She wondered if eagles ever got dizzy.

'You'll feel a bit heavy as we go round this one. Just relax. Ready then.'

Steve pulled back the flight stick and Stella felt herself being pushed back against the seat. She saw the orange sun bearing down on her. Her face was dragged down on to her chest and her breasts seemed to find a new position some-where near her navel. Her body curled, bowl-like. She thought of the sad faces she used to pull as a child, but she was sure that if she had a mirror this would surpass all her previous attempts. The weight on her chest became unbearably heavy, and then began to lift. She breathed. It had taken so long, she thought that Steve must have passed out. She had no idea how anyone managed to stay in control during such acrobatics, but she was glad they could.

'We'd better get back to base,' said Steve cheerfully. They circled down in an elliptical spiral, and touched down on the twilight grass.

Olga wakes again and draws closer to Estella. They get up and piss into the salty sand. They can faintly hear the plashing of water on the beach. Estella swings the billy and they eat breakfast watching the birds once again.

'Want to come for a walk?' says Estella.

'Yes. Just wait while I get my sunglasses.'

They walk across the sand towards the water. Estella is trying to follow the solid ground, but it's hard to tell where the soft patches are. She places her feet carefully, walking as flatfooted as she can, trying to distribute the weight evenly.

'Wait,' she hears from behind and swivels to see Olga sinking into the mud. Estella walks back to her. 'Don't stand on one foot, or you'll sink further.'

'How come you're not sinking?' Olga pulls a squelching foot from the mud. Her thongs are coated brown. She removes them and walks forward gripping Estella's arm. They walk together, Estella, like a Jesus bird, is unaffected by the mud; Olga sinks in with each step. They reach the water's edge where it is a little firmer. Olga washes the mud from her thongs as gulls dive for fish in the still water.

To their right, behind an arm of water, is a line of sand, superimposed by a line of white salt, and behind it further stripes of more sand and more water. It forms a landscape like an abstract painting, parallel lines, decreasing in width as you approach, from above and below the central line. Lines of blue and brown and white.

'Strange, isn't it,' says Estella. 'Every time I go a long way from the cities I see landscapes like paintings. It's like all the people who watched the solar eclipse on TV, because they were scared they'd go blind.'

'What did you do?'

'I went to the zoo with a friend.'

Stella and Kay met at the zoo gates at three. It wasn't very crowded even though it was a Sunday. There was still a bit of time before the eclipse would be visible, so they made the most of the quiet and ambled from one enclosure to another. For once the koalas were awake. They thought it was sunset, although it was only just after three.

All the animals were behaving oddly. Some, like the koalas, were waking up; others were moving towards their sleeping places. The animal keepers were trying to placate them with extra rounds of food.

The shadows were lengthening quickly. The monkeys were making a racket as Stella and Kay walked by.

The air felt strange as dusk settled too quickly on them all. They were leaning on the wall near the orangutan enclosure as darkness fell on them. The orangutan walked up the tree trunk and stood there with his face lifted to the sky. Then he took in a huge breath and began beating his chest. The sound rang out like a tom tom, hollow and eerie. As the darkness increased it became louder. He beat his chest all during the darkness, as if it was the beginning of the world. Everything was silent but for the beating of the tom tom, like the first beating of a giant heart.

Steve and Stella were going up to Mike's farm. It was on the edge of a state forest, and as they rode in, Stella was reminded of all the descriptions of country cottages she'd read. It was a small cottage with a tree in full pink blossom leaning towards the front verandah. Inside there were raw timber walls turned dark with age.

She liked the farm with its green paddocks and the bush not far away and wished that she could spend more time there. But she'd been arguing with Mike since they arrived. She'd been telling them about the CR group she'd just joined. 'Consciousness raising group,' she had to explain. Mike had treated it as a joke. 'Just another gossip group,' he said. And Steve slipped from being vaguely supportive of her to being outright rude.

'They should burn all these feminist books,' he said. 'All they do is wreck marriages and relationships.'

'Only those that would crumble anyway,' said Stella. 'It depends what you want.'

'What do you want?' said Mike. 'Another woman. You want to be a lesbian or something?'

'No, I didn't say that. I just want some respect for my needs. Honestly . . .'

'Well, I reckon you should stop reading those books. We only started to argue when you began reading them,' added Steve.

'I think you're going too far,' said Mike. 'I mean, you've changed.'

'What's wrong with that? If I don't, I might as well put on concrete boots and throw myself into the Yarra. Isn't that what life's about? Change.'

'Yeah, but not like you want,' said Steve. 'I mean, you want *us* to change, just because you want it. I reckon *we* should be able to decide when *we* want to change.'

'In that case, I might as well go and get those boots on, because it'll be a l-o-n-g wait.'

They all sat staring at the fire.

'I'm going for a walk,' said Stella.

She walked towards the fence that separated the farm from the forest. She climbed over the fence near a post and jumped down on to the crackling leaves. The air smelled of eucalypt. She walked straight ahead, following no path. She walked thinking about their stupidity, about how they thought they could have everything. It made her so angry. She sat on a log and stared at the leaves at her feet for a while, her mind empty. She could hear the occasional rustle of something in the bush, and not far away she heard the laugh of a kooka-burra. Uncanny, she thought, how they always know when to laugh. She went on, walking in a circle, eventually turning back towards the smoke rising from the chimney. I wonder if they feel guilty enough to cook dinner, she thought, smiling.

When she walked in, she removed her boots and said as she entered the kitchen, 'Mm, that smells good.'

They were both standing there smiling with pride at them-selves. She didn't spoil it for them, they looked like two little boys who'd been playing with the saucepans in their mother's kitchen. In fact, the dinner was nice. Mike had had to learn to cook, up here on his own.

'It's nice having dinner made in a wood stove,' said Stella as they finished eating. 'We're going to have to head back soon, before it gets too late.'

'Yeah, I guess so,' said Steve.

They left just as twilight darkened into night. But some-how it changed after that weekend. For a while their lives rolled on as though neither noticed the change, but with Stella becoming more and more impatient with Steve; Steve rebelling against what he called Stella's demands: demands for time to herself; demands that he do half the housework ('Why isn't it enough that I fix the car and put the rubbish out?' he asked); demands that he shave off his moustache because it didn't suit him; demands that he respond to her demands. Stella went out more, spent days with her women friends. Steve disappeared for whole weekends up to Mike's farm, where he blew his mind on mushrooms and dope.

They'd never fought much, but now it seemed to happen all the time. They disagreed on the colour of some object and it turned into a fight. They disagreed about which movie to go to, about which channel to watch.

Eventually they had to agree that it wasn't working any more. But then each thought maybe it could work and they moved to a new flat in another suburb, hoping that a change of scenery would help.

Steve moved out two weeks later leaving Stella with a rent she couldn't afford, and so she moved too, forgoing the bond.

'When Steve and I split up,' says Estella, 'all our joint friends sided with him. They dropped out of my life as if they'd never been there. I'd gone too far. But you can't reinvent love once the worlds you inhabit separate.'

Further along the lake shore the combination of sand and salt has formed sculptural shapes. Life seems to burst out of every crack in the sand. The footprints of black swans lead them to a small sandy arm that stretches out into the lake. As they approach the swans move gracelessly into the water, hooting and lifting their red beaks to the sky.

They paddle in the shallows out from the arm and head back towards the shore. There, among the samphire they see a dotterel. It begins to lift one wing and hobbles away from them.

'Poor thing,' says Estella. 'Its wing is broken.'

'It's a trick they play,' says Olga. 'If we look near here we'll find a nest.'

'Now how did you know that?'

'Christoph.'

They begin to walk back to the campsite across the reddish soil a little further from the lake. Olga puts her hand out across Estella and they stop. She points. About ten metres away a thorny devil is sitting perfectly still at a right angle to an ant trail.

'They like ants,' whispers Olga.

Just at that moment the devil's tongue flicks in and out picking up ants as they pass.

'Conveyor belt dinner,' chuckles Estella.

They squat and watch the devil eating its dinner and then creep away backwards and turn again towards the car.

'How about some tea,' says Estella when they arrive back.

Olga sits on a blanket and watches Estella make the tea. 'I love watching you be efficient,' she says. 'But just in case you get too efficient, how about a kiss?'

We gather together our nets and food and head towards the peninsula that lies between lake and sea. We walk over marshland, insects buzzing busily around our legs as we disturb them with our tread. The sun climbs higher bringing warmth and later a heavy heat. We continue to walk despite the heat. As the sun reaches its zenith we sit and rest a while. Even the insects are lulled by the heat. We eat a little food and drink some water. In the late afternoon we round the last bend of the lake shore that takes us out on to the peninsula. We wade through the shallow water that separates the two land masses. The land here is slightly higher so the marshes do not extend on to it. We collapse under some banksia trees and watch the sun make her way towards the horizon.

A cool breeze springs up rustling the leaves in the trees. We rise and climb the dunes that separate us from the sea. We look out across the deepening blue. You race off down the slope leaping like a huge frog. I follow you. We run, splashing, into the sea, diving, ducking, dodging the waves that come to greet us. My body wakens. I tingle all over with the sudden touch of cold water on my skin. The water rolls over me.

You dive and grab my feet, pulling me off balance. I fall and the water covers me. I escape from you and dive for your ankles. But you are too quick. Instead we meet like fish, underwater. Our eyes and faces ripple through the water. The last rays of sun form rippling lines across your face so that you resemble an angel fish. I surface and begin walking towards the shore, the water dripping from my body. I shake myself and sit down on the sand. I watch you frolicking in the waves and the dance of sea spray in the last arc of sunlight, little rainbows of colour appearing and disappearing. You come to join me. We sit and watch the sea darken.

20

*I sit by the lake. I can see jelly fish floating lazily in the water,
moving slowly, like pullulating umbrellas. Their bodies, trans-
parent white, like coagulated spit, billow. Like a moebius strip
inside and outside are indistinguishable. Their innards are
shaped like four leaves of a clover. From beneath they resemble
vulval flowers.*

*We walk along the foreshore between sea and lake, collecting
small objects such as shells, pebbles, driftwood for the fire. We
follow the movement of the tides, the comings and goings of the
various birds – cormorants, gannets, gulls – watch a pelican
drifting across the silky lake at sunrise, gathering fish in her
pouch-like bill.*

*We fish in the evenings as the setting sun flares on clouds
and water. We spread our nets early in the day in a part of
the channel where sea and lake meet. As the sun begins to
sink we return.*

*From the shore I can see dark shadows massed but shifting.
The shadows condense and disperse rhythmically. Sometimes
it appears as a single unit, complete and solid. Then a small
shadowy form flicks out of the mass. In a moment the water is
full of small flickering shadows. I try to count them, but they
are too numerous and their movement too fast and unpredictable. I could count a single fish ten times and not know it.*

Sometimes they will surface briefly, blowing bubbles and creating rings of expanding concentric circles.

A fish leaps through a ring on the surface briefly entering the world of dry air leaving only a quiet plash of bubbles. The net billows in the currents produced by tides and fish, the knotted cord connecting each part to every other, is drawn first one way and then another. There is a moment when it appears to be still, but as soon as I am aware of this it moves.

The setting sun is dancing in orange lines on the water's surface. In an instant I see a vision of pearls of light, each pearl a knot in the net. I see the form of a huge woman rising up out of the water, a shawl of pearls falling around her shoulders, then she is gone.

I stand and wade into the water. In silence you and I gather up the net. We roast several fish over hot coals and set the rest out to dry in tomorrow's sun.

We are watching the mirror-smooth lake like two narcissi blowing in the wind and stare into the polished mirror surfaces of our selves. Although we are joined in some sense, our identities do not merge; we overlap without being submerged, and slowly drift apart. We move towards the exteriors, we inhabit our skins. I feel the blood rushing through the capilliaries, feel the air pressing into the lungs. I am aware of a fresh wind blowing across my face and I look out at the world and see the light of the stars twinkling out across the light years, their light captured in a single blink of my eyelids. We are ready to leave.

On our last morning I walk along the beach. I watch the waves rising and falling as they roll towards me, as they break and roll up the sand formed by the tide during the night. The water settles briefly in small pools that reflect the pale morning sunlight but which then contract and are gone.

At once I see three pools like gems on a string. They gleam like white gold. The water seeps into the sand and in a moment they are gone. Nature is so ephemeral. If you miss it you may never see it again.

Stella was relieved to be home. She'd been at the Halfway House all day and she was exhausted. She found the children easy to deal with, and so spent much of her time in the backyard playing with them. The yard wasn't very big, but at least there they had a chance to scream and yell. Inside the women sat around talking about what they'd gone through, why they'd left, and whether to go back to him or not. Some said, 'Never.' Others wavered, made excuses for him. Talked about how he'd been under pressure from his boss, or how there were too many debts. The women drank a lot of tea and coffee, and sometimes too many whiskeys. New women came in, sometimes in a state of shock; often with distressed children, confused about why they were there, sometimes believing it was a holiday. There was always emotional static in the air.

Stella made some spaghetti and collapsed on her bed. She'd been re-reading the university handbook and getting excited about the courses she was doing. She'd begun her exercises for Greek and had managed to translate the first two scenes of *The Agamemnon*. She was thinking about the play and the women at the Halfway House. Not much has changed, she thought. But this year she would learn Ancient Lesbian!

Stella's work at university was giving her trouble. She kept thinking that so much was missing. In her classics essays she was trying to write about women, but there was hardly any information and they didn't like her interpretation. One of her lecturers said that classics was no place for politics. It was like beating her head against a brick wall.

In June she decided to go to the Women and Health conference in Sydney with Julia. They sat up on the train overnight and talked their way to Sydney. Julia was studying Zoology and was trying to work out ways to turn it into a feminist discipline. It was harder, even, than classics.

'How about you write an essay for them called, "The Anatomy of Feminism: A Protozoic Life Form",' said Stella. 'Then they'd have to think again.'

'I've got a good one,' said Julia, 'What about "A New Model of Origins of the Patriarchal State: The Beginnings of Cell Division; Progress or Regression"?'

'The title's a bit long. You could try, "Early Forms of Feminist Consciousness: The Evidence of Protochordates", or maybe we could write one together on "Aristotle and Axolotls". I'll do the Aristotle bit and you can do Axolotls. It'll be a collaboration. Isn't that what they like in science?'

Julia grabbed her hand. 'You know,' she said, then paused. 'Never mind. I just wanted to say that I'm glad you decided to come too.'

Stella felt pleased.

When they arrived in Sydney they went straight to the conference and met up with the women who were billetting them. It was late by the time they got there that night.

'In here,' said Jackie, and led them into a room with a double bed on the floor.

They lay separated by what seemed to each a vast expanse of sheet. Tentatively Stella reached her hand out to touch Julia.

The night stretched out like an expanding universe and extended into light years. Is this really happening? thought Stella. She had contemplated it with Julia, but hardly dared to think it possible. Thought she'd be rejected.

It had never been like this with Steve, even with all his good intentions.

As the night dawdled on they talked, made love, slept, woke, made love, whispered, laughed and worried about waking the others.

'Let me infiltrate your body,' whispered Julia, beginning all over again.

Dawn came too, eventually, its pink-tipped fingers prying open the curtains.

Stella wrote in her diary the following day:

On a timeless day,
long ago or yesterday,
in the immeasurable void of space,
there occurred a remarkable event:

a woman lay, with her self,
a lover a woman,
together she made love with her/self

together she brought forth,
created the universe,

created too the galaxies whirling through space
>the diamond planets
>the music of the spheres
>the rings of Saturn
>the cloudy veils of Venus
>and the moist fertile earth

The big bang theory is really a story
about one woman's orgasm.

I think of you and a cell somewhere in my body goes ping with a memory and the rest begin a clamouring for more. The memory of you is in everything: in my eyes and my ears and my nose and my arms and my legs which curl around you and in my back that feels the touch of your fingers running up and down the spine and there in the seeking tongue. The taste is sweet like quince, like pomegranate, like red heart of fig.

Olga and Estella feel refreshed by their day at the lake in spite of the mud. Olga is worried that the nuts on the tyres are going to loosen themselves and every now and then she gets out to check how tight they are. Estella is more interested in photographing the plants, or the salt crystals that are visible at the side of the road. The landscape is becoming more stony.

Just before lunch they reach a town with a population of two, where they stop and buy lemonade icy-poles, soft drinks and chocolate. Estella tops up the blue water container, groaning as she lifts it into the back of the car.

They drive on through a landscape that is now mostly red. Some of the dry lakes are not salt pans but vast expanses of red earth and rock. A few tyre marks show the road. In some places it has been graded, but mostly you have to follow your nose, or your instinct.

A solitary dingo walks across the flat bed of a dry lake. It stops, faces them and then walks on again, hardly visible against the red earth.

Estella is running down the bank of another lake where cattle graze near the shoreline. This one is different, not blue, but muddy brown, like the dam she swam in as a child. A few straggly mulga trees lean over the water, and wildflowers – budding but not blooming yet – are scattered on the bank.

Olga photographs Estella standing thigh high in the water with the wind blowing her hair across her face.

The land has become flatter and drier again. Dried mud, cracking like broken chocolate, is what they are driving on now. The horizon is beginning to bend again and the late afternoon colours shine.

After the dried mud orange stones, pink clouds, blue sky stretch into infinity. Then come the humps of earth, as they approach the underground town, holes in the hills with doors.

'It'll be nice to sleep in a bed,' says Olga. 'And just think, a shower.' Their friend, Teresa, had offered her dugout to them which they find at last with its geraniums and portulacca flowering.

They go out that night, and eat roast meat and drink wine for the first time in weeks and feel the effects much sooner than is usual for them.

Estella rings Coral in her new flat in Melbourne to say hello and ask her how Christmas and New Year have been. She doesn't mention getting bogged, just that they'd had a flat tyre and had fixed it. Olga rings her parents in Vienna and exaggerates the hardships. 'They like to worry,' Olga says when she finishes the call. They go home and fall into bed and sleep in an instant. It is totally dark when they wake. No sun shines through any window. Olga switches on the light and stretches. 'I could lie here forever.'

Stella decided to go home to Coral for part of the holidays. The rivers were full and during the night the front paddock had flooded; they heard the river break its banks with a roar. By the time the sun came up no land was visible, but the sun looked wonderful rising over the floodwaters. Stella had woken early and had gone back to bed to read about black holes in the *National Geographic.* She read how black holes break all the laws of physics. Once something has fallen into a black hole there is no escape. The gravity is so great that mountains the height of the Himalayas would not be greater than a centimetre. Her mind tried to comprehend the force involved. It seemed unbelievable. Then there were 'singularities'. The entire thing seemed so weird. And yet the fascination exerted a kind of force. She lay back in bed trying to imagine what it might feel like, got up, and looked out across the submerged paddocks. The sun was reflected in the water, which was now mostly still, not like the roaring sound that had woken her earlier. These earthly furies were so small compared with a black hole.

At breakfast she talked excitedly about her new discovery. It seemed like it was hers . . .

She fell. Fell from her chair for the first time in years. Her breakfast got cold on the kitchen table as she fell and kept on falling. Her tongue throttled the breath in her throat, she gasped and bit into the tongue that swelled in her mouth and bled. Coral tried to free it and Stella bit into the bone of Coral's finger. She sank further into unconsciousness, thrashing about in the black hole behind consciousness.

When the convulsion had passed, Coral carried her to her bed where she slept and slept. The sun shone through the window and fell on her face, but Stella did not wake since darkness held her in. Her muscles no longer moved, she was utterly still. Locked in. She could not rise, having no will to rise. The force of unconsciousness pressed upon her. Time did not exist. All memory was gone.

Outside time passed. Hours passed and she lay there, stirring to neither sound nor light. Then her hand moved, a mountain heaving up through the earth's crust.

Coral was sitting beside her and whispered her name to her. She leaned close to listen for the breathing. It was regular. 'Stella,' she whispered.

Her eyelids fluttered, opened slightly. Stella's eyes saw Coral, but nothing sparked. She looked out of a skull, indifferent to the world. There was no pleasure, no caring, no recognition of the image before her eyes.

Coral saw the empty eyes, the blank look, wanted to reassure her, but there was nothing to reassure – simple emptiness.

Stella's eyes closed again. A shadow passed through her mind like a thought, but there was nothing to hang on to – it was like being in a cave far away from the world. The shadow settled and her eyes opened again. Bewilderment and confusion. Where was she? Who was she? Her lips moved in a memory of speech, but no sound emerged. Stella wanted to speak. She saw the other lips move; she felt her own open, move instinctively. But there were no words for the tongue to curl around, no thoughts to form into words, and no words in her head. Her bulky tongue searched as though words might be found in the corners of her mouth. But there was only emptiness, confusion. Her eyes settled on the face she knew, but found no word, no name for it. She closed her eyes again and fought for her will, to regain something that had fallen.

Coral saw the change in her face before the eyes opened with a weariness that worried her.

Stella lifted her hand, feeling the word 'mother' return to her mind. Another word struggled out, 'What . . .'

A space, a vacuum.

'What happened?' And as she asked, she knew it had happened again. And in the relief of that knowledge she sank into sleep.

Stella woke briefly and noticed that night had come. When Coral walked in the door Stella saw her as if from a huge distance, a figure coming towards her and reached in to find some words and grasped at the few that were there. 'I'm tired,' she said.

'Do you remember anything?'

'I remember you.'

'What's your name?'

'Um . . .' Stella laughed embarrassed. 'I know it, I just can't remember it right now.' She searched again. 'Stella, that's it.'

The struggle to dig for her name, to remember herself, was exhausting. Her eyes fluttered and closed again.

Stella slept until the following morning. Sun streamed through the window. She lay there confused. When was yesterday? What did she do? Her mind was struggling to right itself. She remembered Coral coming in last night and asking her a difficult question. She'd had a fit. But when? She didn't know.

The door opened and Coral poked her head in. 'Awake, dearie? That's good.'

'I had a fit, didn't I?'

'Yes.'

'When?'

'Yesterday morning.'

'Yesterday morning? What happened in between?'

'You slept.'

'Really?' She looked at Coral in disbelief. 'For a whole day?'

'I'll bring you some breakfast,' said Coral. 'You stay here a bit longer.'

It was so long. She knew she hadn't had one since she was six or seven. Why had it started again? She pushed the blankets back and, in a wobbly way, stood up. She looked out the window and saw water. That's right. The river broke its banks. They'd had a flood like no one here had ever seen before. She remembered getting up yesterday morning, really early, and watching the sun rise over the water. She and Coral had heard the roar. But before and after that it was still blank. She walked to the bathroom, pissed and returned to bed. She was already tired again. Coral came in with a tray. Stella sat up, picked at the cereal and toast and put the tray on the floor. She was asleep when Coral returned for the tray.

She woke again to the sound of snipping. Coral was pruning the roses. Stella got out of bed and walked out into the sunshine.

'How are you feeling?'

'A bit better but still tired.'

'Why don't you sit in the sun on the verandah?'

'Okay,' said Stella. 'I'll just get my book.'

She came back with a rug and a book.

'Do you remember what you were reading yesterday morning?'

'I hadn't thought about it.'

'Do you remember the night before?'

Stella sat for a minute in silence. 'Yes,' she said finally. 'We watched that old movie on TV. What was it?' she mumbled to herself. 'Marilyn Monroe was in it.'

'That's right.'

'Oh, it's so frustrating, I can see them on the beach in front of a big Victorian building. I know, *Some Like It Hot*. And it was after that we realized that we'd probably be flooded in.'

'If you remember the morning tell me, okay?'

'All right. If.'

It took Stella another day to remember the article she'd been reading about black holes the morning before her fit. And it was three days before she managed to stay up without sleeping.

Coral and she went for a walk down the paddock. Coral said, 'You know, I thought you were going to die. You stopped breathing.'

Stella turned and looked at Coral. She'd dealt with death before, but the knowledge of her own mortality was another matter. But now, thought Stella, it could happen anytime: while you were eating breakfast, lying in bed, or walking down the street. Without warning. Snuffed out like a candle. It frightened her that she was so defenceless, that any day could bring death.

Voice

21

I am building a repertoire of stories and images. I have heard a story of mountains in the east, the peaks they call the Three Sisters. In the days when the earth was taking shape, when women roamed freely over all the lands, three sisters travelled across the sea. They flowed with the ocean currents and in this way travelled across the great ocean until they came at last to the eastern shores of this island.

The change, from the ease of water travel to the effort of walking, tired them and they soon stopped to rest. They built a fire and settled down for the evening to exchange thoughts and retell old stories and talked and talked but could not sleep. The moon and the stars moved across the sky. The sun came and went, the moon circled, the stars shifted position in the sky, and the women sat on, whispering and sleepless but too weary to move.

The seasons changed and birds came to nest on their heads and in their laps, snakes found hollows to curl in, and plants grew where earth had settled. The three sisters hardened to protect themselves from wind sun and rain, though their hearts remained soft. I have heard that if you sit quietly at the feet of the pinnacles you can hear the sisters whispering.

Olga and Estella shop in the one supermarket in the town. They buy provisions for the next ten days: tinned tomatoes, salsa, tortilla chips, more avocados, onions, garlic and some artichokes for lunch. They also stock up on drinks, yoghurt and fruit. By the time they have completed the round the trolley is full of food, drink, chocolate, anything they have craved, or might crave.

They go to the one-hour photo shop and arrange for their films to be developed by late afternoon and then wander around looking at the half-submerged buildings. Even the Catholic church is underground. A shaft of coloured light, refracted by the one stained-glass window near the entrance, falls in a rainbow of colours on the stone floor. The church, like the houses hewn into the rock, is cool and shady inside. There is a small stone altar and niches have been carved for the representations of Christ and Mary that flank the altar. A bowl of purple bougainvillea has been placed on a ledge behind the altar.

'This is what churches should be like,' says Estella. 'It makes much more sense to dig them into the ground.'

'It reminds me of a section of the Church of the Holy Sepulchre in Jerusalem,' says Olga. She remembers the church with its warring denominations: the Anglicans celebrating communion in one corner; the French Catholics upstairs singing a hymn; the Greek Orthodox drowning both out; and the Ethiopians in the tower. Beneath all this confusion she found steps leading down to a crypt. Right at the bottom was a small cavern that was so full of holiness that Olga had stepped back from it, feeling the intensity of something beyond her. 'The walls there were smoother,' says Olga, 'but it wasn't unlike here. Cool and quiet and rather sombre.'

Eyes were looking at her from above. They were brown and blue and brown again . . . and, like the stars in the night sky, there were too many to look at all of them. There were shoulders too, some stooping, some straight, but the eyes were still staring. She did not not know whose eyes they were. Among them there was no face that she recognized. Not one.

Why would all these people look at her? A woman . . . an old woman . . . an old woman in black. Close to her. Her eyes (she is one of the brown eyes) are just above her, and very close. She is holding her hand and stroking it, and she is saying something in another language. Then some of the eyes moved. What a strange room. Where do all the coloured boxes come from? None of it made sense. Stella's mind grappled for something, but she didn't know what it was searching for. She felt wet. She was lying in a pool of water. It didn't make sense. Some of the eyes talked above her. There were children, there were grown men and women, and there was the old woman in black with brown eyes stroking her hand. But who are they? And who is she? And where is she? She turned her head to the side and rolled it into cold wet-ness. Her head returned to its original position. The back of her head was flat against the concrete floor. She turned the other way and saw a row of spaghetti packets, toilet rolls and, just down a bit, tins of cat food. She turned back. Most of the eyes were still there, milling around above her. The fog was still in her mind. The old woman pulled at her, urging her to sit up. She did and saw the open door to the street with the coloured plastic strips hanging down, blowing in the wind. Several children were tangled in the green, orange, yellow, blue and red strips. Beyond the door it was dark. She turned around and saw the counter of the milkbar, the part where ice-creams are scooped on to cones and milk-shake makers stand unused. The old woman in black was smiling at her. Her whole face was crinkled, softly, like a late-summer peach. The old woman was pointing towards the door and the eyes of the others had followed her hand. The first familiar face – one that she knows though has no name for – came bustling through the door. She, the face, came over and put a warm arm around her shoulders and moved her towards the door. Stella wanted to turn and thank the old woman for holding her hand, for caring, but she could not. She felt the eyes penetrating her back as she left.

'How long was I gone? Did I go to buy milk? We didn't get any before we left.'

'No, you went to ring Alva,' said Julia.

'Oh god, did I finish the conversation? She must think I'm so rude, cutting out on her like that. I'm so embarrassed. How can I go and buy milk again from them? They threw water over me. I'm all wet. Why did they do that? Can you go and ring Alva for me, please? Tell her we were cut off, and I didn't have any more money.'

'Why not let me tell her what happened?'

'I'd feel vulnerable . . . I don't know. Maybe she knows anyway. I don't want to talk about it with her. If you tell her, tell her that too. Okay? Everyone will be staring at me when I go down the street now.'

'They won't stare. They'll forget.'

'What's that siren?'

'I don't know, let me look – there's an ambulance there.'

'They won't forget. Are there still lots of people there?'

'A few. Look, I'll go and explain things, then I'll ring Alva. Will you be okay?'

'Yeah, sure. I'll be all right here.'

How am I going to face them again? Why did it have to happen there? Oh shit. I'll have to go and buy things from that other place around the corner.

Julia came back in. 'It's all right,' she said, 'I talked to the ambulance men, assured them I knew what to do, that you were just tired but that you'd be all right.'

'Did you ring Alva?'

'Yes. She said she thought you'd been cut off.'

'Well, I was, sort of. So you didn't tell her?'

'Yes, of course.'

'Oh . . . What'd she say?'

'Nothing much, just said it made at least as much sense as Telecom cutting her off . . . or ASIO.'

Stella slept heavily. She did not dream. It was like the sleep of the dead. When she woke up she remembered the night before. She felt like some huge eye had opened up and was gazing straight through her. Exposed. She couldn't think what she'd say when she went there again, which she knew she'd have to do, if not today, then tomorrow.

When she went back to the milkbar the grandmother was standing behind the counter. She smiled at Stella as soon as she walked in, showing the gold in her teeth. Stella braced herself to speak. The grandmother called to Despina through the door, 'Despina, *ela.*' Despina came out.

'Hello. How are you today? Better?'

'Yes, thanks, I'm okay now.'

'That's all right. We were a bit worried about you. Has it happened before?'

'Yes, it has.' But she did not add that it had never happened so publicly before.

'But you're all right now. That's good.'

'Can you tell your mother thanks for holding my hand. And . . . um . . . can I have a bottle of milk please?'

'Here you are.'

'Thank you.'

Later that day, Stella was walking back from the pizza shop, past the low rise commission flats that overlooked her back-yard, trying to replay what she remembered. There was not much to go on: a series of images, the eyes encircling her and the confusion of that first conscious moment; the old woman's hand on her hand; the sense that someone did not wish to harm her; and the image of being dragged home, corpse-like, along the street. Yet she knows she walked.

She looked up. Two little girls were standing looking at her.

'That was funny what you did last night, falling over in the shop,' said one of them. The one she recognised.

'Yes,' she said, 'yes, I suppose it was.'

She felt the pinprick of childish openness and didn't know what to say to this small girl. When she tried to say goodbye brightly it fell weakly from her lips.

Olga and Estella are sitting on the verandah eating artichokes.

'That must have been something of a shock to your dignity,' says Olga. 'It's one thing to have some kind of illness, but when it flares up so unpredictably in public, that's something else.'

'What helped most, was telling people. The worst time was the first time I told anyone. I really half expected them all to get up and leave, even though I trusted them, at least enough to risk telling. I remember shaking uncontrollably, my voice too. It was like being laid bare.'

They had been meeting as a consciousness-raising group for four months. At the beginning there were six of them, now, regularly, there were four.

They were sitting on Judy's bed. A lamp with a blue day-light globe gave an eerie colour to the room. It was a big bed, lumpy with unmade bedclothes beneath the pulled up quilt.

Judy took over. She was good at that, without being bossy, and she was straightforward. Stella wished momentarily that she could be too.

Judy looked straight at Andrea and asked, 'What happened to your leg? Were you born that way?'

Andrea hesitated a minute, 'No. It developed that way. It's my bones, they didn't grow properly. My mother used to force me to do exercises so that my left leg would grow straighter and stronger, but I hated the exercises and didn't do them, I just pretended that I had. I'd go to my room and lie on the bed and read for ten minutes. If my mother came in, I'd say that I was just resting for a minute. I would have the sandbag weight strapped to my leg, so that she wouldn't know.'

They were all silent.

'If you'd done your exercises,' Stella said hesitantly, 'would that have made a difference?'

'Probably. But it's too late now.'

'Do you mean,' Mary said in her rather tactless way, 'that you wouldn't have to use a stick?'

'It's not so terrible.'

Stella remembered the first time she'd seen Andrea. She'd noticed her stick, and she always walked into lectures five minutes late, as though she wanted to be noticed.

'Are you all so perfect?' Andrea asked.

Stella's heart began to beat fiercely. I've never told anyone.

Judy broke the silence. 'No. Far from it. When I open my mouth, I see the change in people. That's when my working-class origins show. Before that they see my blonde hair and go for me, and . . . well, you know when it happens.'

'It happens to me too,' said Mary, 'when people find out that my parents are Italian. They think I'm Australian because I'm called Mary. But I was named Maria and then when I got to school everyone started to call me Mary, because Maria was a wog name.'

Stella's heart was pounding wildly. 'I have . . . something too . . . but I've never told anyone.' She was remembering the night at school when they told secrets. 'I . . . well . . . you see . . . it happened when I was born.' She stopped. The others were not saying anything. They were listening. She pulled at her hair. Time seemed to be moving very slowly. She wished this would pass. 'They pushed me back in because the doctor wasn't there. He was eating his lunch.'

'That must have been painful for your mother,' said Judy.

She'd never thought of that.

'What happened?' asked Judy gently.

'Well . . . I'm epileptic.'

'What happens to you when you have a fit?' asked Judy without even pausing.

'I don't really know. Julia said that I just fall over and I shake a lot, but my mother says I turn blue. I haven't had many. They stopped for a long time. But they've come back, just recently. I had one on my holidays, and then a little while ago I had one in the milkbar.'

'Alva said something to me,' said Mary.

'You knew?'

'It doesn't make any difference.' Stella found this hard to believe.

Judy grabbed her hand and squeezed it. 'It's okay,' she said. 'It takes guts to say things sometimes.'

'How about a coffee?' said Andrea.

'Or some port?' said Judy.

'It was easier after that,' says Estella. 'Not easy. Not a matter of flippancy. But I knew I wouldn't die of shame if I talked about it.'

'These artichokes are great. What's in the sauce?'

'Butter, a squeeze of lemon and lots of garlic.' Estella removes another leaf, gradually spiralling her way towards the heart.

'I was seduced once,' says Olga, 'eating artichokes with a woman. It was the most extraordinary seduction ever. She had it all planned and had invited me to dinner. Artichoke was the entree. Every time she sucked on a leaf she looked at me and by the time we'd reached the heart we were both laughing and kissing.'

'There's a great poem by Willyce Kim about eating artichokes. I think it's a lesbian tradition.'

You tell me that the shape of the universe is a spiral. You say it is the only form that is finite yet limitless, continuous yet bounded. You say that the spiral universe takes account of the motion of time. It combines the cyclical and linear perceptions that we experience daily. You say that this is why spirals have always been sacred. You point to the many reflections of this in nature: the whirling spiral galaxies, the growth patterns of leaves on a stem, the helical molecule of life. You say that you feel it in your own being, all is reconciled in that form. It is a single form made up of many turns, an infinite unending angle that may or may not repeat. It expands and contracts yet retains its original form. It is dynamic. It changes and is always open to return, to repetition.

Stella went to hospital. The doctor said she needed to have her medication stabilised. What he meant was that he didn't like the way she lived. She arranged to go during a week when she had essays to write but wouldn't miss any classes.

She took with her all the books she had wanted to read for the last few months, *Orlando*, *The Four Gated City* and Bertrand Russell on 'Vagueness' for her essay.

The neurology ward was a strange place. One of the women there, Marj, talked about her operations – from what she said it sounded as though she had no organs left, just pins and metal and plastic.

Margaret was given a private room because she was so troublesome. Stella heard the nurses talking about Margaret. 'She's faked it again, you know.'

Faked it?

Stella heard a scream. She walked down the corridor trying to work out which room Margaret was in. But only the four-bed wards had their doors open.

That night she heard the scream again and the soft shuffle of nursing shoes along the corridor. It came from the direction of the bathroom. She got up and headed towards the bathroom, hoping no one would challenge her. All she saw was the closing door of the corner room. As she passed she heard the sound of struggling.

It was quiet the next day and the one after and Stella thought Margaret must have been released.

She started on the jigsaw Catherine had brought in. She was finding it difficult to follow the picture, to work out where the pieces went. She concentrated instead on the shape of the pieces, trying each piece against the last.

As she looked up, George, another of the patients, walked past. He was wearing a plastic helmet for protection. George was about sixteen, but it was hard to tell, with the helmet covering most of his head. Compared to him, Estella felt like an imposter. For her the fits were intermittent. For him they were a daily plague.

She went back to her jigsaw but was startled by a loud thump. All she could see was George's legs kicking in front of the door to her ward. She sat there, transfixed, watching the beat of his legs against the linoleum. Nurses ran from every direction and once the kicking stopped they raised him and led him away.

A part of her had wanted to jump up and go and watch, but another part had held her back; she didn't want to stare at George the way the people in the milkbar had stared at her. She also feared confronting herself. She preferred to imagine herself fitting. So she sat and watched only the kicking of George's legs.

The next day she got up and went down to the hospital library. She had to get out of the ward, it was depressing her, and sometimes she was frightened by it.

Daily she took the pills they gave her. They'd raised the Valium dose to 20 mg a day. It made her tired in the mornings, but it didn't help her sleep at night. Instead she lay listening to the sound of Margaret in the corner room. She glimpsed her only once – when she thought she'd gone. They led her past the ward late one night. She was wearing a blue candlewick dressing-gown and was moaning loudly.

'Dr Rapin will be coming round this morning,' the duty nurse told her at 6 AM. 'So don't disappear like you did yesterday. All right?'

'I didn't disappear. I said I was going to the library. They just forgot.'

'Okay, okay. I thought I should mention it. Just stay till he comes.'

Stella didn't like him, and she liked him even less after her time in hospital. They didn't even know her dosages half the time. It was she who had to remind them what she had. And he was so patronising and contemptuous towards the patients.

She sat on the floor and continued the jigsaw. She had realized the day before that the picture on the box was different from the picture on the jigsaw. Now that she knew the box was no use, she was progressing at a great pace. Everything was falling into place.

Dr Rapin appeared an hour late.

'Well, Stella, how are you today?' he said, looming over her. He used his full height to his advantage.

'I'm okay,' she said, standing up and brushing the dust from her dressing-gown. 'No different from when I came in.'

'Yes, well your levels haven't really stabilised, have they?'

'What do you mean?'

'They're lower than when you came in. It's very odd.'

'No it isn't,' she said. 'You've changed my entire routine. The food I have to eat here is the most unhealthy rubbish I've had to eat for years. And besides, I got my period on the fourth day.'

'Now don't upset yourself, Stella.'

'I'm not upset. I'm angry. And for good reason. It's been an utter waste of time being here. You don't know anything more about me. If you listened to me you'd find out more than by disrupting my life, drawing up charts and making me have unnecessary chest x-rays.'

The other patients in the ward were staring at her. The registrar had taken her by the shoulders and led her from the room.

'It's only one more day,' he said after closing the door. 'What's the point of getting upset?'

'I want to be told things. I want to know what you've found out, if anything.'

'It's not so easy. It takes years to learn how to read EEGs. Dr Rapin is one of the best. You're very lucky to have him.'

'You'd never know. I shouldn't have to get angry to find things out. He says there's still evidence of activity there. What does he mean?'

The registrar fumbled through some files and spread before her the EEG of her brain. 'See those peaks there . . . '

'Mmmm . . . ' hummed Stella, following the red ink tracks across the page with her eyes.

'That's what's meant by activity. It's more irregular. It comes and goes. See that bit there – the long slow waves – you get more of them in a normal patient.' He flicked over several sheets of similar patterns. 'Those ones, on the other hand, like the ones back on that earlier page, they're the spikes. Everyone has them, but epileptics have more of them and the amplitude is greater.'

Stella nodded and stared at the patterns. She wanted to know more, but she didn't know the questions to ask. 'Why wouldn't anyone tell me this before?'

'We didn't know you were interested.'

'Dr Rapin did. I've plied him with questions from the start.'

'Well, he's a busy man.'

Stella went home the next day. She had finished her jigsaw and almost written her essay on 'Vagueness'. She packed up her books and sat on the bed waiting for Julia.

'That was the year Julia went overseas,' says Estella. 'She'd finished her degree and about a month after my sojourn in hospital she left. Six months she planned to go for. I didn't think the relationship would survive.'

The night Julia left she stayed at Catherine's. Stella lay awake for hours wondering how she would get through the next months. Half way through the night she realised that she'd left her pills – Dilantin and Valium – at home. She spun into a panic. She tried to fill the panic by writing love letters in her head to Julia, wishing she had thought of saying these things before Julia had gone and wishing that the panic would subside.

It was too far to go home for her pills and the next day was worse. Her legs seemed to melt into jelly and when she walked to the shop for an ice-cream the world seemed to spin by her. By the time she got back to Catherine's she could hardly talk for fear. She sat in the chair near the fire and held herself in tight control. Catherine finally said she thought her mother might have some Valium and went off to see. Stella sat on, completely still, terrified that if she relaxed a fit would sneak in and catch her unawares. She wished that Julia were there too. Julia had always been able to pull Stella out of such states with her irreverent sense of humour, and seen Stella through the resurgence of seizures. Catherine returned triumphant, with enough Valium to get Stella through to the next day.

Estella gazes out the car window across the moonscape of rocks and sky that seem to bounce off one another, reflecting the hot brightness of the rocky earth. The memories of that time intensify. The rocks are much the same colour as the orange carpet in the room she rented at that time, and the blue sky. Orange and blue like the wallpaper in her room. An unbelievable combination – and floral. The wallpaper had become a symbol of the chaos in Stella's life. As the university year drew to a close with exams and essays, events in Catherine's life made Stella doubt the importance of anything rational.

For Catherine had fallen into chaos. She came to visit one night, cracked up and remained. She lay in Stella's bed for

184

days, neither moving nor speaking. Some days when Stella returned home from uni she found enigmatic phrases and indecipherable symbols written on the mirror next to her bed.

Stella sat on the bed next to Catherine telling her about her day. Catherine remained silent. Words having failed with Catherine she wrote long letters to Julia which became an anchor as she forced the chaos into words, giving them a shape, a form that could be manipulated.

You tell me of the connection between number and sound. You say, picking up your pipe, that if you double the length of the pipe from any point, you halve the frequency of the first note. The two tones are the same differing only in pitch. You say that this is fixed and immutable. You say that the doubling – the twoness – creates the matrix from which all other notes come. The octave leap is the mother of all music. Duality creates images in mirrors, the two sides of the body and the brain, the complementarity of colours.

You say that the thirteen lunar months coincide with the thirteen-toned scale of two octaves. You play the yearly round for me on your pipes and draw diagrams on the earth that I only half understand. They seem to make sense while you are speaking, but without your guidance I am lost.

Stella was writing an essay on colour. She wrote: Kandinsky (1914) wrote of the psychic effects of colour: '. . . in highly sensitive people the way to the soul itself is so impression-able that any impression . . . communicates itself immediately to the soul and thence to other organs of sense . . . This would imply an echo or reverberation, such as occurs in musical instruments which, without being touched, sound in harmony with some other instrument struck at the moment.'

Stella turned round to look at Catherine, who was lying in her bed on the floor with the sheet up over her chin and mouth, only the eyes peering out. Catherine had ceased to speak and hadn't eaten for five days. Stella was beginning to worry about her – not the eating, but she wished she could get her to drink.

She turned back to her essay and wrote a few more paragraphs, finishing with Kandinsky's classification of the colour orange, 'red brought nearer to humanity by yellow.'

She was getting hungry thinking about Catherine, and went downstairs to the kitchen to make a tomato omelette. She took it upstairs with her and re-read what she'd written so far: red, yellow and orange.

The sun began to shine into her room in the early afternoon and it made her sleepy.

She had a weird dream about food and churches in which everything was orange; the room was chilli-powder orange, even the walls. She dreamt she was in South America, travelling in Chile where the earth was an unfriendly red-orange and the buses were filled with glaring people who kept mouthing her name.

Then, she was in a church and considering what she could steal. The priest approached silently from behind, so she pretended to be admiring the silversmith's handiwork. Back in her hotel room she found she'd been robbed. The manager tried to placate her with a plateful of cream cakes. She joined the feasting. Afterwards, she went to the local beach, but the water was yellow with urine, and she began to menstruate. The water turned orange. When she returned to the orange room, the sun was blazing through the window and two unknown people were floating around the room on psychic energy.

Stella woke up next to Catherine, who was staring at the wallpaper, and wondered what she'd been dreaming and thinking behind those frightened eyes.

That night there was a big fire at the shoe factory down the street. Stella went to watch the flames leap into the air, orange against black. There was the noise of fire engines and the whispered horror of those watching, whose houses could go up in flames at any moment. Stella returned to her room and Catherine and told her about the fire and the people and the houses that didn't go up in flames, and how close it had been.

The next morning Catherine unexpectedly rose from her

bed, and putting on Stella's dressing-gown, walked out into the street. Stella followed her, worried that she might get lost. She walked towards the factory fire and stood in the street looking at the blackened remains of the factory. They were like predatory shadows, incongrously black against the morning sunlight.

They pull up at the creek just as the sun is setting. The trees are silhouetted against the flaming sky.

22

When they wake the trees are green against a bright blue sky, the ground is simply brown earth and they breakfast quickly because the drive ahead is long. They stop at the bright pink roadhouse and enquire about the roads. They are given hand-drawn maps marked with grids, gates, bores, fences, waterholes and places where fuel can be bought, or repairs done to supplement those they already have.

A group of Aborigines come in to stock up for a trip to relatives some hundred kilometres away. They buy meat, matches, butter, flour and sugar, and ice-creams for the children.

'You're going to run out of money before the end of the week, Elsie,' says the woman behind the counter, checking off Elsie's purchases against her account.

'No matter, I'll be with that other mob over Primrose Hill way. We'll have a big feast of tucker. Be back next week.'

'Okay, just thought I'd let you know.'

Stella was poring over a map of Europe. Although there was still chaos in her life, she felt she needed a holiday and had finally decided to join Julia, now that she had her results.

She rang Julia and bought her ticket the next day. Julia was in London still, so they'd start there and go perhaps to

Paris, Berlin, Vienna, Florence, Athens. She liked the sound of the names and she examined the map for the the links between them. A grande tour, she thought, like my great aunts in the twenties. Dora talked about it last time I saw her as if it was yesterday. Not as brave as the other great aunt who travelled to Iceland in 1904.

She filled the next two weeks with detailed fantasies of where she and Julia would go as well as turning the fantasies into graspable realities: a Europass, travellers cheques and farewell coffees and dinners. Coral came to see her off and, amid tears and smiles and a jar of Vegemite, she flew out.

You are teaching me the ancient iconography of this land: the coils, circles, spirals, figures and shapes drawn in the sand. You are teaching me the language of the landscape: to follow the routes to waterholes and hilltops. Later you will teach me how to find my way across the desert.

I draw shapes in the sand, reciting stories of the land in my head. The earth is my paper, my hand the pen. I am learning the ancient art of memory.

They pass the edge of a station, where a small community of Aborigines live. There is an old woman, dressed in a dusty purple dress with huge flowers printed on the fabric, standing with her hand shading her eyes gazing out across the plain. She looks as though she has stood there for all eternity; as though she could stand there waiting until all the souls of the old ones have returned to their places in waterholes, hollow logs, boulders and gullies.

The road is intermittently rocky and sandy, becoming gradually redder and sandier as they progress. Vegetation-covered dunes rise in a series of humps. They go up and over, up and over until their stomachs are ready to fly, then it flattens out again as they drive across a red lakebed. White everlastings are dotted around the edge of the lake and salt bush and grasses grow in clumps between the everlastings.

The day was bright by London standards when Stella arrived at Heathrow. Stella searched for Julia in the crowd and panicked a moment before seeing her.

Stella didn't see a thing from the back seat of the double-decker bus that took them into London, not until Boadicea and Big Ben. Her gaze was fixed on Julia. They talked breathlessly about themselves, interspersed with wordless looks that said all the unsayable things.

Stella talked of Catherine who had finally landed in a psychiatric hospital a few weeks earlier. 'I thought she'd come out of it after a week or two,' said Stella. 'It's been two months now. Just before I left I took her a jigsaw puzzle *with* a picture, and we laughed.

'And you?' asked Stella, after a pause. 'How was Ireland?'

'Beautiful. Cold. Green. We stayed in a cottage that was owned by a friend in the squat. Saw New Grange, which is amazing, covered in spirals – the outside has three interlocking spirals and when you go in there's another right at the back where the sun comes in on winter solstice and hits the centre of the spiral. We missed the solstice, but it was stunning.'

'What about Helen? Did you sleep with her?'

'How'd you know?'

'Something you said in a letter.'

'No, I didn't.'

'Why not?'

'She refused.'

'Were you upset? Are you upset?'

'I was. But she left here a couple of weeks ago. It's okay.'

The bus pulled up and Stella heaved her pack on to her back.

Julia took her keys out of her pocket and opened the blue door. 'This is our room.'

It was a big room, with a window that looked out on to the walled-in garden.

'It's so cold,' said Stella, rubbing her hands. 'It's hard to believe in cold when you're coming from somewhere hot.'

They picnicked on the floor of their room, eating bread rolls filled with salami and cheese. Julia leaned over and kissed her and they collapsed back on the bed. Stella felt her body drifting away in a time lag that swamped even the desire. Struggling against sleepiness she gave in to everything. She woke hours later with the smell of dinner wafting into the room.

The first week in London was spent walking, and riding on buses and trains. They went to hear Joan Armatrading at the Old Vic with standing-room tickets. They walked around the galleries and took a bus to Salisbury to visit Stonehenge. They walked along the Embankment and were glad of their squat, which seemed luxurious in comparison with the cardboard coverings of those under bridges. In Charing Cross Road they walked into almost every bookshop in the street, and they spent hours moving from floor to floor in Foyles.

They decided to take the Magic Bus to Amsterdam because they'd heard there was going to be a women's dance in Hamburg the following week.

That morning, half an hour after getting up, Stella tumbled forward on to the bed on the floor. Julia held her until the fit subsided and then tucked her into bed, hoping she'd be awake by the time she returned from the dentist.

'Still can't remember it,' says Estella to Olga. 'All I remember of the entire journey is queueing for the bus. And by then it was dark, so even that memory is shadowy.'

Estella sees a fork in the road ahead and takes the left one, hoping it's the best option.

'Watch it,' says Olga. 'There's a heap of sand coming up.'

Estella slows down, tries to move into low gear but, as she does the car jolts to a stop. She checks that it is firmly in gear and accelerates slightly. The wheels spin, but the car does not move.

'I'll have a look,' says Olga, getting out. 'Have another go.'

Estella pushes her foot lightly on the accelerator.

'Stop,' yells Olga. 'These arcs of sand look great, but you're not moving. It's just sinking deeper.'

Estella gets out and goes down on her knees. 'The sump is stuck in the sand, no wonder I'm not moving. Looks like we'll need to dig.' She goes round to the other side of the car and kneels to dig. 'Can you bring the towel, this sand's so hot.'

Estella slides out from under the car, covered with sand. 'It's really stuck,' she says. 'I think we'll need some sticks and grass. Can you do that while I dig?'

'Sure.' Olga walks off and begins to drag branches back. 'Do you think we should go forward or backwards?'

'Backwards has the advantage of at least knowing we'll make it back as far as the fork. But the track on the other side may be no better.'

'Perhaps we should walk it,' says Olga.

They walk, measuring the sand with their eyes until they reach the point where the forks join. Someone has rigged up a barrier of branches with beer cans strung from twigs as a warning to drivers coming from the other direction.

'Someone else seems to think the other track is better,' says Olga.

They walk on. Greyed branches and sticks are buried in the sand ahead of the car. 'You're right,' says Estella. 'If we go forward we'll get stuck here.'

Olga continues to collect an assortment of leaves, grass clumps, sticks and branches which she strews along the track behind the car. Estella tosses sand in arcs over her shoulder, as though throwing salt for luck. From time to time she pauses to shoo flies that have settled on her nose.

Olga lowers herself to the sand to help with the digging and leaps up immediately. 'How can you bear it?'

'It's like sleeping in a pool of cold water, if you don't move the surrounding temperature of the water changes to your body temperature. The sand and I have adjusted to one another.'

Bloody hell, thinks Olga, this is useless. But out loud she says, 'I think you should stop, or you'll be fried to a crisp.' Frustrated by the enervating heat, Olga stalks off and sits under the shade of a nearby acacia. She watches as Estella, molelike, heaves sand. Guilt soon forces her to resume collecting sticks and grass. All she really wants to do is sit.

Estella is into the swing of it and is determined to clear the sump. She sees Olga resting and feels like telling her to get off her bum and help. But she doesn't. No point in doubling the crisis by having a fight as well. Estella is worried that they won't get out. And there are no homesteads this time.

'I'm having lunch now,' Olga says, dragging the Esky from the car. There's no response. 'Come on, Stel. You'll do yourself in.' There are sweat tracks running crisscross down Estella's neck, like lines on a map.

'All right. I'm coming,' says Estella reluctantly.

They eat lunch in the shade of an acacia.

'Did you see the lizard track?' asks Olga.

'No. Where?'

'Just over there, where you walked.'

Estella alternates a mouthful of salmon, a bite of tomato, a swig of leftover breakfast tea, still warm and with a tanninish taste. She leans back against the tree and listens to the buzzing midday heat. Olga has slid back on to the shaded sand. The air is tense with heat. Flies crowd the jagged edge of the tin and brush their forelegs over the liquid lying in pools on the bottom of the tin. A flock of galahs sweeps over, unseen and unheard in spite of the racket. A wind blows across the sand picking up grass, leaves, sand and sticks, including some of Olga's little heaps. Ants are making tracks towards the salmon. They gather around it like cattle at a trough. Taking up the tiny pieces they march back to the colony a hand span away from Olga's left foot. The lizard pokes its head from the hole, moves forward, stops, moves forward again and crosses the track it made before the noises came. Olga opens one eye and touches Estella softly. Estella opens her eyes and sees the lizard move across her line of vision. She points. Olga sits up. The lizard stops. For a minute all three sit in utter stillness.

'Shall we have a go at moving it?' Olga says.

Estella stretches her spine forward, arching her back. The lizard ducks for cover in a clump of grass. 'I think I've dug as much as I can.'

They add to the line of sticks and grass and Olga puts the foam rubber mattress behind the back wheels.

The car edges back, and Estella is sure they'll make it. It stops with a clunk. 'Shit,' yells Estella, stretching the word out and thumping the steering wheel. She leaps out and peers under the car. 'Bloody hell.' An axle at the back is caught on a mound of sand. The front wheels have sunk into the holes the back wheels have made. And the foam mats have rolled themselves up like curlers in front of the back wheels.

'What'll we fucking do now?' asks Olga.

'Dig,' and she means it more as a command than an answer.

'Those mats weren't much use. What else can we use?' Olga asks herself out loud. 'I know,' she says, 'the brown blanket.'

'My beach towel,' says Estella. 'It's pretty big.'

Estella is carefully flattening the sand behind each wheel and checking for sand mounds. Each tyre has a thick layer of grass and sticks to run on to, and Olga has laid out the blanket and towel behind the back wheel.

'Okay, you ready then?' asks Olga.

Estella starts the engine and sits for a minute trying to see them rolling backwards out of the sand. She lets the clutch out slowly and feels the weight of the car shifting. It's moving. Olga has run to pick up the blanket now in front of the car and is standing there beaming and encouraging Estella to keep going. Estella's legs are shaking on the clutch and accelerator. She hopes it won't stall. She's over the worst now but keeps backing until she is about twenty metres past the fork in the road, where it is firm. She opens the door and lowers herself carefully to the ground, hoping her legs will hold.

'We did it. We did.' They are both dancing through the sand in jubilant swirls that finishes in an embrace.

'Now we just have to get through the sand on the right track,' says Estella soberly.

Instead of following the wandering course of the river we strike out across country. At the end of the second day we come upon a huge rock, perched on a hillside which resembles an egg split in two.

There are images on the rock of an egg-shaped circle. On its left are long curved lines that look like a snake ascending into the sky, or descending to earth. We walk around the rock, examining its form, feeling it with our hands. We stand inside the shelter formed by one half of the rock, leaning against the other and decide to spend the night here.

Julia and Stella travelled in trains at night to save money on accommodation. Most of their adventures and encounters with the locals were on the trains. In Germany they learned to speak Bahnhof German: *Wann fährt der Zug?* [What time does the train leave?] *Von welchem Bahnsteig?* [From what platform?] and signs that said SPUCKEN VERBOTEN [Spitting is forbidden].

On the metro in Paris they were spat at for holding hands.

In Italy they invented ways of protecting themselves from the attentions of Italian men. They travelled the entire distance from Venice to Florence without mishap in a train that was so crowded that sleeping bodies lined the corridors. They had chosen to share a compartment with a man and his huge black Newfoundland which took up all the floor space. For Italian men the corridors were preferable to sharing a compartment with two women, a man and his big black dog.

Nuns were safe travelling companions too. Seemly behaviour is the norm in the presence of a nun, even one who laces her coffee with cognac. By the time they left the nun at Brindisi they were tired of train travel. They went to Greece by boat, and for days saw nothing but the flat sea surface. Turning in a circle on the upper deck was like looking at a silicon blue dome. Inside they drank Ouzo to wash away the horizon altogether.

The road ahead cuts through the moonscape in converging parallel lines. There's a track and an invisible point at which the track ends. Barely grassed, an occasional outcrop or dip in the land provides a sense of three dimensionality. At the edge of the horizon lie a few low weathered hills, older than human imagination.

Dust flies in flurries, like a bridal train in the wind, behind the car.

There are patches of bog, which, if it rained, would be impassable. Salt crusts, covered where the earth is thicker, show through in these places.

Olga looks at the map, counting the bores, fences and gates they have passed. 'Not much further, I think,' she says to Estella who has been driving most of the day.

Suddenly there are palm trees, rising like phoenixes, from the ruins of an old homestead.

'If the map's right, it's only another seven kilometres. Or maybe it's ten,' she says. 'Seven and then three to the springs.'

Crete was another world. They spent a day in the Museum at Herakleion staring in wonder at the riches there.

Julia had given Estella a labrys, a double axe, for her birthday, which she wore on a leather thong around her neck. In the squat in London, Roberta had told her about its origins in pre-patriarchal Crete. In Italy she'd been advised to hide it, since Mussolini had appropriated the symbol in the thirties and many Italians still associated the labrys with fascism. In the museum in Herakleion there were whole cases filled with tiny gold ones; huge tarnished bronze ones on long poles; others painted on the sides of pots and pithoi, along with birds and snakes, flowers and octopi.

They visited the palace at Phaestos that overlooked the plain with its wide steps and corridors. Stella, still experimenting with her new camera, was taking photographs of double axes engraved in stone. The stones seemed to lie any which way, as though they had simply fallen there.

Stella was reading writing engraved on stone. For all her Greek she couldn't decipher more than a few words, though she could follow the continuity of words that started on the left side, turned and returned across the stone from the right. A continuous squiggly line that imitated the way in which an ox ploughs a field.

Stella was developing her own errant theory of writing, from the Phaestos disk to the boustrophedon of this stone. It's all snakes, she thought, whether they coil in a spiral or slither in curves down the page.

But Julia was sceptical.

You teach me that ancient memories are encoded in stories and patterns. You tell me stories that will be my guide and teach me the story of devil woman. You teach me how to

*recognise new tracks, how to know when I have passed from
one track to another. You recite the story of devil woman who
captured dingo.*

*You take me to the place where devil woman chased the two
women and their dingo. You show me the fallen trees, the track
to the burrow, the track to the hollow log and the place where
they emerged. You show me how to use the story as a map and
squat down and tell the story again. You draw circles, lines,
coils as you speak. You draw tracks, hills, waterholes and the
shape of women sitting.*

They travelled from Crete to Thera by boat. The island of Dia
lay like a woman floating on her back: breasts, belly, thighs,
knees, feet in profile. Phaedra's island, she thought. As far as
Phaedra could go without losing her claim on Crete. Gulls
followed in the wake of the boat, like protective sprites.
Behind, there was nothing but the meeting of the parallel
lines that formed the wake and the curved blue of the
horizon.

'You know,' said Stella, 'it's like the desert. Here the desert
is the sea, the endless horizon that seems to extend even
further than the eye can see.'

Julia rose and walked a funny sideways walk across the
deck and disappeared down the stairs to buy a drink.

Stella sat musing on the horizon, a thin line separating sea
and sky, almost indistinguishable. What is it, she thought?
Sealine? Skyline? What's the definition of a line? The closest
straight line between two points? But does it have to be
straight? What about the curved line that forms the flight path
in high latitudes, the polar arc. A line on a circle. A line on a
sphere. What's the difference? The shape of the container. If
the earth were cube shaped would we think differently? But
the earth is a sphere. The waves are curved lines on a sphere
(earth) that moves in a spiral around around a central point
(the sun) that whirls through another spiral (the galaxy) that is
part of an infinite boundless universal spiral. So to talk about
the shortest distance between two points as a straight line is
ludicrous. Nothing, from the smallest particle to the galactic

arms moves in a straight line. Bodies appear to move in straight lines but they are only approximations – a series of jerks, of infinitely small curves. Watch a person, a cat, a bee, move – a series of curves shifting from side to side – keeping balance, keeping symmetry, and giving the illusion of moving in a straight line. Lift one leg, place it down and as you do lift the other – a series of almost circular movements. The sinovial joint moves in a circle. The spherical bone moving in a loose circular area of bone and fluid. A circle within, making circles without and giving the illusion of moving in a straight line. The boat ploughing through the waves, moved by an engine in circular motion, giving the illusion of moving in a straight line across a straight horizon. Watch a person walking on a boat. The circular motion of the sea beneath gives the walker a swaying motion. No illusion here of walking in a straight line. Instead a series of sways, sideways movement, swaying back. Circles within circles, swaying circles, sinovial circles, wave circles beneath, the endless circle of the horizon which seems to extend beyond the circle of what the eye can see.

'Thanks,' said Stella as Julia swayed over her and handed her an iced mineral water.

Later that day they sat on the balcony of their room surveying the view over the caldera. Below them the domed roofs gleamed white in the sun against the indigo deep sea. Before it blew up the island had been round, like the full moon, now it resembled a crescent moon. Its arms, once the rim of a volcano that jutted from the sea, seemed to reach for one another in an eternal attempt to rejoin. In the centre of the sea/lake that now existed was a small island from which sulphurous smoke rose refracting the late afternoon light into orange pink and red.

'Let's go to the volcano tomorrow,' said Stella. 'I've never been so close to a live volcano before.'

'I was, once,' said Julia. 'I went to the island of Hawaii, with my father, on a stopover from San Francisco. We went up to the rim of the volcano. Inside it was bubbling away and steaming. It smelt like the chemistry lab at school. I remember seeing flowers spread out near the lip of the volcano. It didn't occur to me at the time but, now I think about it, they were probably offerings to Pele.'

'This would be the perfect place for an Icarus jump,' said Stella stepping forward to lean over the railing. 'I suppose people hang glide here these days.'

They rode the small boat over and walked on rocks, once thrown high in the air, now scattered randomly on the ground. The smell of sulphur was thick in their nostrils. Stella imagined the rocks tumbling through the air, the earth groaning and throwing spurts of lava skywards, and later the red rivers of lava flowing into the bubbling sea. In her mind's eye she saw the tsunami, giant roiling waves, flowing out in a huge circle from this tiny island. The Krakatoa of the ancient world, perhaps Plato's Atlantis. She peered at the small sulphur flowers at her feet, breathing in once again the sulphurous vapours.

She wanted to stay on this island forever, gazing out over the caldera every afternoon; she imagined getting old here, wondered could she ever become one of the old women in black? She knew she couldn't and they had a plane to catch in a few weeks' time. But the smell of sulphur flowers stayed with her.

The setting sun is turning rocks and ground a deep orange when they arrive at the springs. The waterhole is surrounded by trees that lean over the water, reflected in its clearness. There's a sign beside the pool that says that this water is three million years old. From the moment rain fell somewhere on the east coast, then seeped into the ground and travelled here underground, through the fissures of rocks.

'It's so nice to be hot,' says Olga, 'and know that the water will be hot too.' Olga's toes touch the water. She lowers herself in from the rocky edge. 'It's like a big hot bath. Come on in.'

'I'm coming.'

The droplets of water, older than anything their bodies can imagine, hold them up and they float like old islands of bulrushes on the surface of the water. Like the floating islands of Lake Titicaca.

Olga is swimming backwards across the waterhole to the other side. Estella follows her, forwards. When they reach the other side, worn out by the combination of effort and heat, they cling to a branch and kiss wet kisses on wet faces.

23

You tell me stories that may not be retold. You tell me things that only women know, that only women can know. Some are elaborations of stories I already know, some are new. We sing and we dance, we repeat the words, we dance the words into the ground.

Listen to this: 'Pornography is the fantasy, rape is the practice.'

'Well that about sums it up, doesn't it?'

'Yeah, but how can we stop it?'

'I don't know, but I do know that we've got to help some of the women they're practising on.' Stella was one of six women sitting in an upstairs room of a Collingwood shop-front that they used as their base for the Rape Crisis Centre. 'You know that woman who rang yesterday,' said Stella, 'the seventeen-year-old from the country who came in here, well, her case is coming up for committal next week. I want to go along to the court. Does anyone want to come with me? I don't really want to go by myself.'

'What happened to her?'

'Almost textbook, the sort they like, she was raped in one of those lanes off Little Bourke Street in the middle of the day by a bloke with a record. He was out on bail at the time.'

'What day is it on?' asked Jane.

Stella gazed blankly towards the middle of the room.

Jane tossed a box of matches at Stella. 'Hey, dreamy, when's it on?'

Stella fell sideways, knocking her knuckles against the brick wall.

Jane leapt to her side. 'Oh, god, what've I done?'

'Looks to me like she's having a fit,' said Sarah calmly.

'What do we do?'

'I don't know.'

'Why don't we call Lisa?' Wendy said.

Jane had moved over to the wall and was cradling Stella's head in her lap. 'I thought I'd knocked her out,' she said to no one in particular.

'No, it missed and whizzed past her ear,' said Julie. 'I noticed because I thought what a good shot. Anyway I think she was already out to it by then. Look at her hand.'

Julie lifted Stella's hand and pointed to the grazed knuckles. 'At least she didn't have far to fall.'

'Yeah, she'd have come down with a real thump, I reckon, if she'd been standing up.'

They sat, waiting for Lisa.

Stella opened her eyes and couldn't work out where she was. She looked at each woman without recognising any of them.

Lisa walked in with her little black bag and looked at her. 'How do you feel?'

'All right,' mumbled Stella, 'A bit tired.'

'Has it happened before?'

'Yes, a few times.'

'How long did it last?'

'Ten minutes.'

'No, it was more like two minutes.'

'I'd reckon about five minutes.'

'You lot wouldn't be much help in a court of law.'

Olga and Estella have decided to have a rest day at the water-hole. They rise and eat a leisurely breakfast of fried eggs and the last of their bacon. They sit for a while, leaning back against the log that someone, perhaps a ranger, has brought in from elsewhere.

'You want to have a swim?' asks Estella.

'No, but you go in.'

Estella removes her clothes and walks to the water's edge, sliding into the amniotic warmth of the pool. She floats quietly for a while, resting her head on the pillow of water. Olga is sitting gazing absentmindedly at Estella. She sees her arms lift and her body thrash and sink. At first she just watches, then suddenly she leaps up running towards the water, yelling, 'Stel, Stel.' She jumps into the water and swims towards Estella, still limply thrashing. Olga stands and lifts Estella's head above the water, holding her, cradling her a moment, then draws her as quickly as she can towards the edge and, with a strength she didn't know she had, lifts her on to the ground. Estella's body is still. Her face is a grey-blue. Olga's heart is racing as she rolls her sideways, listening for breathing. There's a flutter. She blows air into her mouth and listens again. A rasping sound in the throat. Water flows from Estella's mouth. She blows air into her lungs, whispers to Estella and tenderly kisses and blows again. The breathing becomes more regular. Olga holds Estella, crying, saying, 'I thought you'd gone. Out here. Gone, just like that. I know you're breathing now, but wake up. Please wake up.' She sits there rocking and whispering and talking to the unresponsive body in her arms, rocking, holding, rocking through an eternity of waiting.

My devil woman has chased me here, flapping her wings loudly behind me. I jump with fright into a tree. The tree falls, I fall and fly off again into the void, trying to escape her. I cry out, sensing her close on my heels, I cry out and froth at the mouth. I crawl through hollow logs, through tunnels in the earth. I leave my devil woman behind clawing her own darkness.

Stella's eyes open. Olga looks at the eyes that have lost their sparkle, that are flat, like the eyes of the dead. 'Hello,' she says. 'How do you feel?' Estella does not respond. She gazes flatly at Olga. She sits up, vomits and collapses.

A few minutes pass. Olga tries again. 'Do you know who you are?'

'Olga,' says Estella.

'Not me. You. Who are you?'

'Olga,' she repeats.

'I'm glad you're back. I'm Olga. Do you know who you are?'

Estella regards her. The skin above her nose puckers in a frown. 'Olga,' she says again.

'It doesn't matter. You can be me for a while if you like.'

Estella is struggling with her mind. She is without consciousness, wordless, like the void between one thought and the next. The sky is bright and blue above. She is outside, somewhere. Galahs fly overhead and settle on a branch on the opposite side of the water. Water? She looks at Olga. She knows her but is puzzled by her funny questions. She rests on Olga's arm and sinks back into sleep.

My muscles ache with inertia and my tongue has blossomed in my mouth, swelling. There are holes, ridges, pockets of blood in my tongue. My teeth puncture the flesh of my tongue, bite into it, leaving tracks along one edge. The tongue bleeds and swells into bulkiness. It swells and spreads into all the cavities of my mouth until it no longer feels like my tongue. It is there, hugely, but it is not a part of me.

Stella opened her eyes to the sunlight that streamed through her easterly bedroom. She rolled over, wondering what to read next. She picked up *Gyn/Ecology* and re-read some of the parts she had marked. She loved its word play and the mix of poetry and prose. She picked up *Woman and Nature*, which was lying on the same shelf.

They'd talked a lot about these two books at the conference yesterday. She reached over and put both books back on the shelf and got up to make a coffee, stood listening to it bubble up through the metal bit in the middle. She liked lifting the lid and watching the first trickle come through; it was rather sensual, like the first seeping of blood each month.

Stella dressed and walked her bicycle to the front door. She raised her leg over the bar of the bicycle and the whole thing collapsed. She lay in the centre of the road, the bicycle quivering above her.

By the time the neighbours reached her, she was still, and so was the bicycle, except for the mad spinning of the back wheel. They had worried looks on their faces as they carried her through the front door and settled her in a chair.

Mrs Bernardino went to make coffee, while her husband sat and kept an eye on his strange young neighbour.

'Do you think she'll be all right ?' he shouted, as though his wife was deaf. 'That was a heavy fall she took – didn't seem to be able to stop herself. I hope she hasn't got concussion.'

Mrs Bernardino came in and stood while she waited for the water to boil. 'Hmm. She looks all right,' she said. 'She hasn't cut herself anywhere, just dazed. Are you all right, dear?' she asked

Stella nodded.

'Good. You watch her Joe, while I get the kettle.'

'Now dear, here drink this. It should make you feel a bit better. That was a nasty fall you took.'

Stella nodded again, frowning. She drank slowly. Where'd this coffee come from? How'd I get here? What fall?

'What fall?' Stella asked.

'You fell off your bike. Don't you remember?'

'No.'

I don't know these people. They seem to think I know them. She looked at the cup of coffee. Shit. I suppose they just saw me fall and assumed I'd knocked myself out.

'Did your foot miss the pedal?' asked Mrs Bernardino.

'I suppose so, I'm not sure.' I've got to get out of here.

'Probably too many late nights,' said Mrs Bernardino. 'You should go to bed early.'

'Mmm,' said Stella. She finished her coffee and stood to go. 'Well, I'd better go, I'm already late.' Late for what, she wondered. 'Thanks for the coffee.'

She headed out the front door and was surprised to see her house next door. She hadn't realised they were her next-door neighbours. She wheeled her bicycle to her own house and leaned it up against the fence.

'I just have to get a few things,' she added. 'Thanks.'

Stella went into her house and rummaged through her bag to find out where she was going. The conference programme was there. For a few moments she was confused, not remembering. Then she remembered the workshop she'd been in the previous day. All those amazing women, writing books and directing plays. I'd better go. But I wish my head would stop hurting. She put the programme back in her bag and left for the second time.

When she came out she noticed that the mirror on her bicycle had been smashed.

'I have to move my arm,' says Olga. 'It's going to sleep. Can you sit up by yourself?'

'Mmm,' murmurs Estella groggily.

She moves awkwardly, swaying, and leans against the log.

Olga gets up and pulls the foam mats and sleeping bags out of the car. 'I'll make up a bed for you in the shade, and you can sleep for a while. Okay?'

'Mmm.' Estella is almost asleep again, sitting up. 'What happened?' she asks.

'You nearly drowned.'

Estella's eyes widen.

'You went for a swim,' continues Olga. 'I wasn't taking much notice of you. When you went down at first I thought you were just playing around. But then, I don't know what it was, I realized you were having a fit and I jumped in and dragged you out, surprised myself. I must have done it pretty quickly because you were still breathing – just – when I got you out. But I gave you mouth to mouth just in case.'

'God, I could be dead now,' she mumbled across the ridges of her swollen tongue. Her mind is paralysed by the thought. Not again. She falls into a void in which her daily existence is threatened by this quirk of electrical disorder. She tries to pull herself up into the light, but the shadows smother her will.

'I thought you were, for a moment. I really did. Here.' Olga offers her arms as support and Estella drags herself toward the makeshift bed. 'Come and lie down. Maybe you'll sleep again.'

Estella crawls into the sleeping bag and is asleep almost immediately.

I am sitting near the creek. Orchids and centaury are in bloom. You have lit a small fire and sit behind me. I can feel you behind me, you and two others, I can feel your hands though they do not touch me. You begin with a chant of my name.

The world tilts to the left and the hands ascend, the sound patterns change, my breathing deepens and the world shifts again. My eyelids become heavy and close of their own accord and my heart pounds in my chest. I feel a constriction in my throat, gagging, choking, then the air flows freely. I feel a burning sensation in the centre of my forehead and I join in the chanting. I feel my mouth relax, opening, broadening, a desire to smile, but I withhold. My head opens to the world, the subtle breezes flow through the crown, the wheel spins and opens and I laugh, a great wide open laugh. I feel the world rushing towards me, flowing through and out the other side. The petals unfold.

Estella wakes, confused again. She looks at Olga reading, leaning up against the log that is now in the shade. Estella pushes the sleeping-bag cover back. It's hot and she is sweaty inside the down-filled bag. Then she remembers she'd had a fit, that Olga'd said she'd nearly drowned.

She remembers the film she'd seen once of the epileptic drowning in the bath, remembers the brightly coloured bathing caps she and Fiona had always worn at the beach, and understands now why Coral had insisted on them.

She sits up. Olga looks up from her book and comes over. 'Thanks.'

'I did it for me too, you know.'

'I'm not ready to go yet. And yet I know that it could happen any day. No warning. Just gone in a moment of unconsciousness.'

Everything can help to build the rainbow bridge across the void.

24

I imagine an ancient journey with me in it. I am travelling with you from a land across the waters in the north. We are sisters travelling across the sea, carrying all that we possess in our full baskets.

I see a dolphin that is splashing along beside us and there are dugong and green-backed turtle. My tired arms drag like the arms of the sponges drifting in the sea. I can also see the feathered edge of the mats in your basket.

You wake and look into the sky, searching for the morning star. We toss about in the waves using our paddles to keep on course. You smell it first, the land we are approaching. Geese and ducks come to greet us as we near the shore. The red sun rising turns their feathers red, like blood.

We sleep under trees that spring up to give us shade and drink fresh water that gushes from the land as we approach. We gather shells and eat the soft flesh inside. We name these places, singing as we walk, marking them out as special to us. The rainbow lorikeet follows us everywhere, crying out from time to time and when she does we open our baskets. A daughter or two emerge, making our baskets lighter. The lorikeet leaves feathers in the places where daughters are born until our baskets are empty.

The daughters we have brought with us spread out across the land. They carry with them the knowledge of these special places. They sing and dance and paste red feathers on their bodies.

You tell me story after story, again and again until I can see things beyond the words you speak. I see the landscape taking shape and attend to its rhythms. I listen to the meanings that hide between the letters, behind the words, in the silence from which they come. I attend to the colours of existence.

You speak of the rainbow. You tell of the great rainbow whose body stretches from one end of the world to the other, encompassing every dimension. All time is held in her embrace. You speak of the rainbow bridge between the worlds, the bridge that spans the measureless abyss. You speak of the rainbow tracks.

You say that the rainbow tracks are the shortest distance between points on the earth's surface or between universes. You say that they were used in the days before the white mastered ships came. You say that the memory of these routes is passing, though the tracks remain. You say that the tracks have been travelled by some, that you are one of them. You say the Old Woman entrusted it to you, in a dream, in some kind of seizure that lasted several days, when you recognised only your companion.

After three days you woke, hearing the world as if for the first time. You saw the white cockatoo long before she flew over, dropping feathers on your head and you sang in a new tongue, or so others said. You picked up a large stick brandishing it at all except your sister, your companion. You say that in your dream, in some kind of seizure, you were entrusted with knowledge of these tracks. You say you are the bridge between the worlds.

Estella reaches across to Olga as the sunlight washes like liquid across her face. Olga opens her eyes and beams at her.

'Hello, Cheshire cat,' says Estella.

'Hello, my little lorikeet. How are you this morning?'

'I'm all right. I have a slight headache though. I dreamt about lorikeets. You and I were walking. We walked for ages and everything was red, which is why I think they must have been lorikeets.'

'Where were we walking?'

'We started at the sea, as the sun was rising and were walking to the centre somewhere. There were all sorts of birds and animals around us, like those cards you can buy with Australian animals perched in every available space. There was a dog with us too. She was talking to me, telling me how far we had to go. When I turned to ask her why she didn't usually talk to me, she stopped, pricked up her ears and looked at me. It was as though an awareness of that magical thing prevented it from happening. But we walked on, stopping for picnics that we carried in magic baskets that never seemed to empty. Just before I woke up, I saw all these red figures on the horizon, red boas or feathers – and there was red water flowing across the land like a river of blood, and the moon in the sky was red, and everyone was dancing, even the moon.'

Olga squeezes into Estella's sleeping-bag with her. 'What'll we do today? Have another rest day?'

'No, let's go on. I'd want to swim, but I'd be too scared to. Maybe it was the warmth of it. I think I'd like to go on. But not too far.'

They take their time over breakfast and packing up, and it isn't long before Estella is asleep again.

'It must be pretty weird out here when the rains come,' says Estella looking at the map after she wakes. 'The main advantage would be being able to count the creeks as you cross them. There's a line of cliffs we passed through. I hadn't noticed them before. Did you see them?'

'Yes. It was when you nodded off, just before we got to the Possum Waterhole.'

After leaving Duck Ponds the earth becomes redder and they drive over a series of red sand dunes pocked with grass and mulga. The sand is firm, but Olga takes no chances and drives as fast as she can in the lowest gear. 'I feel like I'm driving on water. The hot sand is like liquid.'

'Just imagine you're driving across the Red Sea,' says Estella.

They stop for lunch at Bloods Creek, which will run parallel to their route this afternoon and sit in the shade of a red mulga tree eating tinned tomatoes and tuna straight from the tin. Olga leans over to wipe a trickle of tomato juice from Estella's chin. 'It was blood I wiped from your chin yesterday,' she said. 'You really gave me a fright.'

'I don't want to be aware of it all the time, and if you can't forget, or at least pretend to forget, how can I? Sorry I gave you such a fright.'

'No, no. I'm not asking for apologies. Don't be sorry. It just happened. But be careful, for yourself more than for me.'

'I'll try. But I have to be able to be foolish too. You see what happens. You remember it. I don't. I have to make up memories of it. I have to try and picture how it might be. I don't really want to do anything else. I don't want to see it. I hope I never will. It's too confronting. I don't like the idea of being out of control, of dribbling and vomiting on people. At least I've never pissed myself, but I know it could happen, does happen to some.' Estella turns and touches the bark of the mulga tree behind her. It curls around her fingers. 'Isn't this bark wonderful,' she says turning to Olga. 'It's like the little curls on your head, except yours have flattened out in this dry heat. And it's almost the same colour.' She reaches over and runs her hand through Olga's hair. 'Softer.'

Stella was sitting in the garden, reading. It was Sunday and she relished the prospect of some time to herself, some time to relax while Julia was out. She stopped short at the words, 'Anne Marie died from an epileptic fit . . . '

She panicked.

The only stories she'd ever heard or read about epileptics were ones in which they died or were regarded as mad or exotic. On the positive side, there was Dostoyevsky's idiot, or Van Gogh. There are endless stories of spectacular fits that lead to death. What of those who scuba dived or parachuted, and survived? What of the unspectacular lives, the day to day confrontations of life and death faced by epileptics? *We* don't all die from epilepsy.

She turned to Hippocrates who challenged the notion that epilepsy was sacred, but he was of no help. Then she remembered the priestesses of Delphi who fell into a fit and returned with enigmatic words and no memory of what they had said. Their oracles determined the lives of the Greeks for centuries. Did they ever fear the outcome?

She tried to learn to come to grips with her fear of sudden death. Sometimes it paralysed her, and she would lie on her bed tense with it. She feared the lack of warning and preferred to think she would die conscious.

She had a sense of having returned from death several times. Coming to. Emerging from the void. It's not like sleep, there are no dreams to people the silence with, only an unscalable inertia.

Olga drives all day. They come to an unreadable sign-post, pointing in two directions. The first three letters are missing, something that might be a broken N follows and the rest is so worn it would be harder to decipher than the boustrophedon engravings on rocks in Greece.

They arrive at the permanent waterhole in mid afternoon. It is hot and still and Estella walks into the water and sits on a submerged log. She dunks her hat into the water and tips it over her head. Water runs down her face and over her shoulders. Olga makes up a comfortable bed in the shade of the coolibah. Estella can't help singing 'Waltzing Matilda' to herself. It might have been written for this place, except there are no sheep. She settles in next to Olga. The water prickles as it dries on her skin. There is a sudden rushing of sound. She looks up and sees a willy-willy build. It whirls, picking up leaves and sticks and red dust. It jostles along, lifting and spinning and twirling through the trees. The water ripples in a quick circular waltz as it dances across the surface until gradually it loses vitality. Entropy and inertia reassert themselves. The afternoon is still once again.

Stella enjoyed her part-time job teaching English to a group of Arabic-speaking women. They were irreverent and the classes were a mix of hilarity and seriousness. Children ran in and out, disturbing the occasional recitations or the usual conversations about cooking or shopping or children's illnesses.

She took in her cookbooks, which had pictures of lentils, sesame seeds, chick peas and an assortment of vegetables. Once, they had gone to the magistrates court to watch the trials, another time to Myer's. That day they had teased her. Teaching her words in Arabic. Getting her to say them and breaking into an uproar of laughter because her predictable mispronunciation of a word had resulted in her saying the word for penis instead.

She was nervous about the class today. She had hired a magnetic board with removable body parts from the Family Planning Clinic. Only the torso was depicted and the removable parts included breasts and nipples, and lower down, the labelled inner and outer genitalia of women and men. The ovaries, cervix, vagina, labia minora, labia majora, clitoris. None of these words was familiar to them. Yet all had been pregnant, had been to doctors, had needed these words.

She started with the easier bits: the upper torso. The penis was hardly necessary, they all knew that word, though only one knew the word 'testicles'.

'Do you know the slang word?' asked Stella.

'Balls,' said Fatima.

As Stella reached to remove the magnetic penis from the board they all laughed. 'Good idea,' said Mary, chuckling. 'All my children accidents. Five accidents too many.'

'What's man's operation?' asked Hasna.

'Vasectomy.' Stella put the male internal organs back. 'They cut this bit here,' she said, pointing to the vas deferens. 'The sperm can't get through then.'

They spent a long time talking over the female anatomy. When Stella pointed to the clitoris, naming it, they began talking to one another. Fatima, whose English was pretty good, explained. 'In our countries, bad things still happen. They cut it out. It's very bad for the woman, but the men, they say it is better. That we behave better that way.'

'In English it's called a clitoridectomy,' said Stella, writing it on the board. 'Do you know if it happens here?'

'Yes,' said Fatima. 'There are doctors who do it to young girls.'

At the end of the term they had a wind-up party for the Arabic women's group and brought food and strong Turkish coffee.

Fatima tied a scarf around her hips and another around Stella's. 'Can you belly dance?' Fatima asked Stella.

'No. Can you teach me?'

Fatima and the others moved to the music, swaying their hips. Stella tried to imitate the movement.

'Keep this bit still,' Fatima said, moving her hands vertically down Stella's torso. Stella tried to move her mind into her hips and although she felt as though she was keeping the upper part still, Fatima smiled and spoke across the music, 'Too late. You need to learn this when you are child.'

They laughed and danced until the time came for the women to pick up their children from school.

25

Stella dreams that she is drowning, that she is sitting at the bottom of a pool several metres deep. She has been up for air once and has trouble getting down into the depths again. She releases all her air and gradually sinks. But she has lost the ability to remain underwater without breath. Something has changed. A huge woman appears from nowhere and lifts her like a limp rag doll, then leans over her, slits her throat vertically and scrapes out wads of dust, gathered there like dust in a vacuum cleaner. Stella feels no pain as she floats overhead bodiless. Afterwards she can hear her throat echo like a hollow chamber. The woman takes her to a cafe and Stella begins to sing. They nod their heads and take her into a room darkened by thick curtains. There is a stage and several tables with empty chairs. On the table at the front they place a large flagon filled almost to the neck with liquid and tell her she must make the liquid move to the top of the bottle. Stella sings and wraps her breath into small balls which she places into the flagon until the liquid in the flagon rises and spills over the lip.

Just as they are about to leave Olga, in her daily check of the wheel nuts, notices that the rear tyre is flat. 'I suppose there's nothing else to do but change it,' she says.

Estella walks off to find something, a rock or a log, to back the car on to. There's not much to choose from, but eventually she finds a flat wide piece of wood.

Olga has pulled the jack and the tools out from the back of the car and is sitting in the driver's seat. She backs the car on to the the piece of wood with Estella's direction, pulls on the handbrake firmly, gets out of the car and lies down in the sand, pushing the jack under the weight-bearing point near the back wheel.

'I'll loosen the nuts,' calls Estella. 'You stay there for a minute.'

'No way,' says Olga. 'My father lost a finger changing a tyre. I don't want to lose my head.'

'All right. But I'll loosen them, okay?'

'Sure.' Olga wriggles out backwards like a snake.

Estella thumps at the wrench with her foot, rhythmically moving it from one nut to its opposite, to its next nearest opposite, until she has completed the star-shaped movement several times, and the nuts are loose enough to turn by hand. 'Okay, you can start winding.'

Olga turns the handle of the jack. The car lifts and the tyre turns in the air.

'You know,' says Estella, 'we should have got the spare tyre down before we lifted the car.'

'Do you think the car's stable enough?'

Estella pushes the car from the side. It doesn't budge. 'I think it'll be all right.' She picks up the wrench and begins pulling at the nuts on the spare tyre. She swings on the wrench and feels like a child again. She places the three nuts in Olga's outstretched hand and puts her arms around the tyre as if to embrace it. 'God, it's heavy.' She holds it close to her chest, jiggling it off the bolts. 'No. It's all right. I've got it balanced,' she says as Olga tries to help her. She bends her knees and allows the tyre to drop the last few inches. A puff of dust rises as it lands. 'Okay let's get the other one off.' Estella lowers herself and embraces the second tyre. She pulls it towards her, holds it for a moment and then drops it. Olga takes it and rolls it, leaning it against the tailgate. 'I wish these tyres weren't so big,' says Estella,

217

struggling to get the bolts through the holes on the wheel.

Olga directs. 'Left a little. A bit more. Now right. That's it. Okay, fine. Push.' The tyre goes on easily and Estella lets out a long breath.

The nuts are turned and hand-tightened, the jack is lowered and Estella tightens the nuts as far as is possible, kicking the wrench with her foot. She bangs the hub-cap into place. Olga is back under the car, removing the jack.

'Last bit,' says Estella clutching the flat tyre to her chest.' She lifts one knee under the tyre to give it some support, but it's not high enough to get it on to the bolts. Olga lifts and by chance they get the tyre on to the bolts in one movement. Olga pulls the nuts from her pocket and screws them into place, picks up the wrench and tightens them.

'Done,' says Olga, finally.

'You know what,' says Estella, 'that's the first time I've changed a tyre. I've never owned a jack, so I've always rolled into a garage or called the RACV.'

'Me too,' says Olga, joining the confession. 'I've had jacks, but I could never be bothered.'

'I knew I could, but I didn't imagine the first time would be with such a bloody big car.'

Olga looks at Estella. Dust is clinging to her sleeveless T-shirt and there are ridges of dust on the folds of her shorts. 'You look like you've been in a dust storm.'

Olga and Estella drive with their fingers crossed that they will make it to the homestead. They are driving without a spare on a road that is not much more than a track; there is no one (unless by chance) for a hundred kilometres or so and the day is stinking hot. People have died out here with fewer complications than these.

Estella pulls up, and Olga gets out to open the gate across the road.

They drive on through a gibber plain that gradually becomes less and less stony. A few purple and yellow flowering plants are spread across the increasingly dusty plain. The earth is hard baked and red. Possibilities for shade increase and they see cattle grazing on the ironwood leaves. The dust turns to bulldust and Estella is driving like a bat out of hell. Fine dust billowing up and falling like red rain. She sees the road split in two and stops. 'We'd better walk it,' she says. They jump from their seats and land in little clouds of dust. They walk, kicking the dust up with their feet, like children running through autumn leaves, laughing. The bulldust settles in their hair and in the creases at the corners of their eyes.

'You have a red moustache,' says Estella, 'to match your ochre hair.' She runs her finger lightly across the top of Olga's lip.

Some cattle low, others are tearing young leaves from the lower branches of the trees. But Olga and Estella are oblivious to it. They walk on arm in arm, occasionally separating to jump in the dust. The walk is longer than they expected, but the track that looked worse at the beginning turns out to be the best option, with only a short stretch of soft dust.

Within an hour they reach the homestead, its wide lawns wallowing in the spray of sprinklers. Tiny rainbows arch about a metre from the sprinkler head. An adolescent boy, escorted by dust, rides up on a motorbike.

'Hello. We were told you'd be able to fix a tyre, if necessary,' says Olga.

'We're mustering just now,' says the boy. They look at him in silence. 'I'll see if I can get my father for you.' He rides off leaving a trail of dust in their faces.

They pull an orange each from the box in the back and begin peeling. Olga digs a hole in the skin and sucks, as if from from a gourd. Estella peels in a spiral, just as she always has. There are runnels of orange juice cutting trails through the dust on her hands. When she finishes her hands are sugar sticky, so she wipes them on a clump of grass. Black cockatoos, their tail feathers glowing red and yellow like traffic lights in the desert, are perched on a wire fence about fifty metres from where Estella and Olga are sitting. Black cockatoos are Olga's favourite bird. Estella points and whispers, 'Look, black cockies.' Olga, who hasn't noticed them in her afternoon tiredness, looks and turns to Estella again, smiling with all the sparkle of a small child. She grabs Estella's hand and they both sit there watching the birds fly down on to the trough to drink, then back to the wire again. The cockies make a lot of noise:

rasping and screeching, their raucous cries spattering the landscape. Two dogs come and sit right next to them, as if there wasn't any other space. The tail of one thumps up and down on Estella's shoe. Neither Olga nor Estella moves until they hear the sound of a vehicle, looking up, the dust rushes forward to meet them. Three men alight and soon set about fixing the tyre. One does the heavy work of lifting the rim, another simply watches. The third directs and checks the work of the first. Before long the tyre is patched, bounced a few times and lifted on to the bolts on the back of the car.

Olga pulls out ten dollars, and despite the resistance, pays them for their efforts.

They wave and drive off, once again surrounded by dust.

All around is the flat whiteness of the salt pans. The white brilliance is blinding. The absence of colour and variety of form causes my mind to create them. As the day goes on I see spectral colours and forms dancing against the white flatness. The colours are elemental, like the sharp edge of a knife against flesh, and spectral forms seem to drift in the stillness before my eyes. Nothing else moves. The silence cuts through me. The absence of all other movement is disconcerting, as though I am walking in a dream. But I feel the warmth of the sun and hear my own breath, my tread of feet on salt white crystals. I am aware of the procession of the sun overhead. I am dazzled by the display of brilliance, the reflection of the sky in the colours of the land as the sun sinks in the west.

I hear a distant cry, like the call of a trumpet. I see far away in the western sky an outline of black against red. Black swans rising into the sky like a net. They fly towards me. I hear an echo in my mind of words almost forgotten: I will only look up . . . The swans sweep round and circle immediately overhead just once then continue their flight towards the east. I imagine them flying over the ring of mountains I have left behind. I glimpse the mountains far off, beyond the horizon and imagine I am still ringed by them, an invisible circle of safety. I follow the line of the swans' flight from the west, feel a breath of freshness against my face and go on a little further.

I see a dark pool of water a little way off, feel hard rock beneath my feet. I have crossed the salt pans. The water is only slightly brackish so I settle into the cleft of a rock and drink.

Stella and Julia began to fight. Sometimes there were enormous differences of outlook that they had hitherto ignored; at other times they were ridiculous small things, like the day Stella said to Julia, 'Didn't you clean the stove?'

Julia, irate at the accusation that her stove cleaning wasn't good enough for Stella, exploded. But Stella hated fighting and decided not to go on with this one. Instead she turned around and stormed out the door.

She returned after she'd walked round the block to calm down. As she walked past the milkbar she wished she had remembered her wallet, then she could have had an ice-cream, but that meant going back inside. When she went back in and asked Julia if she wanted an ice-cream, Julia was sitting sullenly on her bed, leaning up against the wall, reading. 'No,' she said sharply. So Stella went to the shop and bought an ice-cream and bought a couple of bars of chocolate in case Julia improved later in the day. Then, when she got back to the house Stella changed her mind and gave Julia one of them. Julia grunted a thanks, and Stella could see her soften. She knew her weaknesses, and chocolate was one of them.

That night they went to a movie, and the day ended placidly. But it wasn't over.

In the weeks that followed they argued about a lot of silly things. At least Stella thought them silly. Julia accused her of cutting off from her, of burying herself in books and papers and not wanting to talk any more.

In turn, Stella accused Julia of hanging on to every difference between them, of emphasising those differences, of not appreciating her for who she was.

Eventually Julia said, 'I don't love you any more.'

'What do you have in mind for me then?'

'I want things to change.'

'And if I don't, then it's just too bad, I suppose.' And as she said this she remembered Steve's rebellion against her demand that he change. Things, even words, come back at you, she thought.

Julia moved from Stella's bed to her own. Stella lay awake thinking how empty the future looked without Julia. She loved her groundedness, something she lacked, and her weird sense of humour that changed your perspective. And though she liked her stubbornness in dealing with the outside world, she didn't like it when it was turned on her. She thought about Julia's arms not being there, not reaching for her in the night. What made her so furious was that Julia would be asleep now, contented, while she lay here angry and lonely.

She slept fitfully and lay in bed for a long time in the morning, feeling the knife edge against flesh. She imagined that cutting your wrists must feel like this, a hollowness inside as the blood seeped from your body. But she was too frightened to contemplate actually doing it, too frightened of the pain.

If Julia came in now and crawled in beside me, would I refuse her? A small vindictive part agreed it would be fitting to say no. But she knew Julia wouldn't come to her. She knew that somehow she had to sit through the terrible feeling of cracking open, of fragmentation. She felt it just above her breast bone.

Stella realized in a long walk through the park that it wasn't fear of loneliness, but the knowledge that she was no longer wanted.

To still the terror of abandonment, Stella took up dancing.

'Don't think,' called Mrs Monacelli. 'Fee-eel what you're doing.' She walked around the room while bodies of assorted sizes and shapes danced across her field of vision. 'Open the heart chakra. Like a flower. A rose. Remember the Rilke poem. Be there.' Sometimes Mrs M was silent and they simply danced to whatever music was playing.

Stella enjoyed the classes, it made her feel totally in herself. Mrs M had played Allegri's *Misereri* one night, had given them thin tallow candles as they entered the room spiralling from the outside in, forming a huge snake coiling in on itself. Stella rode home that night feeling as though she had learnt to fly.

That night she dreamed that she was flying in a contraption made up of various strange elements and pedalling, as if on a bicycle. In one hand she held an umbrella, which gave her control over vertical motion, in the other she held a rainbow-striped child's windmill, which gave her control over her horizontal motion. She was wearing a gown made from coloured feathers which contributed to her power of flight as it lifted or fell in the air. She was aware that some kind of music was playing in her ears and as she floated gently earthward she saw a woman with a cello playing against the setting sun on a wide plain. It was as though the rays of the sun were the strings. Dust puffed from the ground as she landed, and a flock of birds lifted like a tapestry, separated and flew off in every direction. When she looked at the ground all she could see was a thousand egg stones.

I am an egg falling endlessly through the sky, like a star. The falling goes on forever until I am floating on the sea. The sea washes my shell and waves break over me. I am washed up on to the land, carried by a wave that rises higher than all the rest. It carries me to a dry place far inland and leaves me perched on the edge of the world, spreading white into the far distance.

The egg splits open and my innards escape. I watch in astonishment as a myriad stars fly from the broken edges of my shell.

I grow in wisdom seizing the secrets and the mysteries of the world. I comprehend the illusions of space and time. I know that existence is as illusory as it is real; that my hard exterior is an illusion; that my inner being is soft and fluid. I comprehend the truth of myself, of my inner reality, of the external dream. I drift into the mind of this young woman resting in the shelter of my embrace tonight.

Dogs greet them at the entrance to the town. There is dust and the broken down walls of houses. A woman and perhaps her daughter walk towards the car speaking in their own language. They walk past the car without looking up.

The local policeman, whom they've been told to speak to, is out on a shooting trip. So they head for the Coke machines on the verandah of a building on the other side of the street.

223

Olga pushes a dollar of mixed coins into the machine and presses the button labelled Coke. A can of orange-and-passion-fruit-flavoured mineral water comes out the bottom. They press whatever is nearest at hand. None of the buttons matches the cans inside. But they are cold. They cross the street again and open the door to the telephone box. Estella lifts the receiver, but the phone is dead. 'I guess we'll ring when we get to the next service station.'

Children are running races in the main street and three men sprawl on the bonnet of a rusted-out car. Several other battered cars are parked irregularly around the town.

They leave quickly, feeling like intruders in their white skins and drive directly into the westering sun. They camp beside the road near a large orange rock that Estella approaches, and rubs its surface with her hand. It is smooth but too hot to touch on the northerly side. She walks backwards looking at the change in shape. The further back she goes, the more egg-like it becomes. She stops. Across the stretch of fine red dust it is incandescent. The earth looks as though it will light up in a kind of spontaneous combustion. She walks back to the rock and around to the other side. Again she runs her hand over it. The south side is cool. White paper daisies are growing around the edges at each end of the rock. There are indecipherable white marks under the lip of rock at the western end.

Stella talked of moving out and was saving. She had decided, quietly, without giving Julia the chance to talk her out of it, to buy a car and move to the country.

Stella sat in a café, writing. She was working out if the money she had would last. How long would it last living frugally in the country? Somewhere near Catherine, perhaps. She wanted time to think, to breathe, to read and perhaps to write.

She'd try to get some part-time or casual work. It didn't matter what. She'd have a go at anything. But she'd have to tell Julia. She was amazed she'd stuck it out so long. Knowing she wasn't going to stay would help her survive the next month or so.

She spent her weekends driving her new, very old, Morris Minor around the countryside just beyond the city limits. On the third weekend she found a place she could afford.

While I walk I remember the story you told about the egg-rock. You said that long ago the rock broke from the ground like a mushroom, having pushed its way up through the earth. Eventually it rested like an egg on the surface of the earth. One day the great snake was passing overhead. She mistook the egg-rock for one of her own and wondered why it had not hatched. Fearing some evil she darted down from the sky like a bolt of lightning and cleaved it in two. Out of the rock came women, who stretched their bodies, grew wings and flying away, spread across the land.

26

Stella settled easily into her new house. She loved waking to the bright silence of the morning, knowing that the day was spread out before her, empty of markers except those she created herself. Each day was like a journey into the unknown; each day except Thursday, which she reserved for her weekly social life. Thursday was the day she had chosen to drive into the city, visit Shrew – the women's bookshop – drink coffee with her friends and go to some event, a film, a concert or dinner with friends. It gave her one regular marker in her life, like a pillar of sand in the desert.

Stella, luxuriating in the space, rolled over in her bed diagonally, so her feet touched the ground even though she remained horizontal. She stretched, raised her feet, dropped them again and stood up in a single movement.

She wandered out to the toilet which overlooked the garden and then walked up to the chookpen behind the Cootamundra wattle and opened the latch. Three chooks and two ducks scrambled over one another like a panicked crowd in a theatre, eager to get out and scratch around the garden or eat the remaining food scraps from yesterday. Lysippe, the cat, ran past the chooks, teasing them with her speed. Stella had never worked out how they had determined their relationship, but somehow they had, and the pecking order seemed flimsy. She sometimes found Lysippe and the three chooks all sitting in a line on the rail of the back verandah, dozing comfortably together. The chooks sometimes wandered into the kitchen and pecked at the cat's pebbles, and the ducks would waddle up the front steps announcing their arrival with loud quacks and the inevitable splat of shit on the front doorstep. Stella tried to encourage them to remain outside, but they knew that inside was warmer on wet days, and cat, ducks and chooks all knew how to open the back screen door, even when it was closed.

She had come home one wet day from a quick trip to the local post office to find the ducks and chooks huddled under the copper in the bathroom. So she compromised. The living room door, which opened into the bathroom, remained closed. She had no intention of letting them share her living space that intimately. Mostly they remained outside.

After breakfast Stella went for her daily walk. She walked down to the creek and sat and watched the birds flying in and out the windows of the old green FJ Holden that lay askew in the creekbed. It had become a part of the environment. Birds nested there, and one day she had seen just the tail end of a snake disappearing into what once had been upholstery. Since the hot weather had ceased, everything had come to life. She had forgotten the energy of autumn. The bees were swarming the red ironbark near the fence, and she'd found some tiny greenhoods nodding in the breeze a couple of days ago.

Each day Stella walked through the fifteen acre block, becoming familiar with the plants, noticing the things that changed from day to day, not like the city where the movement of pavements and roads is visible only after long time lapses. She watched the sky, noticing the shape-shifting clouds and changing weather patterns.

When she stood up birds fluttered low through the trees. She stepped over the clump of maiden-hair on to a rock and drew herself up the bank with the help of a tree trunk. As she walked back to the house, she collected small pieces of dead wood. She took only those that had not lain a long time on the ground, that were not full of colonies of white ants and other insects. When she reached the house she picked up the

227

axe and began chopping the large branch she'd collected on the weekend.

Stella sat in front of the open fire reading a book about astrophysics, trying to understand the physics of spirals. But instead she found herself taken by the poetry of the language and wondered whether it was because looking at the stars was such an old art. She wrote into her notebook:

> spiral structure has something to do with pitch
> the pitch of our galaxy is 20-25 degrees
> and there are resonances
> near resonances non-linear effects are very
> important
> resonances create spiral patterns
> the way in which spiral waves are created is like
> forcing a semi-infinite (what's that?) stretched string
> fixed at one end and forced at a single point.
> Somehow and somewhere between the points a
> standing wave develops and that makes a spiral!
> in order to keep the spiral going there has to be
> self-gravitation (what's that?)

She put the book down and pulled at an end of wool on her jumper. She tried to break it, but it unravelled as she pulled. Eventually she got up, found the scissors and cut the end. She tied the two ends together and started to make the patterns she'd learnt long ago at school.

Cat's cradle, she thought. She bent over her book: a stretched string, fixed at one end (over my thumb) and forced at a single point (my index finger pulling). She tried to imagine it without her hands doing the work. But the string's not semi-infinite, whatever that means. She wondered if it mattered that the string was doubled. She made coathangers, witches hats, a cup and saucer and went to bed wondering about how these things were invented.

They rise before dawn, cool and crisp with desert dew, forgoing breakfast in order to reach the canyon before the heat rises.

The car moves through the landscape like a willy-willy: dust swirling and blowing along the track, leaves and grass lifting with its passage. Then silence settles again, and it's as though nothing has ever been through that country. The land, with its egg-shaped stones and intermittent patches of grass, wildflowers and mulga, goes on for ever. A meteor could hit it, and it seems that nothing would change. Yet, underneath the stillness and the silence there is teeming life: ants trail their way over ground in long lines and build interlocking tunnels and complex mazes beneath the earth; nocturnal marsupials, invisible in the sunlit hours, forage during the dew-cooled night; and only the lucky or the knowledgeable will see the frogs who hibernate, not for a day but for years, beneath the earth, until the first trickle of rain seeps through the soil and they wake to life again.

It's early still when they arrive at the canyon. The rocks are glowing in the morning sunlight and throwing thin shadows across the camping ground. They gather the things together that they need for the walk. Now that they're near the end of their journey it doesn't take long to get ready. They set off up the steep incline that leads to the top of the canyon.

'God, it's hot,' says Olga rolling a handkerchief across her forehead. 'Why can't canyons be flat?'

Flat land, in a jigsaw of green and yellow, lies behind them. Ahead are rocks and more rocks, mostly vertical from where they are standing. They drink a mouthful each and continue the climb.

When they reach the plateau, rocks still rise around them, but here they have been rounded by the wind and they huddle close together like low buildings. Between them are wide avenues where spinifex, cycads and twisted ghost gums grow. They twist and turn between the rocks following the labyrinthine path. The wind has sculpted the rocks into wide stairs that go up to a point, like stairways to the sky, and then down again.

229

They reach an open area and sit in the shade to drink warmed water. From where they are sitting there are three low rock knolls with wind carved stairs and beyond them is the abyss of the canyon, a huge gash in the earth. On the other side there is another city of rounded rocks. It reminds Estella of Phaestos.

Estella gets up and walks towards the edge of the cliff. She feels as insignificant as a feather: a wind could suddenly blow up and she'd be gone; she could have a fit on the edge of the cliff, and be gone. She steps back, telling herself that she's safer from a fit today than she was a week ago, because there'd been one in the intervening days and she'd never had them that close. She steps forward again. The trees beneath, on the floor of the canyon, look like bonsai shrubs. She looks up from the trees to the sheer vertical wall on the other side. At the base of the cliff is a strange rock formation that looks just like a Minoan snake goddess. There is an ill-defined head, above a torso with breasts and beneath that a rock skirt that flounces out like the bell skirts of Minoan goddess figures.

I wake to the sound of dawn birds. I sprinkle water on my body which saturates my skin. The pool is deeper than I imagined. I could immerse my whole body in it, but I do not. I see now why it is so fresh. The pool has walls of solid rock, a freak of nature. I remember the birds and am thankful for their sign. I rest for the day before setting off on a new track.

The dust is in my hair and eyes. I am following the tracks of the kangaroo. They lead me from waterhole to waterhole. I remember the stories you told me about kangaroo. Some of them tell of her flight from dingo, of how she outwitted dingo by transforming herself into a boulder. Dingo padded past her boulder body and followed the track of a willy-willy spinning on the horizon.

I remember too, the iconographic maps I have been taught. I look for correspondences in the landscape. I see what appears to be the sleeping body of a kangaroo. I approach quietly so as not to disturb her. I am surprised she has not heard my footsteps. I am ten paces away before I realise it is her boulder. I know there is water nearby. I sit and rest for a while, leaning my back against the rounded rock. I wake to see a group of kangaroos gathered around a small damp depression. I approach quietly and slowly. The kangaroos do not budge. They look up at me but maintain their position. I walk very slowly towards the water, scrape some earth to the side and cup my hands. I drink a little of the water and sit back on my haunches to examine my companions. They too sit and gaze at me. Who is imitating whom?

I sleep curled in a shallow bed of earth. I dream, I am running across a wide expanse of flat open land. My body begins to change shape. I hop. One foot changes at a time. I bound. I have a huge tail and a sense of animal freedom. I am carrying with me a secret power that I hold in my paws. I blend with the landscape. Sometimes I curl my body into a ball and resemble a boulder. I bound off again. Other kangaroos gather nearby. We make contact by looking into one another's eyes. We have to carry our secret power to another place, another time. Gradually our numbers increase. Together we are a force to reckon with.

Stella woke up and wrote down her kangaroo dream. She had to get moving, she was meeting Coral at the train at quarter past ten. Coral had decided that, since Stella was living by herself, she would visit and stay for a few days before going to Sydney.

Stella stood on the interstate platform waiting for the train to pull in. She had travelled this route so many times she could not count them. But this was the first time that she was meeting Coral. She wondered how Coral felt about it.

The train was only a few minutes late. Stella watched the people stepping out from the long body of the train, then she saw the familiar shape of her mother and moved quickly along the platform to embrace her and carry the one small bag. She wondered with a smile if Coral still packed two weeks ahead of departure.

'I thought we might go the Botanic Gardens first,' said Stella.

'That'd be nice.'

'Did you have any breakfast?'

'Only a cup of tea.'

Stella and Coral walked through the Botanic Gardens. For the moment they have each forgotten they are mother and daughter. The path led them through the fern gully. Stella remembered the first time she was here. Stella was in her school uniform, out of school for just a few hours. She recalled the intimacy of that day and relived it. She relished then, and now, the cool green sweeping over her. They have emerged into the sunlight and made their way to the hydrangea beds. Coral examined them, commenting on the number of new varieties, the strangeness of some. Stella had never been very fond of hydrangeas, but today she saw them as Coral saw them, understood something new and was swept up in the complexity of this over-big flower, its hundreds of little flowers, like the eye of a fly. She had always liked the hydrangea for its colour, and its litmus sensitivity to soil, but now the form appealed to her. They hovered, Coral in blue, Stella in purple, like insects over the flowers and then walked on, past the monkey-puzzle tree, crossing the lake again as they moved up the hill towards the bandstand.

'Iris and I used to come here,' said Coral. 'I'd bring my school books. Mum would have a book to read . . . we'd sit here on the grass for hours . . .'

There was longing in Coral's voice. Stella felt it, wanted to reach out to her, her mother again, but cannot.

Stella, regretting the distance that had come between them, the separation of adolescence, the sense of utterly different ways of living in the world, wanted the easy silence that Coral implied she'd had with Iris. And yet, there *was* something, an intangible thread that transcended the differences of politics, some kind of placental connection that ran beneath everything they said.

When they reached the house Coral opened the gate for Stella. Chooks and ducks scattered as Coral shooed them off the garden.

'I've given up on that,' said Stella. 'I've managed to fence off the vegies around the other side, but they can forage here. Occasionally they dig something up, but not often.'

They went in and put the beer and crayfish into the fridge.

'You can have this room,' said Stella, leading Coral into the room she has used as a study. Coral put her bag on the bed and looked at the books packed closely on the shelves. 'Doesn't look like you'll ever run out of things to read. How's Giuseppe these days?' asked Coral, nodding towards the black cat that has just walked in.

'It's Lysippe, not Giuseppe.'

Ducks and chooks cluster around wanting to be fed. Stella goes into the shed and grabs a handful of wheat, which she throws to them.

'Have they got names?'

'Of course. The Austrolorps are called Freda and Valerie. I can tell them apart when they're eating. Valerie always goes first. The silver one is Sylvia. And this is Radclyffe and Alice,' she says pointing to the khaki campbell ducks. 'They're wonderful company, except for when they wake me up too early, because they want to get out.'

'You shut them in every night?'

'Yes. Too many foxes around here. But they're out all day.'

'They lay well?'

'They're not exactly prodigious, but enough for me. But I haven't found a single egg from Alice or Radclyffe yet. Not one. I don't know if they're not laying, or simply hiding them well. But we talk a lot.'

They walked up the hill to the fruit trees, picked some quinces and went down to the creek, which they crossed on stepping stones. Stella was pleased to see that Coral retained her agility and her love of walking.

They sat on the chairs around the fireplace drinking beer, talking about the weather, the plants, the chooks and ducks and Coral filled Stella in on the news from home: weddings, children, deaths and divorces.

'Are you *with* anyone at the moment?' Coral asked.

'No. Not in that sense. Taking some time out.'

'You're not lonely out here?'

'No. At least not yet. I do talk to Lysippe and the ducks and chooks too. But no, I'm not lonely. And I have one day a week in the city.' She paused. 'Were you? Lonely, I mean.'

Coral looked at the print of a solitary desk in a sunlit room, that hung over the fireplace. 'Yes,' she said, 'but then, we had no city nearby. And life was harder. I didn't choose to be alone as you have. It was only occasional, before your father died, but after . . . I really don't know how I got through those years. Both of you away at school. Your father gone. I'd always thought we'd have time together later, when we wouldn't have to work the land so hard. But later never came, for us. I wouldn't have made it without Grace. She was marvellous.' She looked at Stella. 'I *can* understand your . . . the emotional bond with women,' she said cautiously. 'But I don't understand the sexual thing.' She stood up and poured herself another beer and pulled the wrapped crayfish from the fridge.

Stella rose and unwrapped the crayfish, rinsed it under the tap and cut through the carapace.

Coral stood and watched as Stella knifed her way through the hard exterior. 'I think,' said Coral, 'you need a long time to get to know someone, to go beyond mere fondness. Sometimes you need to close yourself also. That's a freedom that's hard to come by nowadays.'

'It's why I'm out here,' said Stella, 'and not living in some communal household in the city. But I think it's different with women too.'

Stella removed the carapace, threw it into the newspaper and watched as Coral gutted the white flesh.

Estella walks to the corner ledge and grips the rock next to her as she leans forward to look down into the gully below. A deep blue circle of water, surrounded by arching ghost gums lies directly beneath her perch. Lush and oasis-like, the vegetation stretches south and westward in a long thin line along the creekbed. Dwarfed by the bulging rocks that sometimes almost meet in the narrow crevices running off from the main canyon, a few hardy gums clutch on to the sheer wall, where a randomly blown seed fell into a pocket of soil. As they go down into the gully the patterns repeat themselves in miniature: mistletoe, with its dangling leaves and elongated flowers, clings to vertical trunks of ghost gums.

234

They descend into the gully and walk along a narrow sandy path, through the cycad fronds to the waterhole at the end of the canyon. The waterhole is cupped by rocks. A narrow fissure on the opposite side is the only visible break in the rocks. They strip and Olga slides into the water on her bottom. The water is cool in the shade and warm where the sun hits it in an open circle of light.

Estella pauses a moment before sliding in – she feels fear running through her bloodstream – before she plunges forward, as her head rises out of the water, tears, mixed with water, run down her face. She moves quickly from the deep water to the shallow edges, feels wide open and terrified that one of her pleasures has been taken from her.

Olga looks at her from the centre of the pool and swims quietly to her side. She reaches out her hand and tugs at it gently. 'Come on. Come with me into the middle. You'll be all right. I'm here. I'll watch you.'

'That's the problem, I don't want to feel watched.'

'I know, but give yourself a chance. This is the first time you've been out of your depth since then.' She tugs gently again and Estella follows her.

Estella pulls her hand out angrily. 'Leave me alone, I'll do it myself.' She swims into the deepest part of the waterhole.

Olga watches her, her heart thumping in her chest, then turns away.

Estella turns treading water and faces the cliff wall. She turns again to come face to face with Olga who has swum up close and who now reaches out her hand to brush the salty tears from Estella's wet cheeks. Olga swims to the edge while Estella remains in the middle, steadying herself, then turns and swims into Olga's arms. As Olga enfolds her and the tears come again, her shoulders lift and shake and she gasps for breath between sobs. Eventually she is silent. There is only the soft lapping of disturbed water on rocks and the buzz of midday flies.

It is hot out on the open track that leads away from the water-hole. A lizard scuttles past Estella towards its hole, then stops. Estella stops too, raises her hand and turns to Olga. Olga has already seen it and is motionless. They all stand completely still watching one another while Olga moves and the lizard darts into its hole.

Sheer walls of rock drop into the canyon and they walk on past low shrubs with small purple flowers that look like a kind of mint. Estella reaches down, rubs the leaves with her fingers and sniffs. She screws up her nose, thinking with it, trying to figure out if it smells like mint. The rock floor flattens out again, still high above the plain and they begin the descent. Ghost gums sprawl in awkward positions, sometimes clinging impossibly to a crack in the rock. Spinifex, looking like inviting cushions, dot the path down. Estella remembers the sharp needle of the grass from the school trip to the north west. She could still feel the spinifex's sharp needle. Right at the bottom of the path reeds cluster in damp hollows. Three black cockatoos are perched in a leafless tree near the car.

Stella was sitting at her desk. In one corner the desk was piled high with boxes containing papers and notebooks, a kind of makeshift filing system. She had surrounded the desk with pictures and knick-knacks of different kinds that appealed to her. Immediately in front of her eyes was a photograph of Saturn with its six moons. The frisbee rings encircled Saturn, which was dwarfed by the moon Dione in the foreground. The other moons, Enceladus, Rhea, Titan, Mimas and Tethys, floated in the silent blackness of space. To the left of the photograph was a winged woman, strung from the ceiling. She swung over the moons effortlessly, in the breeze from the window. Winged, and with a fish tail, she appeared to be in some kind of ecstacy. Next to her was a glass crystal that caught the morning light and scattered rainbows on the wall. Stella, spinning it, watched the rainbows dance. Beneath these was an astrological egg, based on the principle of Chinese boxes, but egg shaped, each of the five eggs had different markings. The outer one was dark blue with the golden stars of the zodiac marked at the point where the two eggs separate. Stella pulled them apart. The next two eggs had pictures of the sun and moon at each end and in between were the symbols of the twelve zodiac signs, six on each egg. The fourth egg had the symbols of the nine planets, and the fifth and final egg, which did not open, had a picture of a chook on a nest.

A loud squawk broke the silence. She raced out the front door to the hay bales, peeked over the railings of the steps and saw one black chook squawking and crowing delightedly at the egg she has laid. Valerie stalked proudly out from behind the hay bale continuing with her song. Stella picked up the warm egg and held it in her hand, allowing the warmth to run through her palm. She sat on the steps and watched the chooks and ducks scratch and squawk and quack their way between the plants.

Out on this flat land there is a strange sort of silence. The silence is there, but it is not complete. The spaces between the sounds are great enough to make you aware of the absence of sound. I listen for the next sound to break silence. Until then I listen to the silence. The silence seems to enter my bones, that are bleached by silence, like the bones I have found on this journey across the desolate heartland that speak to me in silent ways. The silence cracks. An insect flutters briefly in the crack and then is gone. I am left to contemplate the sand, the stones, the dust, the silence once again.

27

The days and nights seem endless in this expanse of land that stretches, almost featureless in every direction. I turn in a circle searching for a break in the level line of the horizon, but mostly I just walk, silently, each step a step towards the centre.

'Okay, girls, that's enough. I want my spot back.' Stella walked on to the blanket at the back of the house and went to sit down. The chooks leapt from their places and the ducks, Radclyffe and Alice, quacked at her for disturbing their sleep. Radclyffe rose and waddled off to rummage in the leaves, Alice slept on. Stella reached over and touched her feathers lightly. She liked the soft oily feel. Every now and then she would have to go searching for them down at the creek. At those times she would pick them up and carry them under her arms back to the house, where she would watch them so she could find the hole in the fence through which they had escaped. Their bodies were lighter to carry than they appeared, and once settled under her arms they were happy to remain there.

Stella went back to her book on Fibonacci numbers. The number series, in which each succeeding number is the sum of the previous two, was generating all sorts of ideas. She mentally worked out the first dozen numbers in the sequence: 1, 1, 2, 3, 5, 8, 13, 21, 34, 55, 89, 144 and mused over the repeating patterns of numbers for a while, and then read on. The spiral formed by this pattern was replicated in the growth pattern of leaves on some plants. She got up and walked around the garden looking at the plants, at the way in which the leaves grew. The roses seemed to come closer to it than some of the others. She wondered whether that was the pattern behind the stems that flowered on the geranium plant. Was there perhaps a secondary pattern there?

Stella had arranged to meet Karen and Jenny in the city for dinner and their three-weekly meeting. They had continued to meet in spite of the distances and had seen one another through a range of crises. One year they spent doing Aikido together, learning to roll, slap their hands against the mat with a satisfying loud clap, and throw one another. Karen's responses were the fastest. You were on the mat before you knew you were being thrown. Jenny's strength was her endurance, the measured calmness in her body, even a two-hour class did not exhaust her. Stella had endurance too. She could do all the exercises and rolls at the pace set by the instructor and the other women in the class. Stella enjoyed rolling along the mats, she felt her body move in the way it had as an adolescent. It was good to know that she had retained that easiness with her body. But the Aikido class had folded and now they were back to thought meetings.

Stella told them about the book on spirals she'd been reading. She wished she understood all the stuff that Jenny, a mathematician, talked about. 'I want to understand maths so I can understand magic,' she said. 'I know it's the last thing any maths teacher would want you to do, but maths has been magic for millennia. It's there in the language too, with irrational, imaginary and transcendental numbers. It's all made out to be so dry and boring at school, they don't tell you any of this interesting stuff.'

'The mathematics of the spiral seems extraordinarily complex,' said Jenny. 'But there are some very simple ways of creating a mathematically exact spiral nonetheless.'

'How?'

'There're a couple of ways. One is what's called the golden rectangle, or sometimes the whirling squares, and the other is the golden triangle. In fact you can use any regular polyhedron. Let me draw it for you.' Jenny drew a rough rectangle followed by a series of smaller rectangles, all with the same proportions. She then drew a curved line that joined the opposite corners of each diminishing square, forming a spiral that looked like a nautilus shell.

'You can also use the isosceles triangle, using the same principle of line lengths,' continued Jenny drawing yet another figure.

'There are lots of possibilities, lots of different approaches. It's like the ideas we have about time. Time appears to be linear, not because it is, but perhaps because it occurs on the circumference of an infinite circle. The circle is so big, we can't see the curve.'

'But you can if you look at little things, at daily life, for instance. I see it with the chooks and ducks, and with the plants around me.'

'But that's an illusion too, to some extent,' said Jenny.

'It feels real to me.'

'Sure, but it's all a matter of co-ordinate systems. If you choose a suitable co-ordinate system you can even get rid of gravity.'

'Really?'

'A feather and a hammer dropped simultaneously in a vacuum will each reach earth at the same time.'

'Theoretically then,' said Karen, 'we *could* fly.'

'I suppose so, though flying is different from falling. But also you'd have to get yourself into the appropriate co-ordinate system, and that might not be one that is consistent with live cells. So there are still are few problems. The idea's been played with in lots of movies. I think that there are more exciting things than flying.'

'Like what?' asked Karen, slightly miffed.

'Like black holes. On the surface of a black hole time is a contradiction. Either it stops, or it's infinite. Black holes break all the rules of physics, but by breaking them, they show how accurate they are. No one's ever seen a black hole, though theoretically you could travel through one – through a worm hole – to a parallel universe.'

'Imagine that!'

'Maybe there is a world out there in which we could all fly to the Pleiades,' said Karen. 'I'd like to go to the Pleiades. The constellation of Taurus seems like a friendly one. Maybe we could reinstate the Minoan reverence for bulls and rosettes.'

They laughed at the direction their talk had taken. They sometimes talked about their relationships, but the repetition of those patterns interested them less than speculating about the origins of culture or of the universe.

It was late when Stella got up to go.

'You can stay if you like,' said Karen.

'I have to lock the chooks up. But thanks.'

She drove out into the country, into the starlight. She could see the Pleiades out the side window of the car. She liked being able to see the stars at night. She pulled into the drive and parked the car. She stumbled round to the back verandah, picked up the torch and went up to the chook pen. She shone the torch in. One, two chooks, one duck. Where are the others? She walked around the garden calling chookchokchokchokchok. She walked into the arc of light from the front light and saw a black body sprawled and dismembered on the path, its head missing.

She went back up to the pen, locked the gate and went and slumped on the arm chair inside, staring at the wall. She decided she would bury Freda in the morning.

Olga and Estella are walking behind Iris and Dorothy. Iris, wearing a bright blue dress with yellow roses on it and an army surplus cap on her head, is explaining how to make kiti, a resin made from spinifex that has been ground and then heated. Iris shows them the hard, cooled result on the end of her dish. Three children accompany the women and they prance on ahead, finding shady places to sit while the women instruct Olga and Estella in their ways. The orange dust settles like a film against the black of their feet. Dorothy is walking, holding her digging stick diagonally across her back and her dish tucked under her left arm. She has two free hands and looks as though she could walk right across the country like that. They walk through the trees, following a well-worn path. Every now and then Dorothy or Iris stops, and picking up a rock that seems to be part of the environment, she explains how to grind kaltu kaltu, native millet, into a powder to make damper, or how to make sweet cordial from the insects that suck the juices out of the mulga tree, or from blossoms of hakea or grevillea. The rock is returned carefully to its place and left until the next group passes through. Dorothy points to the native tobacco plant with its white tubular flowers and scalloped petals, the source of pituri. They talk about fire and how to make it with wood, grass and kangaroo droppings. They indicate the bloodwood tree and the mulga and hand them bush plums to taste, with their slightly sharp flesh and nutty seed in the centre.

The rock is huge and seems to come down and meet them in waves. They sit gazing at the shapes formed by the rock, parts worn down by torrents of water. In the burnt scrub near the waterhole at the base, where they are sitting, crows are stalking, black against the black trunks. The rock seems to fold in on itself, creating shadowy holes. Estella wishes she could wade through the water to see how deep the holes are, but this waterhole is drinking water. They are leaning against one another silently watching as the crows now swoop over the water and land on the rocks. They make their funny two-legged jump and take off again, casting black shadows of themselves on the rocks. Then they fly off.

Estella is thinking about the way the rock seems to be many, and yet it's one. Beyond, on the other side is the one that from a distance appears to be one, and yet it is many.

'Shall we go?' says Olga.

Estella raises herself and offers an outstretched hand to Olga.

Stella woke and then she remembered. She put on her slippers and went up to the chook shed. Sylvia and Valerie were still on the perch. Radclyffe was sitting in the dirt. She went down to the house, picked up the spade and then went to collect Freda's dismembered body from the front. With a heaviness in her, she dug a hole in the vegetable patch and placed the chook inside it, picked up some dirt and scattered it over the feathers and then heaped soil back into the hole. She left a small mound. Then she walked around the garden again, looking for the remains of Alice. But she could find nothing. Somehow, that was worse than burying Freda. At least she knew what had happened. It reminded her of the little dog that she'd dreamt about for so long after she went missing. But Alice, being bulkier and slower than Radclyffe, wouldn't stand a chance against a fox.

Stella went back up to the pen and opened the gate. Lethargically they came out. It wasn't the usual scramble with a racket of clucking and quacking. Instead they were subdued. In shock, thought Stella. She decided that she would clean out the pen for them, as you would for a sick friend.

All day they walked around together, the three of them, never further than a foot or two away from one another. They made no noise, simply fulfilling the needs of survival, eating whatever fell in their path. She'd never seen animals so depressed.

She spun the day out, cleaning the pen, chopping more wood, weeding the garden, stopping occasionally to eat something small. She didn't leave to go to the post office or the milkbar, and all three were back in the pen by five.

She was exhausted when she went to bed. She dreamed disturbingly about Julia, who is with her at a large celebration. There is singing. Half way through Julia stands up and shoots herself in the heart. It passes through her body, the body of her new lover and the body of her longtime friend. They all stagger around the room. The bullet ricochets and hits Stella in the heart. Stella shouts in pain and looking down sees a hole in her chest. 'You'd better not have killed me,' she yells.

They are flying. The plane sweeps over the land. Rocks rise up as if out of nowhere, the many heads of one contrasting with the rather squat body of the other. There are deep fissures that split the rounded rock, creating gorges and in the middle there is a circle of spinifex sheltered by the surrounding domes. The plane banks and flies into the golden orb of the sun.

I have travelled far, beyond the track of the kangaroo and I am following the track of the brolga. I search the sky for signs of her passage. I sing to her, sing of her quarrel with emu.

The heart of the brolga dances. She soars high, singing. The heart of the brolga sings. She flies high, spinning. Brolga wings her grey-feathered way over land parched and dry. Below her people tell stories of how brolga outwitted her sister, emu. They tell of how brolga, mindful of the future, foraged for succulent sedge roots; of how brolga pounded her sedge roots with a stone well-suited to the task. Emu, on the other hand, had no mind for the future. Her sedges were any sedges, her stone any stone. Emu hungered. So she stole the stone from brolga. She swallowed that stone and it lay heavy in her belly. Brolga searched long for her stone. She accused emu. Emu confessed her crime. Brolga threatened her with a stick. Emu cried out, 'Yagi yagi yagi . . . don't . . . don't hit my head. The sky will fall, the people will suffer, the land will be stricken, I will destroy all.' Brolga, mindful of the future, hit her on the back and the stone leapt from emu's mouth. Emu spoke, she said, 'Henceforth I shall run over the plains, I shall rush through scrub and trees, I shall frequent the billabongs.' Brolga spoke, she said, 'Henceforth I shall sing to the melaleucas, the rivers, the creeks. I shall soar high in the air, I shall fly circling, circling. The people will hear my circling song.'

I sing the song of the brolga over and over, imagining myself a brolga, flying in circles. I imagine catching the warm currents of air that rise up from the earth. Lost in a dream I look ahead and see two figures in the distance. They move gracefully about on the plain. I watch them dance and hear a loud brassy call. I see the two figures lift off the ground and soar into the distance.

I walk to the dancing ground. I search for marks, for foot-prints in the sand. There are none. And yet, I saw, I heard.

28

As I walk I finger the bloodwood talisman you gave me. Though it is about the length of my forearm and hand together and roughly the width of the widest part of my hand, I can hardly feel the weight of it. It is carved and painted with symbols. Along the central spine is the image of a snake giving birth.

Scattered on the surface are other symbols: the circle, the spiral, rings of concentric circles, U shapes, ellipses. The surface has been rubbed smooth, apart from the carvings. It is cool and pleasant to touch. I touch and rub it. I gain strength doing this. In turn it takes on my vibration, my spirit, and its potency is enhanced.

I contemplate the symbols on its surface. I begin to understand the power of pictorial representation. I sit in silence, listening to the occasional sounds of the earth, listening to the power of it.

Stella was packing her things into boxes. She had decided to move back to the city. Since the fox, it hadn't been the same. She had found a job in the city, and each day as she let the chooks out she worried there would be another attack, but the pen was too small for them to be locked up all the time.

Lysippe would go with her to the city. She spent three

weekends packing up her belongings and her books. She had found a small house, near the tramline and tomorrow would move. She went to bed surrounded by mountains of boxes and dreamt of high buildings falling into the sea. She felt terrible when she woke up in the morning.

Catherine arrived early and took Alice, Sylvia and Valerie with her. 'You can come and visit them,' she said.

Then Karen and Jenny arrived separately, and the three of them piled things into the three cars. Lysippe crept around the almost-empty rooms, clawing, for the last time, the arm chairs that would remain, and when Stella put her in the car she crawled over the uneven surfaces and sat on the flat piece behind the back seat, miaowing pathetically.

'I wish I didn't have to do it to her,' said Stella. 'She sounds so miserable. When we get there she'll dart under the nearest piece of large furniture and stay there for a day, then she'll prowl around the house like a panther and only straighten up when she thinks I'm not looking. We go through this every time.'

They drove in convoy to the house in North Fitzroy. It was long and dark and there was no garden, only a concrete lawn at the back. She regretted the shift, but knew that it was necessary. That a phase in her life had come to an end.

'My shout for dinner,' said Stella, when the last of the objects had been taken inside. 'How about a pizza from La Porchetta?'

'Sounds fine to me,' said Karen.

'Me too.'

It was busy at La Porchetta, so they bought take-away pizza and picnicked by candlelight in the living-room. After they'd gone, Stella stood wishing the boxes would unpack themselves. Lysippe, meanwhile, had gone into hiding and wouldn't come out, though she called and called.

In the middle of the night Stella woke with a start when a car passed, and wondered where she was. She found Lysippe curled on the end of the bed, and reassured by this fell asleep again.

When she woke she missed the sound of birds and chooks and wished she could see green outside her window.

Being back in the city prompted memories. In her mind she walked the inner city streets that she knew so well. Now and then she stopped at a particular house in a particular street, reminded of some event or person. It was like a kind of map. A mental map of streets and stories, of people and events. She thought about how you could paint it using signs and geometric forms. In her mind the map looked like star-shaped flowers and circles overlaying a faint grid of streets and parks, with large circles for the houses she had lived in. Her new house was just along the street from the blue-and-orange-wallpaper house where Catherine had come to stay with her. From here she could walk to the shopfront where she had worked; and the flat with the line of bricks, where she had sat watching the world do somersaults, was on her way to work.

She wondered aloud where the electricity people were. Still no sign of them. She wasn't too worried about missing work. The public service moved so slowly nobody would even notice her absence. She spent days writing supply orders for outback meteorological stations: 6464 Thermometer, and then signing her ever-diminishing signature. She'd had nine letters in her signature when she started, but signing twenty or thirty forms a day had reduced it to five. She gave up on getting to work at all when the electricity people still hadn't come and it was half past two.

As it was getting dark she tried the lights. They came on. At least she'd had a restful day. But she still had her Warlpiri class that evening. She locked Lysippe inside the house and drove out to the university, listening to the tape and repeating the phrases:

karnta ka nyinami
karnta ka nyina
the woman is sitting down

wangkami kapala karntajarra
wangka kapala karntajarra
the two women are talking

nyarrpajarri kapu karnta
what is the woman going to do?

When Estella tries to restart the car, after taking a photograph of a flower beside the road, it is dead, nothing, as though the battery has suddenly gone flat.

'Well, somebody'll come by eventually,' she says, after crawling into the bonnet to see if there are any loose wires. 'Everything seems okay. I don't know what it is.'

They sprawl on the mats in the back of the car, reading, comfortable in the silence. Olga falls asleep. She is woken by a loud buzzing noise.

'Look,' says Stella. 'A motorbike. Two.' A swarm of bikes comes over the rise.

'Looks like twenty motorbikes.'

The riders pull up and the leader takes off his helmet. They speak Japanese to one another, and a woman steps forward and speaks in English. Olga explains and she and the stranger examine the manual. The men in the party have decided to try pushing the car, but it is dead. Olga and the woman push through the crowd to the car and pull out the fuse box. The stranger examines each fuse and replaces one with a spare.

'I work in electronics,' she explains as Estella starts the car.

On the twenty-sixth day I see round forms against the horizon. They glow red, like blood, like glowing earthbound fireballs. They are far off, but even from this distance I feel them reaching out, drawing me on.

I begin to run. The rocks are immense. They bounce on the horizon as I run towards them. My mind is empty with awe. I am a bee dancing towards her hive. I am pulled towards the rocks by some force. A thread, an umbilicus, connects us. I follow the thread.

Stella looked back through her diary and found the Tarot she'd thrown for this year. December promised a new lover. Who? she wondered. Maybe she didn't know her yet.

Estella and Olga drive on towards the rocks which spread themselves across their field of vision, sprawling like an old woman

249

with lumpy patches on her body, or like one of those ancient figurines that are all buttocks and breasts. The rock, angled towards the sky, is dimpled with spinifex and the occasional green shrub, the brown, the yellow and the green all merging in a kind of repeating mosaic. Some of the rocks seem to lean together for affection or protection or for sharing secrets. They arrive at the gorge and the first plant they stumble on is a desert rose, dangling at eye level with its red heart, lilac pink petals and spotted egg-shaped leaves. The rock walls loom in a V-shape ahead of them. They move towards the V, past round boulders thrown from the rock wall by the forces of heat and cold, large lumpy boulders, like the dough of raisin bread. Above they point to the holes left by the falling rocks.

The V of the gorge is reflected in a waterhole as they continue their way up the path. Estella meanders beside the shallow stream which has cut its way into the rock over eons and gazes down into the valley beyond the gorge, through the spear grass and she drops to the ground where they pass the waterbottle back and forth between them. Seated, the spear grass blocks the view one way, but gives them good shade to sit and admire the view the way they have come.

'Want to do a Tarot?'

'Can you do a joint one?' asks Olga, new to it.

'Sure. We just have to make sure that we both shuffle and cut and think about the coming year as we do it.' Estella pulls out the cards she's been carrying around for the last week. These are the ones she'd given Olga, not long after they'd met. They are round and easy to shuffle. Estella spreads them on the cleared piece of earth. The first card to come up, January, is the Lovers. Their eyes smile at one another. The year promises emotion and sensuality with a Cups card in the centre and three others at different points throughout the year. It is balanced by the Fool of creativity in April, the High Priestess in August, and the travelling Sun in December.

'It couldn't look better,' says Estella after a long silence in which she runs her eyes over the cards. 'This is the year I've been waiting for.'

The earth I run across is dotted with boulders, clumps of spinifex, small bowing shrubs. I feel the force of sanctity in all these things. Every feature of the landscape is steeped in sacred lore. I watch the faces of the rocks changing as I approach. I pause briefly to take in the beauty of the forms, a detail of colour or shape. The shape of the rocks, the caves, the watermarks and depressions remind me of stories I have been told.

There are stories of how women helped with the birth of the carpet snake. I approach the rocks, stopping for a moment to measure my insignificance against the immensity, the durability of the rocks. I walk forward and press the palm of my hand against the hard surface. It is warm, filled with the heat of sunlight. I wander slowly around and through the rocks, touching and pressing There are places where the rocks have been rubbed smooth by contact with the bodies of women who came here to give birth.

I run my hands over the rounded bellies of boulders, which are taut, smooth, warm. I can see the pebbly tears of women, weeping for their still-born children.

I wander further into the circle of rock. There are caves. Some are caves where women sheltered in the days that preceded the birth. There are others where women sat, child between knees. I can see their breasts swollen with milk. I pass quietly in and out of the caves and walk silently between the rocks. I am one of them. I sit and wait for night to come.

They walk down the same path they have come. Stepping lightly over rocks, sometimes holding hands. When they get to the waterhole they sit in the shade of a red river gum. A light breeze blows the water surface into ripples, creating strange reflections in the otherwise still pool. The silver leaves of the tree look like tiny fish darting about. And there are tadpoles, halfway to maturity. Little legs poking out from their oval bodies. The shade is a relief. Not cool, because the air remains hot, but a relief from the direct sunlight.

Olga looks up from the pool and gazes at Estella, who seems to be far away. She loves her for her ability to lose herself in an environment, and for the way she persists in carrying on her life as she wants it, climbing rocks, swimming and so on in spite of the dangers. 'Stel, what're you thinking?'

'I was remembering the day we met. You know, it's just over a year ago now. It's flown, but there were times when it didn't. Like when you were away for all those months.'

'Ditto, for me too. I missed you so much.'

'Do you remember the first time we danced? That's when I fell in love with you. I tried to stop it, thinking that a relationship would intrude too much into my life, take up too much time.' Estella watches the replay of it in her mind, Olga swirling around her, flirting and singing along with the music. Estella could feel the smile she'd had on her face as Olga spun in and embraced her with one arm. Before either seemed to know what was happening they were kissing. At the time Stella thought she had forgotten how, but this was better than she remembered it.

'I resisted too,' she says remembering the emotional crises of the preceding year.

Olga sees them dancing too, sees the magical smile that Estella had flashed at her when they began dancing, sees the way her body responded to the rhythm of the music. She isn't sure if she had loved her in that instant, but it wasn't long after that before she did, and she didn't know who had started it. It just seemed to happen.

A half-transformed tadpole whishes across the point in the pool at which both were staring fixedly. They look up. Estella speaks.

'You know that Tarot predicted you – new lover, December, it said.'

I have not eaten for many days, since my arrival at this magical place. The rocks resonate power. I drink water as I need it and chew pituri mixed with ash, but my need for nourishment has diminished. I spend my days sitting still, waiting for the nocturnal animals to emerge, waiting for something to happen.

29

'I saw it once,' says Estella.

'What?'

'The great serpent in the sky that flies between the stars, devouring whatever gets in its way. It comes by only rarely and then you can see it only when the skies are jewel clear, like they are here.'

There are snakes living in the crevices of the rocks. I have seen their eyes shining in the shadows. I have heard their bodies slithering over stones. I can see them now. I watch. I look into their crystal eyes. I see a movement of a head, a body.

Stella got up early. It was the only way to see the comet.

I watch as one long shining body moves from her nest. She is looking into my eyes. Behind her I see a writhing mass of bodies. Slowly they disentangle, separate and follow her out of the darkness; they approach me, tongues flickering.

It was one thing she wanted to see before she died. So three mornings in a row she did it. The first day she saw nothing. The sky was too light.

I remain. I am still. I hardly breathe.

She got up earlier and drove out of the city on the second morning.

They slide forward quietly. Their sinusoidal movements are hypnotic to watch. There is a stillness in the air despite the onslaught of motion.

She saw it, but clouds kept scuttling by and she couldn't find anything stable enough to give her camera a long exposure. She decided that it was useless to be anywhere near the city, and rang a friend who lived on a farm well away from lights, and far enough inland to be fairly certain that the sky would be clear.

I feel the rasp of reptilian scales against my skin and do not move. I feel their bodies pressing lightly against parts of my body, my feet, legs, buttocks. One snake runs along the base of my spine. I shudder. Tongues flicker and eyes gleam as they slide up over my thighs.

It was cold out at four o'clock, but the sky was indigo clear.

Some of the snakes coil in the sun around the triangular perimeter of my body. One coils in my lap. Another spirals its way up my torso to my head. It coils upon my crown and sleeps. Two snakes encircle my arms like spiral bracelets.

She saw it as soon as her eyes adjusted.

Everything is silent again and still. The snakes sleep. I remain unflinchingly on my still spot. I watch the shadowy movement of a circling hawk. Time stands still. The air shimmers with heat. I am a dream. I am a reality. I am. The air cools.

It wasn't as big as she'd expected, but the tail stretched well behind the head. Fence posts turned out to be an ideal pseudo-tripod.

The spiral bracelets move. They creep down my shoulders and neck. The sun blazes orange and red on the horizon. I feel a tickling in my ears. I hear a faint whispering. Their tongues are licking the skin, the wax of my outer ears.

Like some huge serpent slithering across the skies, she thought, looking at the sprinkle of light points that formed the tail.

I hear a sound like fresh wind blowing in my ears. I hear the distant rumble of waves on a shore. I hear voices, individual voices breaking through the melée of sound. I hear music, spinning, ringing out. A chorus of sounds enters the silence. I hear a voice, an internal resonance, sound sliding over strings, a voice forming words, a voice speaking.

She stood there shivering, wishing that Olga were with her.

I feel the movement of my vocal chords. I feel the words forming in my throat, my mouth. The tongue, the palate, the teeth, the lips all in harmony. I feel the word flutter from my mouth. I hear myself speak. I speak my own name: Estelle.

The rocks soar over them once again. Olga is walking in front. The air is hot again and the grass is searing in the midday sun. She hears a rustle and then sees the tail.

I hear the sibilant hiss. I repeat it over and over. I speak. I call to the rocks.

She stops and Estella almost falls over her, as Olga points her hand in the direction of the tail. It is brown and hardly shows against the rock.

I whisper to the snakes.

They step backwards a few feet, ready to move more quickly if necessary. But the snake remains in its place, only the tail still visible.

I feel the slither of scales on skin.

'You have eyes for snakes,' whispers Estella.

They are leaving. I feel the final flicker of a tail as they return to their nest in the rocks.

Stella feels like she is gumless, tongueless.

I sing the future into being. I open my mouth. The magical sounds flow forth, vibrating, creating. The chords vibrate. The tongue clicks.

The words have gone again. The thoughts are straggling, they do not want to form into meaningful sequences. The synapses have split apart again.

The tongue moves from soft palate to teeth. It furls and unfurls.

No messages are passed on. The words have been seized.

The air whispers as it passes between lips.

She falls into sleep, though the sun is shining directly into her eyes.

The air hums, thrums. The song manifests reality.

She wakes up, finds Olga beside her.

The lips touch.

She wonders how she got here. She should be over there, on the other side of the world.

The sounds from palate, tongue, teeth, lips vibrate like demateri-alised matter.

Where did you come from?'

Matter is sound condensed.

'I've been here all week, don't you remember?

Sound vibrates. Matter vibrates. Matter disintegrates into sound.

'I found you fitting.'

Matter explodes.

'I held you, and rocked you back to consciousness.'

My voice explodes into song, creating matter.

'I waited.'

The world forms in my mouth.

'But where did you come from?'

I spit it out.

'I came back to see you. Had to. I missed you so much.'
'Mmm. Me too.'

I sing to the future.

Stella goes to the airport with Olga, and waves her off. She stands and watches as the plane lifts into the sky.

I am standing in the chamber of rocks. I stand fingering the bull roarer.

They talk and write their way through the remaining months. This thread of connection, however fine, sustains them.

I finger the knot of twine that is attached at one end. My hand passes over the carvings on its surface.

Stella dreams of the time when Olga will share her bed again. When they will lie curled in one another's embrace.

I run my hand along the smooth edge. Slowly I begin to turn. The bull roarer swings in a wide arc around my body. I turn and turn and turn. I begin to spin. One hand trails my body, the other is lifted, grasping the twine in its fingers.

She wakes to the phone ringing.

As I spin I hear the whirring sound of the wood in the wood. This is the voice of the wood, of all women. This is the voice of the blood of women. This is the voice of the blood that splashed on every tree. The sound was in the blood. It is the sound of my blood, of our blood. The blood of death, the blood of life. The sound of the whirring wood echoes through the rocks. The sound expands in concentric circles around me.

She rushes to pick it up and hears the echo of Olga at the other end, so far away. She can also hear, or seems to hear, the sound of the waves, of the oceans stretching between them.

Echoes push memory out. I bleed. I spin. The echo of the blood cry wanes. I am embraced by the ring of rock. The rock is the womb. Silence creeps into the spaces left by the echoes. I am alive. I dwell in her womb, my womb, the womb, the source of silence, the source of sound.

'Only another week,' says Olga, and the goodbyes stretch out as long as the preceding conversation.

My voice brushes past the rounded rocks. It circles the chamber.

The round squat shadows have become long and thin as the sun begins its path down and the rocks begin to glow like hot coals.

It returns to me. It vibrates in the chamber of my ear and is heard. It is transformed into something external and separate from me.

The light reminds Estella of her childhood. Afternoons under the gum tree at the back watching Theo kill a sheep, or watching Coral milk the cow or prune roses. Always getting in their way, but enjoying the sunlight and the smells of bodily fluids.

How can I differentiate these things?

Dead mulga branches point to the sky and if she turns to look the other way, little spots of light form in front of her eyes as she stares at the low sun, creeping behind the rocks.

259

The rocks tower around me. Above the sky is black. No moon shines through the darkness yet, and only the stars break up the blackness of the sky. The rocks around me cast no shadows. Their black forms rise on every side, surrounding me. Nothing moves, there is silence, stillness. I fall into silence.

The moon is shining outside the bedroom window, casting a light shadow on the bedspread. Olga cups her hand over Estella's body. She touches the belly and brushes upwards, breastwards.

The darkness gathers me up as if in a gossamer web, protective but not restrictive. I fall through darkness and silence. My whole being relaxes. The fall seems endless. I sense the beginning of sound, an echo of silence I am in, an echoing silence.

They lie entwined like a coil of snakes, arms and legs curling over and around. Small puffs of breath slide across their cheeks. Kisses curve endlessly like time on an infinite circle.

The quality of silence has changed. There is a hollowness, a reverberation in silence that is echoed. It is like the spaces between the reverberating sounds of a gong, though imperceptible just as the sound is in the silence, in the echo of the silence.

They begin again, but they have never finished. The longing surges up through their lungs and comes out in long sighs that greet the pinkening morning and the call of the wattle birds in the bottlebrush that sweeps across the window pane.

I cease falling. I am seated on the ground. Around me the rocks form a barrier.

The sun has slipped behind the rocks, turning them mellow brown.

I listen to my heartbeat and am suddenly overcome by a longing for your presence. I feel a need for your solidity, your matter of fact manner. You are at ease with the world and with yourself.

Olga and Estella turn to look across the windy valley, towards rocks still glowing in stolen sunlight.

Memories crowd in on me.

A tree is silhouetted against the deepening sky and cockatoos fly over screeching.

I dream of the great snake.

Venus sets and they walk on through the shadows, now black.

There seem to be two of her. A phantom? I feel her circling my torso, coiling in opposite directions. Her heads reach for my breasts. I suckle her.

The rocks are black against a deep blue sky, tinged pale towards the earth.

The rocks loom over me. My mind wanders back over the journey, the passage through the land of the kangaroo, the brolga. I consider my time here in the home of the snake. I am dizzy with anticipation. I could dance.

Looming large, the rocks are like huge bodies stretched out against the sky. Like breast, belly, thigh.

I rise slowly from my seated posture. Legs stretch, my body sways slightly with the shock of movement. I move slowly,

261

tracing the outline of a circle on earth. The blood begins to flow in arteries and veins. I lift my arms, my eyes, see the faint halo of light that precedes the rising of the moon. I shift my weight from one foot to the other, twirl slowly, watching the rocks move in a circular dance around me.

A sliver of moon rises next to Venus and seems perched over the breast rock.

The dance becomes me. I am the dance. I lose track of individual movements, of individual moments. I pass through invisible barriers. I seem to be moving through space. The motion of my body is not smooth. At discrete points in time I am in discontinuous points in space. The rocks dissolve.

It is still, apart from the sound of their breathing and of their tread over rocks. Rocks that extend into infinity, that could be tiny planets or huge atoms.

I am a star, moving, dancing, spinning and twirling through space. I whirl. I am a spiralling galaxy. Time passes through me. I travel the spiralling perimeter of space-time. I bend with it, curling in its embrace. I am a dancing particle of light. I am the waving ribbon of light, penetrating darkness.

Hard and resistant to time. And yet, in the cracks live lizards and snakes and small marsupials.

I wave. I particle. I am an electron. I am a tachyon. I travel faster than light. I am beyond all else. I am infinitely small.

Ants tread crisscross trails over and under her.

I am a hadron
     a baryon
     a lepton
     a meson
     a quark
     a resonance.
I am beyond all division. I pass through all barriers. I tend to exist. I am being. I am doing. I am existence. Pure and utter existence. I am in every place, in every time. I am the moment. I am a point, a wave of light. I glimmer. I twinkle.

Birds swoop, and some dart to pick up ground prey . . .

I am a Blue Giant.
I am a Red Giant.
I am a White Dwarf.
I am a Black Hole.
I am a White Hole to another universe.

others call loudly to the rocks . . .

I am dancing. Like a resonating comet I leave behind me a trail of light. I am a star. I speak my names:
     Stella
     Estella
     Estelle
     Ester
     Esther
     Astarte
     Ashtaroth.
     Ishtar
     Inanna

. . . and the call is bounced back.

The Fall

There are a myriad falling stars. The world is teetering on the edge of annihilation. The Dark One has returned. She presses up against me. I feel her in my nostrils. She caresses me, cradles me in her arms. I leap into the void . . .

She falls.

I am. The light ripples through my fingers. I walk towards the sanctuary where the cunctipotent Dark One presides.

She falls.

I may not enter before divesting myself of the seven veils, seven elements. I tread the winding passage that leads to the centre, leads out again and then to the inner circle. I am struck down.

You fall.

I lie before her. I feel her sightless eyes seeing the unseen. I am stripped to the bone. The flesh falls away. Her cry carries me to other worlds. I hear the echo of her cry revolve in endless circling rings. My memory is washed clean.

You fall.

I am bare, open, desiccated, desecrated. I die a miniature death. Faint echoes of cries from that world sift through the veils that separate us. I hear, momentarily, the cry of another. No other hears her. Night closes in on me.

I fall.
I fall.

I am blind. I am deaf. No heat penetrates my skin, no cold, no pain. The scents, the tastes of the world have no impact on me. My soul is bare, bleached, dark, inert. I have no name. Silence stills my blood. My blood is black.

I fall.

I am a moment in time. I break through the membrane of life. I travel into the vast spaces beyond death. I travel through the darkness. I am a point of light. I am dancing the endless dance of transformation. I dance and spin my way through the matrix of eternity. I exist virtually.

I fall.

I have a tendency to pass out of existence. I have a tendency to pass back into existence.

My existence compliments that of another. My soul vibrates in harmony with another. Together we resonate. Our circles spin and sing in harmony. I am attracted to another. Her field of force exerts a pressure on me. I move towards her. Together we constitute a whole new being. Together we are different. We are formed out of the void. We dance eternally around one another. We meet.

Olga flies into the country at dawn. She watches the sun flare on the horizon, extinguishing the night.

We collide. We fuse. We become indistinguishable. We are the same. A spin in the dance ends. A chance meeting, a fusion, a resonance of song changes us. We separate and travel yet again. Each carries her own rhythm, her own charge. We are particles or stars. We are waves of light or an arm of the galaxy. We sing and dance eternally now. We rejoice at our singularity. We fall into another's embrace, laughing.

They meet. When they kiss their skins merge. They part and move arm in arm toward the automatic doors.

We are defined by our interactions. We exist only for our relations with others. We travel the curved edge of space-time. We spiral through the wastelands of the universe in great hordes. We fall like stars. We are solitary. We emerge into existence again.

Estella and Olga step out into the sunlight.

We sing. We see. We are visible . . . We change . . . we change . . . we change . . .

The new moon is invisible in the sky.

The spiral curls another time . . .

Acknowledgements

page 82
Laurence Binyon's poem "For the Fallen", © 1914.
First published in *The Times* on 21 September 1914.

pages 121–122
Aldous Huxley quotations from *Brave New World*, © 1932.
Edition used: London: Penguin Books.

page 185
Wassily Kandinsky quotations from *Concerning the Spiritual in Art*, © 1914. Edition used: New York: Dover Publications.

OTHER SPINIFEX TITLES

POETRY

Bird and Other Writings on Epilepsy
by Susan Hawthorne
ISBN: 1-875559-88-4

Birds don't fly on leads, I said.
Safety belts are to learn with, not to live with —
I'm safer on the trapeze than crossing the road.
And I do that every day, often by myself.

So thirteen-year-old Avis argues when confronted by the limitations imposed on her at school. From societal limitations to the inner experience of seizures, Susan Hawthorne's poetry takes the reader on a journey rarely recorded.

Many-eyed and many-lived is this poet, as seismologist or lover, bird or newborn child. To the classic figures of Sappho and Eurydice she brings all the Now! Here! sense of discovery that fires her modern girl taking lessons in flight.

— Judith Rodriguez

NON-FICTION

Wild Politics: Feminism, Globalisation and Bio/diversity
by Susan Hawthorne
ISBN: 1-876756-24-1

[*Wild Politics*] is a passionate book offering a kaleidoscope of
ideas, arresting ways of seeing things, and possible solutions for
many of the man-contrived environmental messes across the
violated globe. Its barefaced audacity is its greatest attraction.
Hawthorne has blazed a trail for others to follow.
— Alan Patience, *Best Books of 2002, Australian Book Review*

An impressive and far sighted book which is thoroughly, and
very thoughtfully researched. Susan Hawthorne writes with
clarity, intelligence and humour.
— *Chain Reaction*

[*Wild Politics*] is that rare combination, both intellectually
rigorous ... and clearly readable.
— Carol Anne Douglas, *Off Our Backs*

Australian publishing company Spinifex is putting out some
of the most alternative and exciting topics on the market, and
Wild Politics is no exception.
— Claudette Vaughan, *Vegan Voice*

Non-Fiction

September 11, 2001: Feminist Perspectives
edited by Susan Hawthorne and Bronwyn Winter
ISBN: 1-876756-27-6

So many of us have been waiting for exactly this book! The voices and ideas here are so worldly, feminist, engaged. "September 11" will never pass as ungendered after one reads Hawthorne's and Winter's international collection. I'm going to use this in classes and give it to friends.

— Cynthia Enloe

Unsurprisingly, many Afghan women regard the new political order as a false dawn ... Their concerns, together with some of the best literary responses ... have been consolidated in an excellent book of diverse feminist perspectives, edited by Susan Hawthorne and Bronwyn Winter.

— Scott Burchill, *The Age*

This book is essential reading for anyone who is interested in understanding the ways women are positioned by the global events unfolding around us and shaping the contexts in which women experience everyday life.

— Amanda Third, *Australian Women's Book Review*

NON-FICTION

Cyberfeminism: Connectivity, Critique and Creativity
edited by Susan Hawthorne and Renate Klein
ISBN: 1-875559-68-X

An exciting, inclusive and wide-ranging anthology with contributors from four continents.

The great strength of *CyberFeminism* is the desire to actualize strong critiques of the digital assumptions and promises of the era.

— Tara Brabazon, *Australian Popular Culture and Media Studies*

Fiction

*Car Maintenance, Explosives and Love and
Other Contemporary Lesbian Writings*

edited by Susan Hawthorne, Cathie Dunsford and Susan Sayer

ISBN: 1-875559-62-0

For a lesbian, some things are different. Lesbians are skilled and inventive adaptors. Lesbians have invented a culture through many ages. Contemporary lesbians are inventing at an astounding rate. And writing is no exception.

From theatre and circus to fiction and poetry, this anthology draws on the complexity of contemporary lesbian culture.

NON-FICTION

The Spinifex Quiz Book: A Book of Women's Answers
by Susan Hawthorne

Shortlisted, *Australian Awards for Excellence
in Educational Publishing*

ISBN: 1-875559-15-9

Are you frustrated by quiz shows that ignore women's achievements?

[*The Spinifex Quiz Book* is] funny, instructive, entertaining, and inspiring ... use it alone or in school. I recommend it wholeheartedly.

— Senta Trömel Plötz, Virginia

It should be compulsory reading in every Year 10 class in Australia.

— Alison Coates, ABC Radio

FICTION

Angels of Power and other reproductive creations
edited by Susan Hawthorne and Renate Klein
Australian Feminist Book Fortnight Favourite

ISBN: 1-875559-00-0

In the tradition of Mary Shelley's *Frankenstein* fourteen writers have used the technological developments of their time as their starting point in tracing the consequences of reproductive technologies. They do so, through fiction and poetry, drama and filmscript.

Angels of Power should head the reading list in any course in ethics and reproductive technology.

— Karen Lines, *Editions*

Non-Fiction

Australia for Women: Travel and Culture
edited by Susan Hawthorne and Renate Klein
ISBN: 1-875559-27-2

Explore the history and culture of women in Australia through this book. From the millennia of Aboriginal women's culture to contemporary visual arts, theatre and music, *Australia for Women* is an indispensable guide for anyone travelling in Australia.

Don't be deceived by the title: this is a book for everyone – female, male, resident and visitor.
— Cassie McCullagh, *Good Weekend*

If you would like to know more about Spinifex Press,
write for a free catalogue or visit our Web site.

SPINIFEX PRESS
PO Box 212, North Melbourne
Victoria 3051, Australia
<http://www.spinifexpress.com.au>

NON-FICTION

Cat Tales: The Meaning of Cats in Women's Lives
edited by Jan Fook, Susan Hawthorne and Renate Klein
ISBN: 1-876756-37-3

Happiness is being owned by a cat. — Evelyne Moseley

Women and cats go back millennia – from ancient Egypt, Assyria and India to the contemporary world of women whose lives are enriched by cats. The contributors to this volume explore the ways that cats create atmosphere, how some cats have household staff. There are stray cats and Amazon cats, cats stuck on poles and windowsills, farm cats, feral cats and city cats. There are cats who can open fridges, sign contracts and cats in drag. With contributors from Australia, USA, Turkey, New Zealand, Thailand, England, Germany, Canada and Switzerland these women and girls write about their friendships with cats.